A Marriage of His Convenience

Taylor K Scott

This is a work of fiction. Names, characters, places and incidents are either the product of the author's imagination or are used fictitiously. Any resemblance to actual persons, living or dead, business establishments, events, or locales is entirely coincidental.

Warning: The following work of fiction describes content of a sexual nature. See Author's Note for more information.

DEDICATION

For Fiona, a beautiful, funny, brave, and mischievous little girl.

Dravet syndrome, also known as Severe Myoclonic Epilepsy of Infancy (SMEI), is a rare form of intractable epilepsy that begins in infancy and proceeds with accumulating morbidity that significantly impacts individuals throughout their lifetime.

Current treatment options are limited, and the constant care required for someone suffering from Dravet syndrome can severely impact the patient's and the family's quality of life. Patients with Dravet syndrome face a 15-20% mortality rate due to SUDEP (Sudden Unexpected Death in Epilepsy), prolonged seizures, seizure-related accidents such as drowning, and infections.

-www.dravetfoundation.org

MUSICAL INFLUENCES

Big My Secret – Michael Nyman

The Heart Asks Pleasure First – Michael Nyman

Bittersweet Symphony – The Verve

Music by Vitamin String Quartet

Einaudi Experience

2Cellos

ACKNOWLEDGMENTS

Thank you to the community of writers and readers out there who have answered questions, read my work, given me advice, and shared my work. Thank you to all of you!

To my beta readers, Gabrielle Seaton, Denise Tuxford, Jaclyn Combe, and Mama Sue, who all took the time to read this book during the early stages. Just to have someone read my work and offer their opinion is always so empowering for me. I sincerely appreciate you offering me your time, support, and advice.

I must also thank my poor, suffering husband for supporting me through my obsession with writing. Not only has he had to live with my reading habit, which is becoming more and more consuming, but also has the added bonus of losing me to my own works of fiction. Know that I love you dearly, as well as our two beautiful girls, and appreciate all the encouragement you have given me.

Finally, but most importantly, thanks to everyone who has taken a chance on my novel. I hope it hasn't disappointed, and that you might take a chance to read some of my upcoming releases. Thank you so much again.

Author's Note

I like to write about what inspires me and not be confined to specific subgenres, which is why you will find romantic comedies, contemporary romances, dark romances and now, historical romances in my back matter. I will admit that I am no historian and do not pretend to be. I research my books as much as I can, including visits to English Heritage sites and seeking the advice of those who are more knowledgeable that I am. If I have included details that might not be wholly accurate for the time, know that this is an oversight, not a purposeful distortion of fact. This is a work of fiction, including the characters, the settings and the plot. It is by no means meant to be used as a non-chronological report of the time.

Trigger warnings: This book contains scenes of a sexual nature. It also contains scenes that refer to, and detail, medical conditions, specifically epilepsy.

Prologue

Emily

I can see the whole world from up here, even as far as the church if I squeeze my eyelids together. If I close them up tight, I can imagine I'm a ship's captain, setting sail on my maiden voyage to a new world. Or perhaps I'm on top of a mountain where the snow makes a delicious crunching sound beneath my feet. Or maybe I'm on top of Papa's horse, flying through the park without anyone shouting at me to slow down or to act more like a lady. If only I had been born a boy like Edmund, I could do all these things, and no one would even question it. Alas, the frills and bows decorating my new dress tells me what is plain for all to see. I am nothing more than a girl; a doll to primp and present to society.

"Emily!" I hear them calling for me, but I choose to ignore it for as long as possible. Instead, I tilt my face towards the sun and bask in its soothing heat, all the while pretending to be a million miles away from here.

"There you are," a voice that's a few years older than mine says from beneath where my feet are hanging limp and weightless.

There's a smile in that voice, one that speaks of friendship and camaraderie. A voice who has played with me ever since I was old enough to climb my very first tree. I choose not to move, however; I simply smile with my face remaining warm and relaxed in the mid-afternoon sun.

"Shhh!" I grin widely, listening to him now laughing at me, even though we both know I'm going to be in a lot of trouble when my mother finally catches up with me.

"Come on, Em," he says softly, "not everything will change. We shall still be friends. We just can't be as…affectionate as we once were."

"I love you, Edmund, even if you are lying to me," I tell him with my smile still shining through the sadness of it all. However, it takes only moments to drop the façade and lower my voice to barely more than a whisper when I tell him, "Everything is going to change."

"Emily, turning twelve doesn't mean you're about to be shipped off and married," he says softly when he takes hold of my foot, only to instantly let go again. Such contact will no longer be endured by either of our parents, not now we are of an age when tongues might begin to make assumptions. No matter how ludicrous the insinuations may be; it is simply best not to put oneself in such a vulnerable position. As you may well have guessed, I was given such a speech just this morning. My mother had wished me a happy birthday before laying down a new set of rules for me to follow, all in time for my birthday party.

"It just means you are getting ready to become a lady," Edmund continues, snapping me out of my bitter memories of one of the worst birthdays to date. I had been naively excited about it yesterday. But then, I was a completely different age only last night. "Believe me, Em, I have been given the same warnings and expectations. You must know that as much as I would love to keep playing pirates and explorers of far-off civilisations with you, I can't. Anyway, *you* should be pleased," he scoffs, "I have even less time to enjoy being a child."

"You're a boy, Edmund, you will have so much more freedom than I ever will." I pout when I finally open my eyes to look at him. He smiles softly at me before holding out his arms to help me down from my branch. Saving a damsel from a tree might be the last opportunity for us to touch one another with childhood innocence, and without the watchful eye of a chaperone. How different our days will be now that we are being forced into the initiation of adult life.

With a deep sigh, I shuffle to the edge and reach for his hands, giving into the inevitable moment when Mama will scold me for running away from my very own birthday party. The fancy tea and endless list of guests was all a concealment of the fact that I will no longer be able to live the life I so dearly love. In all fairness, it has been a life most little girls in my position have never been privy to. It has been a blessing to be my papa's youngest and most cherished child; he truly is the best of fathers. Even so, I still feel as though I have been wronged, now that it has come to such a sudden end.

As I shuffle further forward, my father's voice booms from behind Edmund, causing him to look away and completely miss my flailing limbs that are still trying to reach out for him. He does not turn back to catch me until it is far too late, and I am left yelping in the knowledge that I am about to head straight first into a particularly hardy looking bramble bush. The sting of thorns cutting through my right shoulder blade hits me with overwhelming pain. Both my father and Edmund fluster about before my mother comes traipsing across the lawn to make it feel all the more agonising.

"Oh, my heavens!" she cries angrily at the same time as she beats away both men with her bare hands. She reaches for the brambles as if they are nothing but soft blades of grass, then pulls me up with a strange mixture of tutting and soothing sounds of comfort. "Emily, you wicked child, look at what you've done to your new dress! What on earth are we going to do with you?"

"I'm sorry, Mama," I reply bashfully, for I'm more than aware that Edmund is still very much close enough to hear every word of this humiliating chastisement. "I just needed one last hurrah."

"Well, I hope it was worth it," she grumbles while studying my entire body for injury. She soon locates the area that was scratched the hardest and shakes her head. "This one is most likely going to leave a scar. Come on!"

"Goodbye, Emily," Edmund says sadly, for this really was our last moment to be alone as friends together. According to my mother, we are now much too old to be left alone without risking a scandal.

"Goodbye, Edmund," I reply before swallowing back a hard lump of emotion.

For the entirety of our walk back to the house, my mother berates my father for not having had a firmer hand with me and for indulging my whimsical need to act like a boy. She then turns on me and begins to complain about how much harder I have been to educate in all things ladylike in comparison to my sister, Elsie. Not that I am truly listening. If I had been, I might well have told her that to have had that last moment with Edmund, without somebody watching me, was more than worth it. When I look at my father, he smiles with a mischievous wink for me. He knows exactly what I am thinking and is no doubt thinking precisely the same thing.

"Colletta, my dear, perhaps I might teach Emily how to play the piano?" he suggests while I try to hide a sneer over the idea. The arts have never come easily to me, and I simply do not have the patience to persevere through the challenge. "It might do her good to have at least one interest indoors, hmmm?"

"Excellent, George, what a wonderful idea," she beams, instantly forgetting her argument with him. "Starting tomorrow, I think."

"Of course," he replies, even though she is already marching off to attend to the many guests whose names I do not even know.

"I am quite sure I shall be terrible on the piano, Papa," I tell him as we link arms with one another. "You would be better off trying to educate Elsie with such a talent."

"Your sister is already proficient in playing the piano," he says with a hint of firmness behind his words, "as well as needlework, and dancing."

"Of course, she is," I mumble to myself.

"Come on, Emily, you know I hate to deny you, but this time I do believe your mother is right," he says in such a way I feel guilty for pouting at him. "You are a wonderful girl and will make a very fine wife one day."

"I do not want to make a very fine wife one day," I whine, "I want to stay young and free forever!"

"Oh, Em, we all wanted that, child," he says, and when I look at his kind eyes, I cannot help but melt a little in my stubbornness. "Besides, I think you will come to enjoy the piano once you know how to play. You certainly have the long fingers to master such a skill."

"I suppose so," I relent on a sigh, "and it will mean I get to still spend time with you, away from mother lecturing me on how not to conduct oneself in front of others."

"Precisely," he says with another wink. "Emily, my dear, you will fly, and I will enjoy seeing you soar!"

I am not even remotely convinced by his words, but for his sake, I will do all I can to make my parents proud. Even if it does mean that everything which I hold dear is about to change, and simply by turning one day older.

Time to grow up.

Time for the fun to end.

Chapter 1

Six years later

Emily

My mother had informed me that this would happen, that this was what was expected of a lady when being presented before possible suitors at a ball. What I didn't expect was to feel quite so much like a cow being studied for market with gentleman sizing me up amongst the other girls in their feathers, lace, and skirts. Neither did I expect to feel quite so constricted in my undergarments which are causing me to fidget and squirm like one of Elsie's lap dogs trying to escape from her clutches. As such, I've strategically positioned myself on the end of a long line of eligible ladies so I can shuffle around without being glared at. Goodness knows I've had enough of Mama doing that since the moment we arrived at Lord and Lady Cottingham's lavish estate. How she thinks I'm going to manage being married to someone without her supervision is something I've frequently questioned over the years; ever since the moment she hinted at a future union between myself and some lord somebody or other. Fortunately, with my ability to strategically hide myself away from view, this is something I hope I don't need to worry about for at least a few more years. Besides, they still have Elsie to marry off; I'm sure I'm a long way down on her list of priorities.

Speaking of which, my hiding spot happens to also be where I can see Edmund trying not to laugh at me from across the room. Easy for him; he's a man and therefore on the more fortunate side of this ridiculous little dance men and women must engage in. Not that I can stay jealous of him, not when he tried so hard to reassure me earlier today.

"Don't worry, Em," he had whispered to me, "this is only your first ball as a debutante. You are unlikely to meet your match on your first outing."

"How many of these things have you been to?" I asked, still feeling less than convinced by the whole thing.

"Too many to mention!" he laughed and pinched my nose with his usual, restrained affection. I giggled with him until I saw Mother watching on with a judgemental stare. She often reminds me of the warning she had given on my twelfth birthday, and the reasons as to why I could no longer 'play about' with Edmund. She had explained that even though we had grown up together, we were no longer children, and therefore eligible for scrutiny.

"And no one has caught your eye?" I teased, shuffling back so my mother might stop glaring.

"Oh, yes, she has," he muttered without looking me in the eye. I noticed a blush spreading over his usually pale cheeks and frowned at him, waiting for him to elaborate. "I'm just not so sure she's ready for me yet. She's very young."

"I think my sister might be holding out for you, Edmund," I smiled, choosing not to push him on this mystery girl.

Elsie is two years older than me, as is Edmund. One could say she's the complete opposite to me and is very much ready to marry and become a lady of society. You could also argue that part of the reason for this is so she can make all the other girls jealous. I have no such desire for I am a little indifferent to it all. Edmund is still Edmund and I'm still wishing I could run around the garden chasing after my best friend whilst climbing trees. We haven't been like that for a long time though, not since that awful twelfth birthday party when my childhood officially ended.

"Hmmm," he mumbled back before leaving to join his father at the gentlemen's club.

"Stop fidgeting, Emily," Elsie grumbles from in front of me. "You won't attract a husband if you continue shuffling about like a child back there."

"Why do you think I chose to crouch back here in the first place?" I huff back at her.

"Are you ever going to grow up?"

"I wasn't planning to, no," I reply with a small defiant smirk on my face. "Besides, Mother and Father won't truly be worried about me until they marry you off, Sister, dearest. This is merely practise to appease Mama!"

"My lords, ladies and gentlemen," a man with a rather large white wig and a booming voice calls out amongst all the chatter, silencing everyone within an instant. "May I present the Duke of Kent!"

The room erupts into muffled chatter and gasps of surprise, and I have to wonder what is so special about this man, other than the fact he is a duke.

"Elsie?" I whisper shout, only to tut when she ignores me. "Elsie, what's going on?" I repeat, but this time with me tugging on her satin skirts.

"The Duke of Kent is one of the most eligible Bachelors in England," she eventually replies as if under duress, "and rarely attends such events."

"Right, so?" I ask as I screw up my face in unladylike confusion, right before I notice Edmund laughing at me from across the room. He is gifted with a sly poke of my tongue and a ridiculous grin while Mama is too busy looking towards the door.

"So," Elsie's friend, Miranda, pipes in from beside her, "he's obviously on the lookout for a wife. It's about time, he is almost thirty. Very handsome too."

"He is in a perpetual bad mood," Annabeth joins in from the other side of Elsie. "Mother says she is yet to see him even smile. My maid says her sister works at his household and has described him as being proud, angry, and with impossibly high standards."

"Sounds appealing," I mutter under my breath.

"Shush!" Elsie hisses. "You need to stay quiet, or you'll get us into trouble. You could only be so hopeful as to be propositioned by someone like the duke. Not to mention, our very own father has a lot of business dealings with him. Whatever you do, Emily, do not cause a scene!"

With an audible sigh, I quickly look over at Edmund, who gives me a subtle wink before standing to attention in front of this man who sounds about as interesting as a morning at church. Hushed voices and the ladies in front all straightening up to attention tells me the Duke of Has-A-Smell-Under-His-Nose has just entered and officially begun the humiliating process of eyeing up the cattle before him.

"Good lord, he's so handsome," a few of them whisper

down the line, to which I can't help but roll my eyes. I have read many a book with a pretty cover, only to be thoroughly disappointed with the story inside. I have to agree with Father when he tells me that most of the ladies here are completely ridiculous and full of nothing but stuff and fluff in their heads.

A small huddle of gentlemen and waiting staff gather before us. With a sort of morbid curiosity, I watch as Elsie, Annabeth, and Miranda bow down in front of me. Of course, I am out of sync with everyone and end up staring at the small group before lowering myself with the rest of them. I expect Edmund has now fallen into fits of laughter over my bungling performance. More talking ensues and when I stand back up, one of them is pointing right at me; a handsome man with the finest of fabrics adorning his person.

The ladies in front of me, including Elsie, begin to part out of the way to reveal my hiding place. It's so unexpected, I end up looking behind me to see what it is they are pointing at. Strangely, there is nothing but a blank wall. Realising they must be pointing at me, I turn back to look into the icy blue eyes of the man the hall has been cooing over. He stares right back at me without expression. It's deeply unsettling. Thankfully, in the peripheries of my vision, I soon see my father making his way over, hopefully to save me.

"My Lord." Father bows before this man who must be about twenty years his junior. "This is my youngest daughter, Miss Emily Rothschild."

"Delighted." He utters this one worded response as though it tastes bitter on his tongue.

"And this is my eldest, Elise Rothschild. She is proficient in needlework, the pianoforte…well, they both are, but Elise…"

My father continues to sputter from the side of this man whose chilling orbs remain focused on me, causing my cheeks to heat and a deeply uncomfortable feeling to erupt inside of my chest. I have never seen my father react like this before someone; he is always in command, never answerable to anyone.

"Lord Rothschild, I would like to dance with your daughter," the duke demands, still not looking at anything else but me. "I trust this is agreeable with you."

"O-of course," Father replies, though, when I look at him with frightened eyes, he appears to be anything but agreeable.

"Good," the duke says with only a grimace of a smile before he holds his hand out for mine. I stare at his offering like it is a temptation I shouldn't fall prey to. "Miss Rothschild?" he says with an arch of his brow. His expression is one of impatience, but also one that reminds me of a picture I had once seen of the devil.

"Emily, go with the duke, child," Father laughs nervously. I cautiously take hold of his large hand, if only to save my father from his obvious embarrassment.

The duke leads the way onto the dance floor where other couples are being encouraged to join us. Fortunately, chatter soon ensues, to the same extent that it had done before the arrival of the duke. It comforts me for but a moment before he swings me around to begin a waltz, a dance I am not in any way proficient in performing. I even notice my mother wincing when he begins the movements with me. Meanwhile, Elsie has also joined the dancefloor with a rather pompous-looking gentleman. My father is stood to the side, drinking a large glass of punch, and with a furrowed brow of concern as he watches on. Whether this is due to the duke taking interest in me or because of my lack of grace on the dancefloor remains to be seen, though neither scenario fills me with any confidence. Edmund, my usual source of reassurance, has completely vanished from sight, which only has me feeling uncertain all over again. I so desperately want to see his friendly face, to comfort me in this most uncomfortable of situations.

"Miss Rothschild, you are new to this, no?" the duke finally asks me with a confidence that makes me feel even more timid in front of him.

"Yes," I murmur, instinctively looking to the floor when speaking to him.

"I would prefer it if you looked at my face when you addressed me, Miss Rothschild," he says. Against my wish to avoid his devilishly handsome, but painfully stern gaze, I force myself to look into his eyes which are such an icy blue, they make me shiver from their coldness. "I find I can understand you better if you look at me when you speak."

"My apologies, My Lord," I reply, like a well-trained student of elocution lessons. "I am, indeed, new to all of this."

"And what are your thoughts?" he asks without expression. It is almost bewitching how his face is able to remain so passive no matter what is being said.

"I am yet to decide," I reply honestly. "I fear I have not yet secured my understanding in all the things a lady of age should know."

"And how old are you, Miss Rothschild?" he asks, not appearing to care one little bit for whether this is an appropriate question to ask of someone he has just met. "You cannot have been of age for very long?"

"No," I admit, "this is my first ball as a debutante. I turned eighteen just last month."

We suddenly turn and I lose my footing for a moment or two. A heated blush spreads over my cheeks and I feel like I might have cried had it not been for the fact that I can now see Edmund hovering by the side of the dancefloor. I smile at him because he looks worried for me. For some reason, I want to reassure him, even though it is I who is in this precarious situation. When I turn my attention back towards the duke, I notice, for the first time, he is now frowning slightly, as though I have confused him.

"And who is that gentleman? Are you promised to him?" he asks rather bluntly. The question sounded accusatory, and I find myself emitting a nervous laugh, much like I do when my mother has caught me trying to escape outside.

"Who? Edmund?" I ask, trying to mask my giggling for fear of angering him with my immaturity.

"Are there more?" he asks with his frown dipping even lower between his eyes.

"No!" I reply with a hint of indignity.

"Then, yes, *Edmund*," he clarifies.

"Edmund and I grew up together," I explain with the same blank expression he had been giving me up until this strange conversation. "We are good friends, nothing more. Mama had told me on turning twelve that being of age means I am no longer able to keep company with him unless my mother or sister are with me. So, I don't."

"Quite!" he snaps.

"Have I spoken out of turn, Your Grace?" I ask after swaying about with his piercing blue eyes staring at me for longer than is comfortable.

"Not at all, though…" He trails off as he leans in towards my face. The sudden closeness has me tensing between his arms and wondering what he is planning to do in front of all these people, in front of Mama. "Your youth and naivety are more than obvious if you cannot realise when a gentleman is interested in being more than just your *friend*."

His words cause me to instantly look at Edmund and his concerned features, then back to the duke, who is now sporting a smirk that I should find insulting. However, my thoughts have suddenly turned to mush, so instead of telling him how I feel about his observation, I remain feeling limp, shocked, and unsettled within his arms. Fortunately, the music comes to an end, and he bows before me. A few uncomfortable seconds pass before I manage to force my body to wake up from its momentary paralysis, after which I force my mind to do the same. We then step apart from one another, me with my hands hanging down by my sides, him with his hands tucked behind his rigidly straight back. I do not feel relief like I had hoped, for it still feels like the whole room is watching.

"Miss Rothschild, your frame is small, your knowledge of social etiquette is, at best, patchy, and your footing leaves little to admire," he arrogantly assesses me, causing a heat of shame to spread all over my otherwise pale complexion. After remaining silent for a moment or two, he offers his arm and begins to lead me back to where my parents are waiting in nervous anticipation. Unfortunately for me, he does not appear to be finished in his verbal repertoire of insults and continues detailing all of my failings as we walk arm in arm across the room.

"You are young, naïve, and much too forward, which only gives away your immaturity. With that, I bid you good evening."

Whilst I feel a multitude of emotions over his callous

assessment of me, he nods his head to both my father and mother, satisfied with having delivered me back to them, then abruptly turns to leave. My body returns to its former numbness and my mouth hangs open in shock for the entire time I watch his back retreat to the exit. The urge to cry weighs heavily, and tears build rapidly in my eyes, though I refuse to let them fall.

"Em?" Edmund whispers to me from behind; I must have missed him in my state of shock. "Em, are you ok? You do not look yourself."

"I-I-I…" I stutter, even when he passes me a glass of punch to try and steady my nerves.

"Did he say something untoward to you?" Edmund asks, my mother and father remaining silent, no doubt wanting to know the answer to the exact same question. I take in a deep breath, shake away my feelings of unease, then place on my usual happy and relaxed expression; the one I usually have wear when in Edmund's company.

"No, he said nothing at all," I finally reply before returning to face my mother and father. "I'm afraid I don't think I made quite the right impression to tempt the duke."

Whilst my mother looks thoroughly disappointed, my father gifts me with a small smile from behind her and winks. It is no secret that I am his favourite and therefore has no desire to see me married before I am at least twenty. He merely entertains the idea of parading me around to keep my mother happy and with the understanding that this is simply practise for me. Edmund, however, still looks concerned, even when he turns to stare at the duke's retreating figure. The frown upon his usually placid face remains intact for a good long while after.

Tobias

A gentleman's club is the only place in this sort of society where I feel even remotely comfortable. The pomp and circumstance at this evening's ball was enough to drive me to whiskey and lots of it. I have never been one to join in with society's need to parade the wealthy and beautiful people of the upper classes around like an animal market. Fortunately, it looks like Frederick has already ordered the establishment's best bottle in readiness for me. I would thank him if he wasn't currently laughing over my rather dire situation.

"You danced with one girl!" he laughs at me. "One girl who is at least ten years your junior!"

"She was the only one handsome enough to turn my head," I mutter without a hint of interest behind my words, "and she'll do."

"You do not know her, Tobias," he tries to argue, "you need to court a girl before seeking her hand. Besides, she's young. Surely the poor girl needs to get used to you before she is signed over to you for the rest of her life."

"It matters not," I reply, tipping back the last mouthful left in my glass, "she will learn soon enough that I am not the stuff of fairy tales. This isn't some romantic union to read about in a bedtime story."

"No?" he says with far too much sarcasm for me to stomach after attending tonight's insufferable ball. "Not even with that pretty face of yours?" he continues to tease. His playful attitude causes me to slam my glass back onto the table, for I am in no mood for Frederick's smug banter. "Course, you do have that title of yours; I am sure there were plenty of girls there who would kill for a chance to be the new Duchess of Kent! Perhaps someone who is a little more experienced and less likely to crumble under your usual cantankerous mood."

"As long as she looks the part, bears a child or two, I will let her have a comfortable enough life. We will have our separate rooms, show up to the least amount of society events as possible, and speak rarely. I won't even force myself upon her until she is a few years older, and when I do, it will be for the sole purpose of producing an heir. The job is done!"

"You have to ask her father first," Frederik smirks at me, "he looked quite protective of his pride and joy. Did you not notice his nervous disposition when you practically demanded to dance with her? His attempts to sway you towards his eldest child? Not to mention his watchful eye the entire time you were trying to avoid her clumsy feet on the dance floor. Then, there's the admirer, the *friend*? You might even be too late. I saw the fear in that young man's eyes when you showed interest. He's most likely upon bended knee as we speak."

"Precisely why I am going to speak to her father as soon as he shows. Why else do you think I am here, drinking with you, when I could be at home drinking in my own company with a warm bed just a short walk away? Besides, who would refuse a man of my position? Edmund Barton is no higher in rank than her father. He certainly cannot take their family any further up the social ranking than they already are. Best he can do is marry the older sister who looked like she would bore me to tears and is not nearly as handsome."

"So romantic, Tobias, as always," he chuckles.

"What has romance got to do with getting married?"

"Some people like to marry for love," he says with a mocking, girlish sigh. "I fall in love frequently; you should try it sometime."

"Love never helped anyone to get anywhere. She should be grateful; I am doing her a great favour."

"Well, here's your chance, your grace," he says, pointing towards where Viscount Rothschild and Mr Barton have just entered the vicinity. I instantly notice the young pup, who is currently trying to bend the elder's ear. I sigh heavily, gulp back more liquor, and proceed to get up to approach both gentlemen. This should take less than ten minutes, after which, I can finally go home, far away from 'society'.

"Mr Rothschild, we have known one another for many years; I even count you as a second father figure! Our families are close enough to be called one another's already..."

Mr Barton continues begging, all the while gesturing with his hands flying all over the place, which only gives away how nervous he is. It would seem Frederick was entirely accurate.

"Edmund, I know how fond you are of Emily, but she is my youngest daughter, and in my opinion, not yet ready for marriage-"

"Yes, I understand completely, sir, but you cannot deny she is already gaining the attention of many gentlemen. It is only a matter of time before someone asks for your permission-"

"It doesn't mean they will have it, Edmund. She is my Emily, my pride and joy," he argues with a heavy sigh before signalling for two glasses of Brandy. "She is young and so full of life. She-"

"And I would keep her like that! I wouldn't change her for the world! I just want to make her mine before-"

"You see? You want to claim her too! Emily is my daughter and I want to keep it that way for a little while longer. You have to understand, Edmund."

"I do, but if I could just have your assurance that-"

"Viscount Rothschild, Mr Barton," I interrupt for I cannot bear to listen to the pup anymore, especially when he is trying to beg for my bride's hand. I am about to ruin his otherwise lovely day and I am going to do so, so I can be home within the next hour.

"Your Grace," the viscount flusters mid mouthful, just before they both nod their heads at me. I try to hide my smile when I notice how reluctant Mr Barton is to perform such a social nicety.

"Forgive me, I did not mean to interrupt your conversation," I lie, for this is exactly what I intended to do.

"Not at all, we were just discussing my youngest daughter with whom you danced with this evening." He smiles sheepishly before leaning in a little closer, as if not wishing to have others hear what he has to divulge. "She is still learning from her mother. Please accept my apologies for any steps that may have caused you a bruised toe."

We chuckle together out of politeness, though all Mr Barton can manage is a grimace while he looks me over with obvious contempt. I am about to give him good cause for the sentiment.

"Not to worry," I reply as I wave a hand, smiling tightly when I notice Frederick smirking in the peripheries of my vision. "I am sure she will be an expert soon enough. She is very beautiful, and I am honoured you gave me permission to have her first dance."

"It is I who is honoured," he expertly answers. "We do not expect her to form an attachment just yet; tonight was her first ball."

"Well, now that you mention it, I would like to take this opportunity to officially ask your permission for her hand in marriage."

It is almost comical to watch their reaction to my proposal. Both of their mouths have fallen open like a pair of gaping fish. In fact, the younger one has turned decidedly puce in complexion whilst the father now has no colour whatsoever. Be that as it may, I do not lose any of my confidence over it, instead, I remain rigid in my stature and without showing any hint of emotion. We all know the viscount would be foolish to refuse a duke as a future son-in-law.

"Mr Rothschild..." Mr Barton begins flustering but immediately silences under my glare.

"I apologise, I should have asked you when you were alone. Would you mind, Mr Barton?" I gesture for him to leave; however, the young calf remains frozen to the spot, still with his mouth hanging wide open.

"Yes, perhaps you could give us a moment, Edmund," the viscount gasps rather breathlessly without even looking back at Mr Barton. I give him a smile that is more smug than polite, to which he grinds his teeth together and finally turns to leave. *I am afraid you've lost, Mr Barton, my commiserations.*

"That is a very magnanimous offer, Your Grace, though I have to ask, why my Emily? She is young, inexperienced, and not yet confident in the social niceties of the ton."

I can tell he is asking because he desperately wants to turn me down. Fortunately for me, he knows he cannot do such a thing without word spreading. Such gossip that will not only make him look foolish in terms of business, but also to the society in which his wife seems more than keen to impress.

"I can tell she means a lot to you, Mr Rothschild, and with good reason." I smile momentarily, giving him a reprieve to consider my proposal with a more rational head. "She did indeed stand out from all the other ladies tonight. Besides, being young means I can train her into becoming the kind of duchess I require. She will bear beautiful children and will make a fine wife. Trust me, Mr Rothschild, I will take good care of her and make sure she is afforded every luxury she could ever dream of."

"I've no doubt you would treat her well, but…but…but she's my Emily!" he replies with emotion choking at his words. "Did you not see her sister, Elsie? She is older, more refined, more…more ready for this."

"I do not want anyone else but Emily, Mr Rothschild. I'm afraid this is not a negotiation. As for being *your* Emily, I have to question for how long. Her window to marry may have only just opened, but it will not be long before she has to marry, and then who will your options be? I will not wait, Mr Rothschild, and I do not know of any other eligible dukes looking for a wife. I have no need for her dowery, only her. So, what do you say, Mr Rothschild? Do we have an agreement? I urge you to think of Emily's aspirations, as well as your own."

I watch him without word while he orders yet another brandy, which he gulps back in one mouthful. Both Frederick and Edmund remain watching from the side lines with keen interest as the older man in front of me begins to perspire along his forehead. After a moment or two of being kept waiting, something I am not known to respond well to, I sigh and make a point of looking at my pocket watch.

"Erm, well…" he eventually gasps with an awkward smile, then shakes his head as if finally ready to consider his options with a level head. "Apologies, Your Grace, I wasn't expecting this to happen so soon with Emily, and especially not with someone of your stature." I simply smile tightly, still waiting for the answer that really matters. "Of course; you have my blessing."

"Perfect," I reply and tuck my watch back inside of my pocket. Frederick is now smiling to himself while Edmund has abruptly stomped away from the room altogether. "I will call on Emily tomorrow at ten. Please have her ready for me. I will be writing for special permission to marry her before the end of next week."

"W-What? Why so soon?" He wipes his brow as he stumbles over his words. "She will need time to get her head around all of this, to know what is expected-"

"All things I'm sure your wife can help her with over the next few days. I wish to return to Kent as soon as possible, so delaying the marriage will only hold me up unnecessarily. I bid you goodnight and look forward to seeing you in the morning."

"Er, yes, goodnight, Your Grace," he replies before shakily accepting my hand and nodding his goodbye.

Frederick soon stands to join me in finally leaving this God-awful place. I have no further wish to be here, and the call of my bed is much too strong to now ignore.

"Well, Tobias, my old friend, she's certainly a lucky girl!" he laughs as he clasps his hand over my shoulder, just before Mr Barton comes into view.

"Your Grace!" he shouts out as we pass him by without comment. "Your Grace!"

Sighing heavily, I turn with Frederick to face him while readying myself to defend my person with full force should the young calf decide to do something foolish. I would not put it past him to try and challenge me for a lady's hand that is already mine.

"P-please," he stutters, which only has me standing up straighter to my full height, for his blithering is not only irritating, but is also holding me back from my bed. Frederick shakes his head from the side, no doubt thinking what a cad I am for tearing apart this young couple in calf love.

"Can we hurry this along, Mr Barton?" I ask without feeling, just as he looks about ready to let his emotions come to the surface.

"P-please, will you look after her?" he asks in barely more than a whisper. "She isn't...I mean... just please, take care of her."

"Mr Barton, I fully intend on taking care of my future wife. I suggest you find another girl to become yours so you can keep out of my business. I will not warn you again," I threaten at the same time as I take a step towards him. "In fact, I think it best you stay away from Emily altogether. Once she accepts my proposal, she will be instructed to do the same. Goodnight, Mr Barton."

I wait for him to come back at me, to lose his calf temper, but to my surprise, he simply nods his head and remains slumped over. Frederick pulls back my arm, easing my temper and prompting me to turn and finally leave this place.

"Has anyone told you what a cold heart you have, Tobias?" Frederick mutters from the side of me.

"Many," I happily admit. "I've always taken it as a

compliment."

Chapter 2

Emily

"Up, Emily!" My mother chirrups from my bedroom curtains which she has just ripped open with enough enthusiasm to have the whole household up in a frenzy. The sun shines through into my eyes, and I groan in response to the punishing brightness. No sooner have I turned over to go back to sleep, than my mother is at my side, practically hauling me out of bed like my very life depends on it.

"Mother, what is going on? Why are you being more...*insistent* that usual?" I huff while rubbing my eye of sleep. She chooses not to answer me straight away, instead, I am pulled to the bathroom where she begins attacking my hair at the same time as ordering the maids to get fresh water and towels. When she causes me to wince in pain for the third or fourth time, I begin to develop anxiety deep inside of my gut.

"Emily, my dear," Father announces as he appears at my doorway looking tired and grey, "I-I-I..."

Before he can finish his sentence, he is suddenly overcome with emotion. He reaches out and pulls me into his embrace. He holds on so tightly; it reminds me of when he used to do the exact same thing when I was a small child after having fallen from my horse.

"Father, whatever is wrong? Has something happened to Elsie? Are you ill?" I gasp as I begin to feel tears building along my own eyes.

"No, no, nothing like that. It's…good news," he says unconvincingly from over my shoulder before pulling back to study me, still with tears streaming down his cheeks. "I'm just going to miss you, my darling girl!"

"Mama, what is he talking about?" My voice is small, and trembling and I finally give permission for my own tears to fall.

"Emily, what your father is trying to tell you, is you are about to become engaged!" Mother beams at me as she delivers this gut-wrenching blow.

"W-What? Engaged? After only one ball? No!" I cry, shaking my head while Papa finally emits his own whimper. "I don't want to be married yet. Who is it? Is it Edmund? Tell him I'll marry him next year, or at least when I know how to waltz properly!"

"Emily-" my mother tries to soothe me by rubbing at my arm, but I cut her off before she can say anything of worth.

"Please, you have to! Edmund will understand, he told me himself that I am too young, and I promise, I promise if he waits, I'll marry him with open arms-"

"It isn't Edmund!" my father cries over my pleas. His voice sounds stern and resolute, telling me without the words not to argue with him. A voice he rarely ever uses with me, which is so shocking, I momentarily forget what he has just told me. Whoever I am about to be engaged to is someone I do not know; it's not Edmund.

"Then who?" I whisper when I finally make sense of his

words.

"The Duke of Kent has asked for your hand in marriage, just last night," he tells me without any emotion. His straight face and rigid stance tell me he has already agreed to it. Agreed to it without even first talking to me. "He was quite insistent and has even refused your dowry."

"Th-the duke?" I ask with confusion and fear swimming around my head; a concoction that causes me to feel quite dizzy. "That man who said I was small, naïve, and virtually clueless in how to be a real lady?!"

"The very same," Father admits. His stony expression cracks as he looks at the ground with a sheepish expression, though not enough to give me any hope of him relenting in his decision. "He is on his way over here now; he wants you to be wed by the end of next week. I've given him my blessing, Emily."

"No, please, no! He was so horrid to me. Besides, what about Edmund?" I cry with painful tears prickling at the backs of my eyes, and all the while clinging onto my father's arms. I am so overwrought with emotion, I no longer care if this goes against everything my mother has tried to teach me about how to compose oneself before my father, or anyone, for that matter.

"Admittedly, Edmund had asked me before the duke," he says sadly, to which my mother gasps in shock. "However, I told him I was unwilling to let you go, at least, not yet. I told him I thought you were too young. Before we could argue anymore on the subject, the duke brought forth his proposal. He reminded me that he is the best option for you. He also made it quite clear that he is not willing to wait. Emily, you cannot refuse such an offer!"

"But what about Elsie? She is older, more learned, and desperate to marry someone like him!" I try to bargain.

"Emily, I tried to offer Elsie in your stead, but he was insistent that he wants you and only you," he says as he pushes me into my mother's arms for comfort. I let him, for I am now so overcome with sobbing, I can no longer hold onto him. "Emily, I am your father and I insist you accept his proposal, for all our sakes, as well as your own. If you do not, I will have no option other than to show you the very gravest of consequences. Emily, if I let you defy me, I will be just as ruined as you."

"Papa," I cry with so many tears in my eyes, I can no longer see him properly and my throat hurts from sobbing so hard.

"Listen to your father, Em," Mother coos in my ear while she strokes my hair, "this will make you a duchess, and he has promised to take great care of you."

"I am sorry, Emily, truly I am," my father softens, "your mother is right though; you will want for nothing!"

As I stand, cradled in my mother's arms and with my father reaching out for me, even after his harsh words, I finally relent and nod in acceptance of my new fate.

Mother made me wear one of Elsie's ballgowns and even primped my hair with feathers and pearls; it was all pinned up and pulling at my scalp like claws scratching at my head. If I can at all help it, I never wear my hair up. A stubbornness I usually get away with because wearing it back makes me appear more like a grown up; Father has always wanted to keep me looking like his youngest little girl.

As I waddle into the room like an awkward goose, Elsie practically glares at me while Mother escorts me over to perch on the best sofa. I cannot help tutting when I am shuffled about with strategic arrangements of my limbs, but still, my sister will not smile. I have no idea why she is so angry with me; I would gladly swap places with her.

"What time is it, Molly?" Mother asks one of the maids.

"It's nearly ten o'clock, Lady Rothschild; everything is prepared for His Grace," she says with a nod of her head. I cannot help thinking that even she is more primed to exercise social niceties than I am. How am I ever going to survive being a duchess, a wife, or even a grown woman?!

"Good, good," she replies, still looking at me as though contemplating how to make me look even more presentable to the duke when he arrives. Though, in the end, she simply sighs, as though I am a lost cause. I suppose the duke will have to accept me as I am.

"Emily, don't fidget, don't slouch, and do not, whatever you do, shrug your shoulders when he asks you a question."

I notice Elsie finally relinquishing her battle to remain looking bitter as she curls up the corner of her lips, as though relishing in my humiliation. Before she notices me watching her, I sigh heavily and look to the floor so she cannot see my tears building.

"And don't sigh, Child!" Mother snaps at me, but when I look up with a few stray tears escaping, her face immediately softens. "You can do this, Em, you can do this!"

"Can I, Mother?" I whimper. "Because I don't think I can."

She kisses my cheek, seemingly ignoring my question, and

listens for the sound of male voices talking from out in the reception hallway. My breathing quickens and my heart begins to pound inside of my chest. It feels as though it is bursting to get out so, it too, can run and hide. Mother must notice my mounting fear for she takes a moment to show me how to take in a few deep breaths. When I begin to copy her example, she offers me a reassuring smile that makes me feel like I am eight years old again.

The door clicks open, and I bolt upright to face the man who is demanding to make me his. I stand to attention, then notice Elsie sitting in the corner of the room with her embroidery, looking almost as sad as I feel. My father leads the way only to move to one side to reveal the tall outline of the duke with his imposing stature and piercing blue eyes. His other features only come into focus when I gain back some of my breath. Elsie is now looking him over with appreciation for how attractive he is. Like a Greek tragedy, the wrappings are pretty, the story is monstrous.

"Good morning, Your Grace," my mother welcomes him in with perfect finesse. "We are pleased to receive you this morning. I trust you are well?"

"Very, thank you, Viscountess Rothschild," he relies with a stiff nod of his head. "I thank you for your hospitality."

"It is our pleasure to have such esteemed company," she beams while I try not to roll my eyes over the long winded back and forth between gentry. It is a performance I have seen many times before, though never with a duke involved. "My daughter, Elsie," she says at the same time as gesturing over to my miserable looking sister. He barely acknowledges her, merely smiles, and nods before returning his gaze to my mother. Elsie, on the other hand, is now sporting a bright red complexion while looking awkwardly at the floor. "And, of course, you remember my youngest, Emily."

"Of course," he replies, not yet looking at me, but I still bow before him for fear of Mama chastising me in front of this man who is going to be my husband. "Might I have the pleasure of talking to Miss Emily alone?"

Mother looks back at me with worry in her eyes, only to look back at the duke and curtsey in submission. After she has retained her usual stature, she quickly and unsubtly begins to round up my sister and make a move toward the doors. I desperately want to scream for them to come back, or perhaps run out with them, but then I remember my father's words. Against all my natural instincts, I remain rooted to the spot.

When my eyes reluctantly return to the duke, I swallow hard over how intensely he is staring at me. It feels as though he is silently assessing me in the light of day, studying me for imperfections to make sure he hasn't made an error in his decision to take me for his own.

"Please, sit down, Miss Rothschild," he instructs in my very own house. He watches me do as I am told before taking the seat opposite, removing his gloves, and then making himself comfortable before me. "I trust you have been informed of my intentions, Miss Rothschild?"

My mouth has turned bone dry, so I look at the floor and nod. He most likely thinks I am behaving as a child would with my timidity, but it is all I can do to stop myself from running away and hiding.

"Speak, Emily," he instructs with a cold tone to his voice. "I do not suffer fools, neither do I believe you are one. Please do not act as such."

"Forgive me, Your Grace, your presence and intentions have made me a little nervous," I answer truthfully. "I fear you are much too grand for someone like me."

"Undoubtedly," he replies with a smug expression, "though you are beautiful enough to have warranted my attention."

"Thank you," I reply like I know mother would want me to. Not that this was my first thought after he just insulted me. In fact, the words that initially sprung to mind are ones I have never dreamed to even think about before meeting this man.

"I am offering marriage, by the end of the week. I have been repeatedly reminded I need to sire an heir, an inconvenience more than a desire, let me assure you. We will live on my estate in Kent, with separate rooms and separate staff. You will be educated in how to conduct yourself as a duchess; Lord knows your knowledge in social etiquette is severely lacking. You will be dressed in the finest of fabrics and presented at various social events throughout the year. When you are twenty years of age, you will be expected to bear me an heir. Other than that, we will lead very separate lives, Emily."

"Ok," I whisper, at the same time fidgeting with a bead on Elsie's dress while trying not to be sick. Mama's warnings spring to mind but I cannot begin to force myself to stop in my anxious fiddling.

"*Ok?*" he parrots back sternly, just like my governess used to chastise me when I did not know the answer to one of her questions. And like I used to do with her, all I can manage is a slight nod of my head before looking down at my gloved fingers. He merely tuts before taking hold of one of my hands, to which I gasp. When he continues holding my hand without any care for my shocked reaction, I force myself to look up into his icy blue eyes. With his other hand, he produces an ornate looking ring, gold with three emeralds clasped across the middle.

"Do you accept my proposal, Miss Rothschild?"

No, never! I would rather drown in the river than be with you!

"Yes," I murmur, even though he is already pushing the ring on with force before I have finished enunciating the word.

"Good," he replies before getting straight to his feet again. "I will inform your father of your acceptance and make my way to meet with the priest straight away. All being well, I shall see you next Friday, sharp at ten. Have your things ready to leave for Kent that day. I suggest you say your goodbyes before we are married; I will not be left waiting, Miss Rothschild."

I nod my head sadly and follow behind as he walks to the door, obviously being more than ready to leave after having secured his new property.

"And Miss Rothschild?" he says before finally leaving, "The young man with whom you are *friends*?" I look up at him with confusion and a halt of my steps, waiting for him to elaborate before I give any other sort of reaction. "It is no longer appropriate or acceptable to have any further contact with him. Do you understand?"

"May I tell him goodbye?" I ask, no longer caring if this is, or is not, the socially acceptable thing to do. Edmund and I have been friends since childhood; he is like a brother to me.

"You may write him a letter which your father will check before sending," he informs me while pulling on his gloves. "We are officially engaged, Miss Rothschild, and I will not be insulted by you consorting with other men. Should you ever defy me, there will be consequences, understand?"

"Yes," I whisper with a hard lump in my throat.

"Yes, what?" he snaps with his eyes piercing right through mine.

"Yes, Your Grace," I reply, seemingly placating him before he finally leaves.

Tobias

The church is arranged, Frederick is to attend as my best man, and my staff have been informed over our impending arrival by the end of the week. I could have gone to purchase a new suit for the occasion, however, the urge to go and have a drink with Frederick at the gentleman's club took precedence. Of course, now that I am here, listening to him laughing at me over my description of the proposal, I am not altogether sure I made the right choice. However, I am already three drinks in, so at this point, I merely shrug when he teases me over my lack of tact and willingness to sweep a lady off her feet.

"I hear congratulations are in order, Your Grace," Lord Bartholomew toasts his tumbler of amber liquid my way, to which I salute him with a half-smile, half-grimace. "A very handsome young lady too, though, a little young for you, isn't she?"

The stout man with a bushy set of eyebrows, ridiculous sideburns and a curling moustache, questions me whilst frowning over my choice of wife. I am not surprised given he often socialises with Viscount Rothschild, and with him, Mr Barton. I am sure I have well and truly pushed his nose out of joint too.

"She is of age," I retort without much care behind it, "and her lack of years will make her easier to train."

"Quite!" He laughs unconvincingly while looking put out

by my blasé attitude toward the young lady in question. "I remember when Miss Rothschild was still ten years old and climbing trees with my young godson, Edmund. I always believed they would be married one day, so did he."

I smile smugly to myself, now understanding why the old man before me is suddenly so interested in my proposal to Miss Rothschild. I merely shrug at him, looking deeply amused and not at all sorry over barging in between the young couple. Frederick is trying but a little harder to hide his mirth, but is still not making much of an impression on our new audience.

Eventually, after not receiving the required reaction from me, the old man wanders off, shaking his head before re-joining his group of other old, pompous looking gentlemen at the bar. Frederick and I chuckle over the odd glare we garner from one or two of them before ordering another glass of something amber and alcoholic.

"Well, Your Grace, always making friends wherever you go." Frederick smirks at me. "And don't look now, but Lord Bartholomew's godson has just walked in with your future father-in-law."

He pushes his chin out towards the door where Viscount Rothschild and Mr Barton have just appeared, both of whom are looking extremely forlorn. Sighing heavily over the fact I will have to play nice with my betrothed's father, I sit up straighter, and try to look a little more approachable. I have to at least pretend to acknowledge that we are to be family in the very near future. Frederick purses his lips over the sound of approaching footsteps whilst I take in one more healthy gulp of my drink. Only when they are right next to me do I turn to see my future father-in-law, looking at me with a fake smile and pale complexion.

"Viscount Rothschild," I greet him by standing and nodding his way. "I trust my future bride is well?"

"Yes, of course," he flusters before glancing at Frederick for a moment or two. "Though, admittedly, she is a little overwhelmed by how fast everything is happening."

"Well, best to get these things done and out of the way," I reply.

"She was rather hoping to say a proper goodbye to her friends before being taken across the country to her new home," he says, looking briefly to the side to where Mr Barton is now standing with a thoroughly angry expression.

"I feel for her, but I do think it is rather inappropriate for a girl of age to be consorting with a young man, especially when she is engaged to another."

"I understand, Your Grace, but if she were to be chaperoned by her mother, surely it would pose no threat to your engagement," he counters.

I am about to make my feelings on the matter a little clearer, if not with a hint of insistence when Frederick intercepts.

"Perhaps if His Grace was to be present too," he offers, taking no note of my mounting anger.

"An excellent idea!" The viscount practically beams. "Why, we would be more than happy to have you come and visit our grounds whilst the childhood friends say goodbye to one another. They have been like siblings, after all."

"Very well," I grind through my teeth, "tomorrow at two."

"Perfect, I shall inform both Emily and her mother." He

grins after his win. "I shall, er, leave you to your drinks, Your Grace."

He turns to nod at Fredrick as though silently thanking him for intervening on his behalf. I merely glare after him before slumping myself down inside of the armchair. Frederick practically spits out a laugh before holding out his hands defensively in front of him, as if such an action will stop me from gifting him my wrath.

"I apologise, Tobias, but you looked like you needed a little help in maintaining bridges between you and your new in-laws," he chuckles. "Besides, you must have a little sympathy for your future wife. Being married to you is unlikely to be much fun for her."

"Next time you think I need help, please don't!" I growl before getting to my feet and storming out of the smoke-filled room as fast as I can. If I do not, I may well say something that I would later regret. We have said worse in the past, but my patience is waning, and I am tired from acting at all interested in the people around me.

As I walk out into the cold night air with only the sound of my echoing footsteps, I have an overwhelming feeling that someone is following me. Without a moment's pause to think, I slow down, heavily sigh in frustration before I eventually come to an overall stop. If the young calf is about to do something stupid, I at least want to face him before I put him out cold.

"Something to say, Mr Barton?" I voice into the cool night air, making him gasp when I finally turn to face him without any hint of surprise on my face. "Your anxious breathing gives you away."

"I just want to know why," he growls at me, clearly losing

the social niceties with which he would have been educated. "Why Emily? Why my Emily?"

"You forget your place, Mr Barton, she is *my* Emily now," I counter with my jaw tensing up in anger over his lack of respect. "In fact, I don't believe she was ever your Emily, was she? I heard your desperate pleas to her father, as well as his very firm refusal."

"I have loved Emily since the day she and I played make believe weddings, when she was just ten years old," he sighs sadly, looking lost in childhood memories. "I fell from one of the trees in her back garden, so she took off her sash to wrap around my sprained ankle. It did nothing to soothe the pain, but the kiss she gifted to my forehead was enough to make me smile through it. I knew then that I wanted that wedding to be one day real, to be her husband and take care of her the way she had taken care of me."

"Touching, Mr Barton," I finally reply after a moment or two of watching him being lost to his sadness. My heart is not completely black...yet. "But it is exactly that; a childhood memory, nothing more, Mr Barton. In answer to your question, Emily Rothschild is from a reputable family of good standing, and the only girl to have piqued my interest over the last few years. She will bear beautiful children and nurture them just as you have described. That is all I need; I have no other answer for you."

"Please don't take her from me," he whispers with his face pointing sheepishly towards the ground. "You can have anyone, Your Grace. Emily needs friendship, a companion to listen to her wild tales, someone to see her for the amazing woman that she has become. Please, I beg of you, don't take her away from me!"

"Mr Barton, I already have," I reply before about turning and marching towards my coach. Before I instruct my driver to go, I feel a momentary pang of guilt, so I turn towards the window where I see his slumped figure in the darkness. "I can offer you this, Mr Barton, Emily Rothschild will be looked after as well as one can be. She will want for nothing."

"What you are offering isn't what Emily wants. You cannot offer her what she needs," he mutters back.

"Very well," I reply coldly, "goodnight, Mr Barton."

Chapter 3

Emily

I had told myself I wasn't going to do this, that I was going to hold my head up high and not let my future husband get me down during my last few days at home. Yet here I am, huddled against my mother, on my childhood bed, crying with tired eyes and a painful throat. Mother does not offer me any words of comfort, for in all honesty, I don't think she has any. Instead, she strokes my hair and shushes me gently against her lap. I keep waiting to wake up, to realise this is nothing more than a bad dream, something to tell my father about in the morning. We would laugh with one another, and he would promise to never make me do such a thing.

Out of the corner of my blurry vision, I notice Elsie hovering about by the door, dressed in her night gown and an extremely anxious-looking expression. My mother seems to notice at the exact same time and holds her hand out for her to come and sit with us. She virtually runs over to join us in this sad huddle, where she releases her own tears. As much as we bang heads against one another, we do share a close relationship, one that has had us laughing and joking on many occasions.

"Don't cry, Em," she says to me, even though she is now crying just as hard, "you are fortunate to have made such a match."

"If you are to lie to me, sister, at least do it with a smile on your face," I reply, to which she laughs a little. I have always been the brasher sibling, the one who is much more likely to embarrass my mother with my clumsy frame and need to speak my mind.

"You know I would take your place if I could," she says as she reaches out to clasp hold of my hand. "But to marry a duke is the best one could ever hope for, especially on her very first outing. You will be the talk of society!"

"I do not care that he is a duke; he is a vile man who clearly thinks I am nothing more than a commodity!"

"Em, most gentlemen think that. We are commodities to show before society, to make a match of convenience. Papa and Edmund are the exception to the rule. Very rarely are wives and husbands truly friends. Most of them reside in separate rooms, if not separate houses!"

"Thankfully, he has already told me we will be sleeping separately. I cannot imagine having to sleep in the same bed as a man, especially a man like Tobias Hardy. The more I hear of him, the more I am feeling sick over the thought of having to marry him."

As I finish my sorry sounding admission, I notice mother and Elsie exchanging a look, one that doesn't comfort me in any sort of way.

"Emily, darling," my mother begins, "I have never spoken to you about such things because I always thought we had more time-"

"Good news, my darlings!" my father calls up from the

staircase as he begins climbing with echoing footsteps. My heart momentarily lifts with hope, thinking that maybe the duke has called off the wedding altogether. However, when he pops his head around the door with a reddish hue, compliments of the expensive brandy he enjoys at the gentlemen's club, he notices my puffy eyes, snotty nose, and looks sheepishly to the ground. When he eventually lifts his head and seemingly ignores my falling apart, he plants on a grin that is enough to have me start whimpering again.

"The duke has agreed to chaperone your final meeting with Edmund tomorrow, Em," he says with a smile. Though, it is so sad and obviously ingenuine, I decide to ease his guilt by planting on my own fake smile.

"That's wonderful, Father," I reply through shaky breaths. "Thank you, Papa. You don't know how much that means to me."

"You are welcome, my darling," he whispers before placing a soft kiss on my head. "Try to get some sleep, Em. Things will seem better in the morning; they always do!"

"You are right, goodnight, Father," I reply before watching him leave. My mother pulls me in that much tighter, as though thanking me for putting on a brave face before him.

Tobias

Each morning is the same as the one before it, lost in a haze of too much booze from the previous evening, while trying to remember the two women who ever meant something to me. I was merely a small boy when my mother died, not long after having my sister, Genevieve. Complications from childbirth led to an infection she was not strong enough to fight. My father unfairly blamed my sister for his wife's demise and refused to have any kind of loving relationship with her. The man was pure evil when it came to my sister, as well as a ridiculous drunk who lost any sort of rational thought after he had had to bury his wife. I am almost certain he only gave me the time of day because I was his only son and heir. I played my role as the dutiful son by way of attempting to cover his misdemeanours that were usually fuelled by too much booze and a shockingly bad temper, but I never much liked the man.

I refused to shed a tear when he died. However, I did make a promise to continue the Hardy bloodline. He had made me swear on my mother's soul, for if I refused, he would have had no choice but to leave the entire estate to his equally drunk brother. Not only that, but the Hardy fortune and real estate would have eventually been left in the hands of one of my ridiculous cousins; boys who like to gamble, drink, and play with loose women. As much as I find the idea of marriage and fatherhood deeply unappealing, I was not going to let any of those fools take over my mother's house. Besides, the running of the estate does not only affect me, but I also have my tenants to think of. I may have a cold-hearted reputation that causes girls like my betrothed to shudder before me, but I have always taken my responsibilities very seriously.

With my mother dead and my father an embarrassment to me, I only had my sister, Genni, to call family. I loved her as much as I had loved our mother. Even if I hadn't, I would have done all that I could to protect her, for Mother had made me promise that I would, also when on her deathbed.

"Tobias, my darling boy, you must look after your sister," *my mother whispered through uneven breaths. The pain of her* *infection was more than evident with the frequent wincing across*

her face. "You are her brother, the one she can rely on and take comfort from."

"I will, Mama," I promised through my whimpering. I knew she was on her way out of this world and that I would never see her again after today. I was frightened for her, for me, and for the baby sleeping soundly by her side; my sister who was completely unaware of any of this happening.

"You're such a good boy, Tobias." With a shallow intake of breath, she tried to smile at me. "You always have been and always will be," she said as she brushed back my hair. However, her touch was so weak, she was barely able to make it move. "I know you're going to break hearts one day, my handsome son."

Genevieve was born weak, and with an affliction to the mind that would eventually cut her life short. No one knew she was born with such an ailment. In fact, only two other people knew about her condition before she died, myself and her governess. I kept it hidden from others to protect her from medics who may have sought to take her away from me. When I was eventually sent away to school, I had to enlist the help of her governess. It was while she was in her care, she passed on. The fact that I was not there with her has left me feeling guilty ever since. Grief and guilt are thoroughly ugly emotions that leave you feeling impotent and beholden to them. Other than Frederick, I have purposely avoided personal relationships, thus shielding myself from any future risk of their infection.

I still remember my mother though. Her voice more than anything else. She was always singing, and would often sweep me up inside of her arms to dance around whichever room we happened to be in. After she died, I refused to listen to music, and even promised myself that I would never listen to a single melody ever again. A decision I could not uphold due to it being nearly everywhere a duke is expected to attend. Yet another reason for my hatred of societal balls. It almost made me laugh when I discovered my future wife has even poorer foot skills than me. She will certainly need work. A lot of work.

Yet looking at her now, walking with the young pup, Mr Barton, I still find her mesmerising. If I could pin her to my wall back in Kent, I would make her a silent picture for me to look on whenever I so chose to. Alas, I need more than a picture of her. I need a wife to carry on my arm, a woman to give me my heir, and a mother to nurture my children. I do not need anyone to tell me what a cold, callous, and selfish man I am, for I am already more than aware. However, I simply gave up caring the moment my father died. The only feelings I was afflicted with when he passed on was overwhelming anxiety over becoming the new Duke of Kent, and last surviving male heir of the Hardy name on our side of the family. It was as if my heart finally sealed itself shut the moment that he was lowered into the ground beneath. Life had cursed me to lose any woman with whom I had had any connection but was still practically forcing me to continue my father's legacy with a bow and a smile.

"Your Grace, would you care for more tea?" Mrs Rothschild asks while my eyes remain on the young couple ahead of me with suspicion. Truthfully, I do not think my young bride is conscious of having romantic feelings towards Mr Barton, but he has made it quite clear that he would marry her in a heartbeat.

"No, thank you, Mrs Rothschild, I am quite 'teaed' out," I reply with a momentary smile for her before returning my gaze on Mr Barton.

"Forgive me, Your Grace, but I feel I should warn you that Emily is not very worldy wise," she says, to which I roll my eyes before forcing myself to look back at her with a fake smile. I knew this conversation would be coming my way soon, but now that it is upon me, I still don't feel I have enough patience to endure it. "I thought I had more time to school her in such things but, well, I must say your proposal came a little out of the blue."

"You need not fear, Mrs Rothschild, I will ensure she is schooled in all things necessary after we are wed this Friday," I reply tightly, thinking to myself how much the girl has obviously been wrapped up and shielded from the world, simply because she is her father's favourite. I would question as to why she thought it a good idea to present her to society before she was ready, but instead, I smile and hold my tongue.

"W-what I mean to say…" she continues, but then pauses to sigh while blushing so brightly, I have a desire to get up and walk away before she can finish her sentence. "What I mean to say, is Emily is not aware of the physical aspects of marriage."

I stare at her for a long moment, my expression neutral, even though I am enjoying the uncomfortable feeling I am no doubt inflicting upon her with my cold stare. It is only when she can no longer hold my eye contact and drops her head, that I decide to respond.

"She will," I finally reply, inwardly smirking to myself over her shocked expression. I am sure if I wasn't a duke, she would have been tempted to slap me for being so crass about her youngest daughter. "However, I have already explained to Emily that I will not expect her to produce an heir until she is at least twenty years of age. Does that put your fears to rest, Mrs Rothschild?"

"Please do not think I was-" she flusters, looking halfway between embarrassed and angry.

"I think it is time that I go and spend some time with my future bride myself," I interrupt her at the same time as getting to my feet to leave. "After all, she is going to be spending the rest of her life with me."

"Quite!" her mother mutters under her breath, which I leave unanswered while making my way over to the river that runs through the back of the Rothschild's residence.

Emily

Edmund and I had initially said nothing to one another when the duke had escorted me through my own home and into the back garden. It was a strange situation to be chaperoned by a man I hardly knew, particularly when the other party was a boy who had once been like a brother to me. Lord Hardy had kept a tight lip and a set of thunderous eyes on us the entire time. It was more than obvious he distrusts Edmund and was not at all happy about this arrangement. Had it not been for Mama offering to serve tea to him on the terrace, I do not think he would have left my side.

"Tell me, how you are doing, Em? Really?" Edmund asks as we walk alongside the river, trying hard to ignore the continuing cold stare from my future husband.

"Edmund, what would be the point of telling you that when we both know how I must be feeling. If this is to be our last encounter together…" I begin before having to pause to take in a deep breath of air noisily through my nose to ward of my threatening tears. However, it is only after Edmund subtly touches the top of my arm with a warm smile that I manage to calm down. Fortunately, the duke happens to be looking at Mama at this very moment, otherwise I'm quite sure our walk would have been cut short. We smile at one another once more before I attempt to continue. "What I mean to say is, if this is our last meeting for a while, then let us talk of other things. Things that might bring us comfort during the dark times ahead."

"Hmmm, what to talk about to make you smile?" he says jovially as we continue our pacing alongside the water's edge. "How about some town gossip? You've always enjoyed a bit of the ridiculous to make you forget your woes," he says, and I blush over how well he knows me.

As much as it pains me to admit it, but Lord Hardy may have been right in his earlier assessment of Edmund and his feelings for me. However, now is not the time to ponder on such things. Besides, it makes little difference now; Edmund and I are not destined to be together in that way.

"Did you know your sister's friend, Miranda, has been offered two marriage proposals?"

He laughs awkwardly because it is hardly surprising given how flirtatious she is, though it would not be polite to say such a thing out loud. Still, she seems to manage to gain a man's attention without even risking a dent to her reputation. Elsie and I have gossiped many times about how much of a mystery it is.

"I still think Elsie is waiting for you to show interest, Edmund, especially now that I'm…" I trail off sadly.

"I asked your father for permission, you know," he says to me with a hint of embarrassment, but mainly sadness.

"To marry Elise?" I ask, smiling in shock as I do so.

"No, silly, to marry you, Em," he laughs at me, "to be my wife and to live ridiculously in love in London together."

"Oh." I sigh, for him admitting such a thing in the open confuses my emotions somewhat. It forces me to think on it and consider how I really feel about him. On the one hand, I would much rather marry someone like Edmund, my friend. On the other, I am sure this is all Edmund is to me - a friend. I guess it is very rare to marry someone for whom you have real feelings, especially when you are a lady in my position. Status, money, and titles are considered far more important than emotions such as love. In any case, Edmund's unrequited romantic love for me is not something I need to voice, for the match is now impossible.

"He told me he wanted to keep you his for a while longer, that you were too young," he sighs, "right before the duke offered his proposal. I guess your father didn't have much of a choice."

"I know," I reply sadly, sounding only partially convinced. Did my father really have no choice in the matter? Could he have refused if he had really wanted to?

"Em, if your father had refused, he would have been ridiculed for passing up such a proposal, most likely accused of being under his own daughter's thumb," he tries to argue. "You know how dangerous town gossip can be, especially to people in our position. Your father has a formidable reputation, one he has to maintain. Em, you have to understand how reluctant he was. The duke was quite insistent."

"But why, Edmund?" I gasp with exasperation in my voice. I probably sound like a child whining to her mama, but I cannot help being desperate for an explanation as to why this man has sought my hand when he doesn't even appear to like me. With one last pout, I declare, "I do not understand why he had to choose me!"

"Do you really not, Em?" he asks with a soft laugh, now turning my way with eyes that are looking at me as if I am made of pure gold. It unsettles me, especially with my future husband's beady eyes on our every movement. My voice freezes up and I remain stuck still as a statue when he lifts his thumb up towards my cheek to brush away a stray tear. "How can you not know why he chose you?"

"I think your time is up, Mr Barton," the duke says abruptly from behind me. "Say goodbye, Miss Rothschild!"

"Of course, I-I am sorry," Edmund replies uncomfortably, stepping back as he does so. "I wish you both well."

"Edmund…" I whisper, not quite believing this is finally it between us.

"Goodbye, Em," he replies, just as quietly, and as if he is about to lose the battle against his tears. It is so heart breaking, I cannot help but clench my jaw in anger towards the man still standing behind me.

"Goodbye," I mutter, dropping my head when he finally turns to leave, for I cannot bear to look at his slumped body sloping away.

Lord Hardy, however, is still there, stood at my back. He is so close I can feel the heat from his body as well as his heavy breath on my neck. As an act of defiance, I choose to stay turned away from him. In fact, it is not until I feel his fingers clasping hold of my elbow that I make any kind of movement. When I still refuse to turn, he pinches harder at my sleeve, so I have no choice but to face the villain before me.

His eyes are still a cold, icy, body shivering blue which stare down at me with the same condescension that he had had for me at the ball. They judge me without apology or subtlety and are coupled with an arrogant smirk on his face, one that knows how handsome he is but also how cruel. At the sight of that curl of his lip, I fist my hands to stop myself from clawing at his perfectly styled, raven black hair. He waits for me to speak first, to acknowledge him as my betrothed.

"Will you always refer to me as Miss Rothschild?" I finally ask. However, he keeps me waiting for his own response, just to the point of me wanting to scream at him.

"Soon you will be Mrs Hardy, a duchess, and Miss Rothschild will be but a memory of who you once were," he replies with his hands now clasped behind his back.

"A decision I am still unsure as to how you came to," I counter, being both honest and blunt. "You do not seem to even like me or consider me anything more than a painting to stare at. A piece that hangs in a clumsy frame."

"An interesting metaphor, Miss Rothschild," he smirks once again, "one that is accurate. However, a frame can be replaced, much like your less desirable qualities can be trained out of you. Take off your glove."

"Excuse me?" I frown at him over the sudden change in conversation, which I would describe as a demand rather than a request.

"Take.Off.Your.Glove." He instructs me as though I am a petulant child that needs reminding of who her elders are. I stare at him rebelliously, to which he stares right back, arching his eyebrow as if communicating a threat of his own source of punishment if I do not do as he says. I remember my mother advising me to pick my battles carefully when I was younger. I was frequently reprimanded for speaking out against the other girls when they teased me for acting more like a boy. Realising that I am about to live the rest of my life with this man, no matter how intensely I dislike him, I decide to give in and remove the glove from my hand. However, I do so with an audible sigh and a severely irritated expression on my face.

Only when the glove is completely removed does he look

down toward my exposed hand. He then, ever so casually and purposefully, takes his time to unclasp his own hands from behind his back and finally takes hold of it. Staring, turning, brushing the pads underneath, then bringing it up to his nose to smell, he keeps his grip while staring intensely into my eyes. My breathing hitches for it feels much too intimate for a stranger, a man no less, to be handling a part of my naked body in such a way.

His eyes drop down to my mouth, where my lips are gaping wide open, only because I feel as though I need the extra air to survive the sudden intensity of the situation. He leans in closer, which only has my heart now joining in with my rapid breath, terrified yet strangely curious over the idea that he might kiss me.

"Your hands are calloused, Emily," he observes, calling me by my first name for perhaps the first ever time. "Too much running around like a boy. I would place money on the fact your mother made you frequently wash your hands after you had been out galivanting around the woods. Most inappropriate for a lady in your position. I think it is a good thing I came for you when I did."

"A good thing for whom?" I nervously ask, still breathing far too wildly to try and pass for being aloof to his charms.

"For me, it turns out," he says while moving just that little bit closer. "We are to be together a long time, Emily, please do not defy me every step of the way. You do not want to see me lose my temper."

I open my mouth to argue because his arrogance has now offended me one too many times to hold my tongue. However, before I can even utter a single word, he places a finger to my lips and 'shushes' me like I am nothing more than an errant child.

"Until Friday, my young bride." He smiles wickedly before about turning to march across the garden with a swagger I do not enjoy watching. Even with his back to me, he seems to judge without apology.

Chapter 4

Tobias

Checking my pocket-watch for perhaps the tenth time since arriving here, I side eye Frederick attempting to charm one of Emily's bridesmaids. Losing what patience I had, I begin to look about me for any signs of my young bride; it is already five minutes to the hour. The frugal number of guests who have already shuffled inside of the church, had looked me up and down with a range of judgements - awe, disdain, lust. It is not unfamiliar, my reputation for being virtually inhuman to emotion has spread quickly over town, together with my unexpected proposal to the Rothschild girl, who was always believed to have belonged to Edmund Barton. That and inheriting a good mixture of my parent's attractive genes makes people wary of me; the way I like it.

Frederick notices me sneering over my bride's non-appearance so makes his excuses to the young, primped up lady, before rushing to my side to no doubt try and tame my mounting temper. Just as he approaches, so too, does the vicar who laughs awkwardly and invites me inside to take my place. He is met with a look that forces him to face the floor and follow his own invitation.

"Relax, Tobias," Frederick smirks at me, "one would

almost believe you are worried about losing your betrothed. You don't actually like her, do you?"

"I hardly know her, and what I do know needs altering considerably," I reply shortly. "But if she makes a fool of me, I will not hold back my wrath, from either her or her family!"

"Well, for her sake then, it's a good thing her carriage has just arrived," he says, pointing it out over my shoulder. "Tell me, Tobias, will you be, er, consummating this romantic union?" he asks with a condescending laugh, teasing me with his crass humour.

"That is none of your business, *friend*," I mutter as I watch Emily being helped down from the carriage in her pure white gown, making her already handsome figure even more appealing than usual. I do not attempt to hide my gawking at her, taking in all that is mine. I would do the same with a new piece of art for my estate, and as she so rightly suggested, she is my own piece of art to stare at for as long as I please.

"It would be a shame not to," Frederick mutters close by to my ear as he turns his back on the scene, "she is quite the beauty."

"That she is," I concede with a long sigh, bringing my fingers to cover my mouth in case he should catch me drooling. "I best go and legally claim her."

"Your Grace," he nods before leading the way for us to go inside.

Emily

My mother fusses with my veil, my hair, and any other piece of wedding attire on show for my future husband. I almost want to call him my future owner, for that is exactly what he is.

Some of the passer bys stop to stare as we hover around the entrance to the church, including a mother who is pointing me out to her young daughter. The little girl looks at me with awe and wonder, as if I am a princess or something else to be envied. If only she knew how sick I am feeling, how much I am dreading leaving my family to go and live with a man I hardly know. I would give anything to swap places with that little girl right now.

Elsie holds my hand just as tightly as I hold hers, knowing that this is the last time we will see each other for a long while. As instructed, I had said my goodbyes last night, for I feared if we didn't, I might not be given the chance to do so. Mother is surreptitiously wiping away the odd tear from her face while my father looks to the floor, waiting for the dreaded moment when he has to give me over to the duke. I have often thought I should have been a boy, but never as much as I do so now. Those dreams of discovering new, far-off places, or galloping across the park with carefree abandonment, are all gone, all vanished from even my imagination.

"Are you ready, my darling girl?" Father asks me when we finally link arms. I have to fight the urge to scream *no*. He knows anyway, I can see the way he is inwardly chastising himself for asking such a stupid question. What else can he say though? With that in mind, I simply nod and smile for him. At least I hope I do, for I am feeling so nervous, I am not quite sure I am capable of curling my lips in any direction.

Just before we step inside, following my mother and Elsie, I look over to the square to see all the other people going about their daily business. My eyes trail the path of the little girl and her mother, probably going to the market to purchase their groceries before they return home. A home full of love and familiarity. It is at this moment that I see a face I know all too well, watching me with sadness. I wave at him, a last goodbye. He waves back at me before walking slowly away.

"Please," I whisper to my father, knowing that he has seen him too, "please look after him for me."

He doesn't say any words, just simply nods. He more than likely planned on taking care of Edmund in the aftermath of my marriage anyway, but it makes me feel better to know that my last thoughts as a single woman were of my best friend. It might also be a small rebellion against my future husband.

As soon as we step inside the church, which has been decorated with Lily of the Valley and other seasonal flowers, the world around me turns into a foggy haze. I only pick up on certain words and phrases and barely manage to say my parts, albeit very quietly. The whole time my vision is only able to focus in on the man standing beside me. The Duke of Kent. Tobias Hardy. My future husband.

I listen to the priest asking who gives this woman, as if I am worth no more than a piece of meat, and to a man I do not even like. The duke declares he will take me as his wife through sickness and health, good times and bad, and all without hesitation. However, he also speaks without any kind of emotion that would suggest he has any real affection for me. The echo of my own voice, which sounds alien and ice-cold, declares I will take him too. All the while I think to myself that this is only because if I do not, it will bring shame upon not only myself, but also my family. Then, finally, I hear those last dreaded words, *I now pronounce you husband and wife. You may kiss your bride, Your Grace!*

The last time I kissed a man who wasn't Papa, it had been when Edmund had fallen from the tree in our back garden, and I had tended to his ankle. My poor attempts did nothing to help ease his pain, so I kissed his forehead to try and make him feel better. I think I was about ten years old at the time, so the act was far from anything romantic. I would have offered one of the dogs the same level of affection. And now, the man before me, a perfect stranger, looks into my wide eyes, smirks over the obvious fear taking over my rigid frame, and leans in to offer a chaste pressing of his lips against mine.

Once he pulls back, I feel a little shocked to have survived it, to not have exploded in a puddle of shame and embarrassment on the floor. The guests, such as they are, clap for the 'happy' couple while my new husband takes hold of my hand to lead me back outside to where a small carriage is already waiting for us. The world has turned to fog again when he guides me towards it; I am not even sure how I get inside, just that I am soon sitting opposite Lord Hardy with a thoroughly nervous disposition. My parents wave from the entrance to the church looking as though they have just come from a funeral instead of their daughter's wedding.

"Well, Mrs Hardy, we will return to your father's house for a post wedding drink or two, and then be on our way to my estate in Kent," the duke informs me with a formal tone of voice. "Do not look so scared, Emily, I am not planning to harm you in any way. Our ceremony went smoothly and is another matter of business I can cross off my list."

"I am glad it has worked out how you wanted it to, Your Grace," I reply with a coldness I cannot help adding to my voice.

"Please," he begins with a small smile while fiddling with his cuff, "we may as well drop a little of the formalities now that we are married. You needn't call me 'Your Grace' every time you wish to speak to me, Emily."

"What would you have me call you?" I ask, for in all

honesty, I have no idea as to what to call one's husband who is also a duke.

"Now that you are my wife, how about *Master*?" he replies with a completely serious expression while I simultaneously look at him with incredulity. A few moments later, his lips curl up with wicked amusement, then laughs when my expression does not alter. "I am, of course, jesting with you, Emily. Please, call me Tobias."

"As you wish…Tobias," I reply with little to no emotion behind it.

Once inside of my parent's house, my once upon a time family home, I am greeted by all manner of important people, most of whom I have never even heard of before today. Not that this is any different from before I was married; I have very rarely taken any notice of the people my parents or Elsie talk about. Yet, here they are congratulating me on my match to one of England's most eligible bachelors. A man who not only has a title and a wealth that will never run out, but who is also ridiculously handsome too. I blush, I smile, I say thank you, and then move on, just waiting for when my husband tells me it is time to go. I am unsure as to which is worse, the waiting or the actual happening. I guess I will soon find out.

Speaking of my husband, I watch him play his part well, even smiling every now and then, though I can see how much it pains him to do so. The only person he doesn't pay any attention to is me. Not once does he look at me, smile at me, or even mumble the odd word of reassurance. Not that it bothers me not to have to talk to him, but it only makes the long journey ahead of me all the more terrifying.

What on earth will we talk about? Or will we be spending it

in uncomfortable silence for the entire journey? What is expected of a wife? My mother never told me, neither did Elsie. I remember my governess broaching the subject a few years ago, though only because I had begged her to. She had mentioned something about sharing a bed, but before she could go beyond that, my mother had entered the room and all conversation had ceased. When I tried to bring up the subject again, she became cagey and told me to never mention it again. I didn't much care back then.

"Lady Hardy," a familiar voice booms out towards me. As soon as I turn, I see Lord Bartholomew and his bushy moustache comes shuffling up to me, with his well pronounced abdomen reaching me before anything else. "There you are, how are you feeling, child?"

"Hello, Barty," I reply shyly, hoping it is still ok to call him by my childhood name for him. This man has known me since I was in lead-strings, and he is also Edmund's Godfather. "I am as well as can be expected."

"Quite," he mutters under that bushy facial hair of his. "I saw Edmund this morning. He's rather distraught, you know. We always believed you and he would marry one day. Most unfortunate."

"No one feels sorrier than I for Edmund's heartache," I barely manage to whisper. From the tone of his voice and the unimpressed expression on his face, I would hazard a guess that Lord Bartholomew is holding me partly responsible for Edmund's sorry state. Even I know this is neither the time nor the place to have such a discussion, neither do I wish to.

"Yes, well, doesn't make up for his heartache does it-"

"Lord Bartholomew, excuse me, I did not realise you were

here," my husband suddenly cuts in with a distinctive tone of frustration in his voice. "It was my understanding that you were consoling your godson today. I do so hope you are not upsetting my new wife. She is very dear to me, and it would personally pain me to hear if she was being made to feel inadequate, especially at her own wedding."

I feel his hand graze my back the entire time he stares at Lord Bartholomew with a threatening expression, which leaves the rotund old man to fluster about on the spot. His cheeks are now turning a deep crimson and with his mouth gaping open for extra breath, I begin to worry he may become seriously ill.

"Emily and I have known one another since she was a small baby," the old man eventually gasps, "I felt it my place to be here on the day she becomes a woman."

"A duchess," Tobias corrects him with a smug smirk. "You forget your place; Emily is now a duchess, my wife, and I expect her to be shown the same respect as you would show me. Now excuse me, Lord Bartholomew, but I have come to steal my beautiful bride away. She is needed by her family before we depart for Kent."

"Of course, Your Grace," the old man concedes with a disgruntled curl of his lips. "I wish you my congratulations. May you both be very happy together." He nods his head and quickly about turns while Tobias scowls at his retreating form. He removes his hand almost immediately so as not to give the impression he actually likes me in any sort of way.

"We leave in ten minutes, Lady Hardy," he mutters inside of my right ear. "Say your final goodbyes and try not to let anyone else disrespect our name before we go. You are a duchess and a Hardy now; you need to try and act as such. A lady in your position does not allow portly old men to insult her at her own event."

I watch him walk slowly away without even looking back at me once. I hold onto the angry tears building at the bottom of my eyes and begin my slow journey to where my family are waiting for me. As I pass by Lord Bartholomew, he glances at me before shaking his head with disappointment. Rather than follow my husband's orders, I ignore his reaction to me and continue on my path to say my final farewell to Mama, Elsie, and my father.

I follow the stairs up to my familiar room, where we had agreed to meet should my new husband be magnanimous enough to allow me one more goodbye. Once there, I steal a moment or two to take in a scene I have lived with since I was born. A scene that I took for granted. A scene that will never be mine again.

My father is standing by the window, staring out over the garden of trees that used to entertain my childhood imagination for hours. Mother is consoling Elsie who is weeping against her shoulder, which is a sight I never thought I would see from her. I do not let my presence be known until I have planted on my best smile with my teeth showing; the same one I am usually told off for because my mother says it makes me look 'childish and unbecoming'. Though, on this occasion, I am merely gifted with a soft laugh. Mama holds out her arms for me and I waste no time in running over to fall into them.

"I'm going to miss you all so, so much," I whimper, "even you, Elsie!"

"Me too, though not as much," she teases, and I take comfort in my mama tutting over our playful bickering.

"Come now, this isn't it, my darlings. I'm sure Em will be back for visits with the duke, and we will come as soon as we are able to!"

"I know," I whisper, though, in all honesty, I don't really know. The duke seems to be content in his own company and is extremely keen to be on home soil.

"Come on, Elsie, we need to let Em and your father say goodbye."

We hug one more time, as tightly as possible, before she eventually cradles a weeping Elsie away.

When they are safely outside of the door, I slowly turn to face my father who still has his back to me as he continues looking out onto the grounds below. His arm steadies his balance against the window frame, as though without it, he would be collapsing to the floor in his own grief. I know he is crying, but I do not want to see it. Much like when he had flustered before the duke at that awful ball, I only know my father as being the larger-than-life man that he is; a man who bows to no one. Yet here he is, falling apart before me. The tears are falling thick and fast down my own cheeks, and I wonder how I shall possibly get through this.

"There is so little time and so much I need to say, Em," he sobs, "I-I don't even know where to start. Is that not one of the most ridiculous things you've ever heard?"

"Oh, I don't know. Did you hear the one about a duke wanting to marry little old me?" I laugh, though it sounds more sad than joyful. He smiles with me, but it is only for a few moments before he is back to looking more forlorn than I have ever seen him. Even more so than when he heard my mother tell me I was now too old to be running around playing with Edmund, and that I should be engaging in embroidery instead of climbing trees and catching frogs.

"I am so sorry, Em, I didn't want to agree to this, you must know that…" He trails off as he pulls me into his large chest and holds me so tight, it is a little hard to breathe.

"Of course, I do, Papa. I do not blame you for this at all," I continue to sob, "I am just going to miss you so much."

"Me too, Em," he says before letting me go again, suddenly looking me up and down in my wedding outfit. "You look so much older, so grown up; I hate it!"

We laugh at one another, even though we are both feeling a little devastated. A soft knock comes all too soon, telling me it is time to go. Perhaps it is for the best; any more of this and I might end up roping myself to the bed and refusing to leave. We smile once more, silently telling one another to leave this as our final goodbye, for anything else will be much too hard.

Chapter 5

Tobias

Even I will admit that my new wife is hiding her tears well, bar the odd sniff and sad exhale of air. She points herself towards the window so as to avoid seeing any hint of the fact she is now married and standing inside of a bed chamber with her new husband. She refuses to let me see her red rimmed eyes or bear witness to her mouth gasping for air whenever she sighs. I try to keep the slight pang of guilt deep inside of me by resting my forefinger to my lips, though I cannot help staring at my beautiful bride falling apart after I have just ripped her away from her family. I indulge in her forlorn stature and allow myself to feel a modicum of affection for the poor girl. However, it is soon replaced by my old friends, bitterness, and anger. Instead of feeling any kind of empathy for her deep sense of loss, I force myself to question how her misery is affecting me. How dare she make me feel so awful about myself when I can already do that without her help.

"Tell me, Emily," I begin, readying myself to become the cold-hearted man I have trained myself to be, ever since I lost Genevieve all those years ago. "What is your understanding of what a man and a woman do after they are married?"

She slowly looks at me with trepidation and begins

shuffling her gloved hands in front of her dress. She does not answer me to begin with, instead, she releases a deep, nervous sigh through her soft lips. Lips I may have only tasted once but it was enough to have me feeling urgent for more.

"I must admit, I do not know much...Tobias," she all but whispers, and I smile over her awkwardness over using my Christian name. "My governess told me they sometimes sleep in the same bed, while at other times they retire to their own separate rooms. However, I know my parents share only one bedroom; they always have done."

"And what is it they do in that bed?" I continue, poking at her modesty and enjoying the red blush that grows only deeper in colour as I push further.

"Sleep, Your Grace?" she asks, clearly having no idea as to what I am alluding to. Though something tells me she knows it is more than just sleeping. Her fidgeting hands and sudden lack of eye contact reveals that she merely wishes to conceal the fact. She remains silent, as if waiting for me to save her from this awkward conversation, to take the lead as it were. Ignoring the fact that I am a gentleman and should be acting as such with a lady, I only offer a smile. She soon grows more uncomfortable and begins to walk around her new bedroom, one that is only for her. Though, the bed could easily fit the both of us with space to spare.

"Do you like your new suite, Emily?" I question her as she looks around completely awe-struck. She doesn't appear to know what to say and is no doubt afraid I will make her feel even more uncomfortable if she says anything. She is smart; I knew she would be.

"This room is all yours, my darling wife, and this bed is just for you. I will be sleeping in my own room. Does this make you feel better, Emily?"

When she says nothing, I smile and gesture for her to come towards the end of the bed to where I am standing.

"Please, take a seat, try it out," I offer, to which she eyes me with suspicion. Pausing in thought for a few moments, and still wearing her travelling dress, she eventually perches on the edge of the antique bed that had once belonged to Genevieve. "Well?"

"It is comfortable, thank you," she replies, awkwardly looking up at me. I step forwards until I am right before her knees, then kneel before her. Her eyes trace mine, and even though hers are now looking down at me, she still knows who is in charge here.

"Have you heard of the word *consummate*?" I ask as I reach out for her delicately decorated shoe. The pulse in her neck begins to throb with anxiety, and her chest is now breathing in and out at a more rapid pace.

"Faultless," she replies with what appears to be the remainder of any courage she had. "Showing great skill."

"A book worthy answer, Lady Hardy," I tell her, now looking down to her shoe inside of my hand, which I then begin to slide off from her foot. She takes in a deep breath through her lips and holds it in reverence. "However, I did not mean the adjective, I was referring to the verb; to consummate one's marriage."

Emily

All breath has left my body, and I seem unable to form a single word to respond with. I cannot tell if he is teasing or purposefully being cruel to hurt me. My shoe is soon discarded with a simple throw that lacks any elegance or care behind it. My foot remains frozen within his hot hands. When he sees me staring at it, he begins rubbing and flexing the tender skin beneath my stocking. I cannot deny that it feels nice, but also, so intimate I fear I might be sick at any moment.

"Breathe, Emily," he laughs quietly, calmly, wickedly. "I did not marry you only to lose you on the same day." On his command, I somehow manage to emit a slow stream of air that causes a hissing sound to vibrate through my teeth. "Good girl."

His hands begin to travel up towards my ankle, still massaging against my tired flesh, still threatening to steal every breath from my body. They do not stop at my ankle, however, no. They move up my leg in slow, hypnotising circles that cause me to fall into a kind of stupor. My eyes close without my permission and I even suck in my chest to allow myself to appreciate the delicious movement of his hands.

"What married men and women do together is very intimate, my young bride," he begins explaining to me in a low, quiet, formal tone of voice. "It is private and designed to bring each other pleasure. You are aware of how a man and a woman are different from one another; physically different. Are you not?"

I finally dare myself to open my eyes and look to where he has now pushed the hem of my skirts up to the very top of my stocking. His fingers, which have now ceased their heavenly touch upon my skin, are now pinching at the lace, getting ready to pull it down and reveal my naked leg. His eyes hold mine, demanding me to answer his question, one I have to think carefully about, for I am not entirely sure I can recall his words.

In the end, I simply nod. In fact, with a cleansing breath, I begin to remember having caught Edmund swimming naked in the lake behind their country house in Hampshire. We had arrived unexpectedly early and caught him and his brother frolicking in the water on a particularly hot summer's day. My mother's face had been quite the picture, and Elsie had practically squealed with shock. Being so young, I had looked on with curiosity, and felt it perfectly practical to ask what it was that was hanging between his legs. Of course, Mama had refused to answer and instead, gave me a stern talking to; a warning to forget about having seen anything at all.

My husband before me, my new authority, merely gifts me with a wicked grin to my acknowledgement before slowly pulling the stocking between his fingers, all the way down my leg. If I am not mistaken, he purposefully ensures his skin remains in constant contact with mine, all the way to my calf and toes.

The stocking is thrown away with the same grace with which my shoe had been cast, all the while those wicked eyes of his, the ones taunting me for my lack of knowledge, keep looking right into my fearful but curious ones. I am aware of my body trembling beneath his hands, waiting for him to end this terrifying assault on me, even if it does feel strangely pleasurable. He cups my foot within his hands before leaning his face towards my ankle. I emit a shocked gasp when his lips make contact, kissing them with the same lips that had kissed me so chastely inside of the church. If this was not enough, he then uses his tongue to swirl around my trembling skin, almost doing the same job as his hands had done when I was still covered in the safety of my stocking.

"A man and a woman fit perfectly together, Emily," he whispers between his open-mouthed kissing, "*you* and I will fit perfectly together."

Strange sensations begin to take over inside of me, tingling, fluttering, and a throbbing for more. My breath betrays these feelings to my husband, and he smiles with wicked amusement over it.

"One day, my bride," he whispers against my foot before gently placing it back to the floor. He stands before me, leaving me with mixed feelings of relief and bereavement. My cheeks are hot and my chest still heaving up and down before his self-satisfied grin. "Perhaps when you do not tremble at my touch."

"You tease me," I accuse him breathily. "You tease my lack of experience and knowledge, even though you took me before I was able to learn all that I should have."

"Goodnight, Emily," he simply says before turning to leave. I close my eyes through humiliation and shame until he makes a sudden turn back towards me, and with my name upon his wicked lips. My eyes fly open and wait for his cold words to hit my already dented ego.

"One day, Emily, I will need to sire an heir. Then you shall have all the knowledge you need for what happens between a man and a woman behind closed doors. You will know exactly what the verb, *consummate,* means. Until then, I have no desire to teach you."

When he closes the door on me, I already know he has insulted me beyond reproach. Not only that, but he has managed to do so without me having the full understanding of exactly how he has offended me. And yet, part of me is grateful for his beastly behaviour towards me, for had he not caused me to cry until well into the early hours of the morning, I am not sure I would have been able to sleep at all. I have been in his company for less than a day, and I miss my family and home more than I thought possible. Being Lord Hardy's duchess is shaping up to be as miserable as I had imagined. Alas, it will be a role I must endure for the rest of my life.

The morning that follows my move to my husband's estate has me feeling extremely disorientated. From the moment I wake, everything feels different. My eyes are assaulted by the strong sunlight streaming in through the large windows, and the usual sounds of my family are noticeably absent. In fact, the entire place is strangely silent. Not even a single footstep marches past my door, neither do I hear the comforting sounds of London streets outside of my window. There's nothing.

The atmosphere is so uncomfortably strange, at first, I just remain frozen still inside of my bed. I allow my senses to accept what is hitting them in this almost dream like situation. After I feel more acclimatised to the space around me, I eventually move from the centre of my bed to perch upon the edge. With my feet on the floor, I try to make sense of everything that has happened to me in the past twenty-four hours. So many changes in so little time, it almost has me falling back inside of my bed to hide away from it all. But then I look over to the window, where the sun now feels a little less punishing, and the sight of trees growing in the garden below makes my anxiety loosen its grip on my thumping heart.

The morning sunlight and the vivid greenness of everything has me relinquishing my punishing thoughts so I might go and look out into the gardens below. They're beautiful, inviting, and for the first time since arriving in this new home of mine, I find myself smiling. In fact, I almost allow myself to laugh when I think of who owns this picturesque landscape, and how much he contrasts with the warm glow that seems to emit from every leaf, flower, and twig. It reminds me of the Greek myth of Lord Hades, god of the Underworld, who fell in love with a goddess who represented life, fertility, and rebirth. Such a contrast, yet it was one that seemed to work seamlessly together. The thought has me remembering the way Tobias' icy blue eyes had pierced through mine. The way he placed his mouth against my skin as he massaged me so intensely with his large, warm hands. And when he had used his tongue so lewdly, I had felt so…so…I cannot even describe what it had made me feel. In fact, I find myself having to shake the uncomfortable memory away. Alas, I do not think Tobias and I are fated to fall in love; this is no myth where the impossible happens, this is real life.

As if it might help my need to extinguish such thoughts from my head, I get to my feet and begin marching straight over to my wardrobe so I can begin dressing. Perhaps this place can be a new adventure for me, a new land to discover, and a home that might give me the freedom I once had as a child. I might well be the property of a duke, but I no longer have to parade myself about like a doll looking for a proper suitor. As for today, hopefully I might be able to bypass Tobias altogether; I am more than happy to live outside until nightfall again.

Just before I reach the doors to my armoire, a soft knock upon the bedroom door has me freezing on the spot, wondering who it could possibly be.

"Your Grace," a gentle, female voice sings out to me with friendliness ringing through it. "It is your maid, Mary. May I come in to help you dress?"

I open the door before answering and give the girl who is of about Elsie's age a beaming smile, hoping that she might be a friend in this place away from home. On first impressions, she certainly looks kind enough to attempt friendly conversation. Her dark locks have been carefully pulled back beneath her bonnet and her rosy cheeks are full and round from the wide smile she is gifting to me. My heart soars with relief as I open up the door wide enough to let her pass through, at the same time as waving away the small curtsey she dutifully carries out.

"Please, do come in." I gesture to inside of the room with a healthy blush. I almost feel silly over the formality of my words for I have never been so proper at home. Mama would often comment on my refusal to entertain such ceremonial stuffiness. However, I cannot honestly say I know who I am in this place.

"I must say I am quite bewildered this morning. When I woke, I quite forgot where I was."

"That cannot be surprising, Your Grace, it was your first night here," she says whilst heading straight to the wardrobe to begin sorting through my things. "But how did you sleep?"

"Not too well, I'm afraid. It is strange but I think it is because I am used to more noise," I reply with a furrowed brow. "But please, you must call me Emily. I am not used to such a title."

"I'm afraid the duke wouldn't hear of it, Your Grace," she says shyly. "I would be given my marching orders before the day was out!"

"Oh," I reply rather sadly as she begins putting on my long stay, a restrictive garment I shall never get used to. "Might you call me Emily when it is just you and I then? You see, I have left everyone behind, including my sister, Elsie, and I feel a little…lonely."

She pauses in her undertakings and looks at me with a little pity through the reflection in the mirror. I feel myself shrinking over my words, for what a sad thing to admit to a perfect stranger.

"Of course…Emily," she says, and I smile like a giddy child. "Perhaps I may call you Lady Hardy when in the company of others. Does that sound more friendly than *Your Grace*?"

I merely nod my head in response to her kind words,

feeling glad to have at least one companion in this place.

I pretend to be brave in front of Mary when she offers to lead me to the dining room where I am to have my breakfast. At home, this was a place always full of sunlight and chatter, usually with some arguing between Elsie and me, much to Mama's frustration. We would usually end up laughing and poking fun and our poor mother until she'd relent in a small smile. I am not at all convinced I shall ever have this here, especially not with someone as miserable and pretentious as Tobias. He is more likely to demand that we eat in silence and without eye contact.

I am pondering this sad thought when it suddenly dawns on me that Mary has been leading us through so many halls and stairways, that I no longer know where I am. In fact, my head feels quite dizzy with it all and I hardly know how I would ever get back to my room. It will certainly take me some time to have this house memorised, though I can admit, I am in compete awe of the place. I have never seen somewhere so grand before and have to wonder if the palace itself is of the same grandeur. There are so many paintings, I cannot help but question as to who has the time to admire them all. I notice Mary watching my facial expressions with quiet amusement, most likely being more than aware of how breath taking the place is, even to the daughter of a viscount. Our London home seems positively rudimentary by comparison.

It feels as though hours have passed by the time that we reach our final destination. It is an ornate dining room with a long mahogany table laden with fruits, breads, silverware, and fine china, but with only two place settings at either end. No less than four serving staff, all dressed in uniform clothing, are stood about the room, waiting patiently for the man who I now call my husband, to finish eating. It is a strange sight, but not at all surprising given my new husband is a duke, and a rather stuffy one at that.

"Ah, Your Grace, you are finally come," a kindly older woman welcomes me with her arms stretched out before her. Looking over her, I would guess that she must be the housekeeper of the estate. Without any conscious choice in the matter, my eyes bulge out towards this woman. The housekeeper at my family home always made me feel so nervous, like a small child who is about to meet their teacher for the first time. She was my mother's confidant, as well as her eyes and ears, and I soon learnt what her different facial expressions meant. A simple raise of her left eyebrow usually led to a harsh talking to, a slight nod of her chin to the right meant time out in my room, and a quiet, but obvious tut always meant a truly horrible week was coming my way. She is the one person I will not miss; I think the feeling is mutual.

"Do not look so frightened, My Lady, I am Mrs Keppel, the housekeeper of the Hardy Estate. Let me welcome you to your new home."

Her friendliness looks genuine and her monobrow strangely sets me at ease.

"Thank you," I manage to say in barely more than a whisper.

The kindly old woman smiles and nods her head in acceptance of my small response. I relax a little until I hear my husband swallowing back a laugh at my expense. I try not to look at him when Mrs Keppel walks me towards my seat at the same time as instructing Mary to go and prepare something in the kitchen for me. My initial instinct is to reach out for Mary and beg her to stay with me, but I know that is not acceptable behaviour of a duchess, and would most likely land my new companion in trouble.

"I trust you slept well?" Mrs Keppel asks while motioning for one of the serving staff to come and offer me fresh fruit and bread for my breakfast.

"Yes," I murmur, though, even to my own ears, I do not sound at all convincing.

"It was a long day, Mrs Keppel," the duke finally voices as he looks up to meet my eyes. "The duchess must still be recovering from the aches and pains of sitting in a coach for several hours. Tell me, my dear, how is your ankle this morning?"

His taunting smirk flickers at the corner of his mouth at the same time as his wicked eyes seem to tease me over the memory of his extremely intimate massage last night. I feel my cheeks heat up almost instantly, for I have no clue as to how to answer such a question. By the expression on his face, I am sure he is not waiting for a response beyond the shade of crimson he has managed to bring out on my normally pale skin. So, instead, I look down to my bowl and begin eating. I cannot help but wonder with a sense of dread, if all engagements with this man shall be this uncomfortable.

"Mrs Keppel," he suddenly announces with his stern tone of voice, "would you please vacate the room with the rest of the serving staff. I wish to speak to my wife alone."

The piece of fruit currently sliding down my throat makes a hasty descent, which causes me to cough with an instant need to take a large gulp of water, so as to avoid choking on my own fear. Mrs Keppel merely smiles at Tobias before gesturing for the waiting staff to follow her out the door. The click of which echoes so loudly inside of my ears, I have to cease eating altogether. My anxiety is in no way eased by his choosing to remain silently staring at me for so long, I begin to wonder if I should speak first.

"You wished to speak to me, Your Grace," I eventually have to say to break the unbearably awkward atmosphere.

"What I wish for, and what I have before me, are two entirely different things, darling," he says before getting to his feet and walking towards me. An action that makes me dip my chin lower and in towards my neck.

The heavy thudding of his black, leather boots, only causes the thumping of my own heart to speed up in anticipation of what he is going to do once he reaches me. Will he force me into more of his games? Games I do not fully understand. Games that have me feeling terrified and excited all at the same time.

When he finally reaches me, he holds out his hand for mine, which I stare at momentarily before eventually accepting. I am gently pulled to my feet and led to the double doors that give way onto the garden. It is even more beautiful than when I had gazed over them from my bedroom window. I am so mesmerised by all that I can see that I almost forget my new husband is standing right behind me.

"I will be busy for the rest of the day," he says against my ear, causing me to jump over his sudden closeness. "You are not to go beyond the boundaries of that hedge over there."

"Is there any reason as to why?" I can't help but ask. I may feel nervous beside his imposing stature, his intimidating way of speaking to me, but I cannot deny my natural instincts to question rules that do not make any sense to me. Mama had attempted to train this habit out of me, but my father always seemed to encourage my curiosity. And besides, the urge to go and search the forest beyond is calling out to me at a volume no one else can hear but me.

"Many, the main one being I want to know you will do as I tell you," he says with an arrogance no other man has ever used with me. "I also do not wish my duchess to be seen climbing trees by either my staff or my tenants."

"Of course," I mutter sadly, for never have I felt such home sickness as I do now. "Believe it or not, I have not climbed trees for many years, Your Grace. I may not know everything, but I know enough to not embarrass you in such an obvious way."

"I am not sure I can trust you, Emily, have you seen your dancing?" At his cheap insult, I look at him with such shock, his smirk falters a little. "But, if you are patient, I will take you to those woods myself."

"Really?" I ask with surprise, causing his smirk to return to his handsome face.

"I am not a total monster, darling," he says as he leans in a little closer, "and I did so enjoy our time together last night."

He leans in closer again, so close, I can feel his hot breath on my face, and my body begins to tremble without me giving it any permission to. His hand reaches up to my face and for a heart stopping moment, I fear he is going to try and kiss me again. He can see it, I know he can, and it amuses him. Instead of using his own lips, however, he places his thumb to the corner of my mouth and gently rubs away at the skin. It feels strange, but even more strange when he retrieves his thumb and places it into his own mouth to suck on.

"Peaches," he whispers, "delicious. I should let you get

back to your breakfast."

He immediately steps back, leaving me in a quivering state of shock.

"I suggest you make your acquaintance with the staff and explore your new home, my darling wife," he calls over his shoulder as he marches toward the heavy wooden door. "I may seek to quiz you on it this evening if the mood so takes me. Enjoy your day."

Before I can even give any sort of comprehensible response, he has already left and the staff from before are re-entering the room to watch me eat my breakfast in silence.

Chapter 6

Emily

The days that follow that first one, seem to be stuck on a loop, with Mrs Keppel continuing to show me around the various areas of the main house. I have had to ask her to repeat the tour several times, for the building is so large, I cannot possibly take it all in at once. In fact, it is so vast, I always return to the terrace with a set of aching feet, which is saying something, given that I am well used to walking for long stretches. After the first few rooms, they all seem to blur into one another, and I end up getting quite dizzy from marching up and down the staircases. Mrs Keppel always smiles when she sees how weary I become, and usually suggests that I have tea in the garden to try and get over the ordeal. No matter how many times she suggests this, I always feel like I want to throw my arms around her in gratitude for the idea, because although beautiful, the house in no way compares to the gardens outside.

On this particular Wednesday, only five days since the duke and I were married, the sun is shining, the flowers are blooming, and I can hear the hustle and bustle of nearby tenants from the neighbouring village, with some of them shouting to one another in the fields nearby. Bees are conducting a delicious hum from the blooming roses next to me, and the smell of herbs infiltrates my nostrils with a freshness one cannot find in the busy streets of London.

Whilst sipping on my morning tea, which tastes of home and the family I have left behind, I am suddenly accosted by a black dog trying to leap inside of my lap with so much enthusiasm in its bottom, I fear he will soon have the table over.

"Monty!" Mrs Keppel shouts sternly. "You silly dog, come back here at once!"

The dog pays no heed to the angry looking housekeeper, and I notice Mary trying to hide a smirk as she follows behind. The dog, by this point, is beginning to whimper while trying to push his waggly bottom against my knees at the same time as curling its head around to give me a pleading grin. I cannot help but laugh at the poor creature and his desperation to make contact with every part of his body at once. I am in no way afraid of dogs for Elsie has always had a gaggle of pets, though none as large or as handsome as this strapping young hound. My sister's dogs were always little rat-like creatures and were more likely to snap at you with their odorous breath than offer you this kind of love or affection.

Even though the dog before me appears in no way perturbed by me being a stranger, I cautiously offer him my hand to sniff so he might give me his permission before I place it on top of his smooth, jet-black head. We exchange a warming hello to one another before Mrs Keppel arrives to chastise the over-exuberant beast.

"I am so terribly sorry, Duchess," Mrs Keppel flusters. "Monty is the duke's dog, his companion, but he is still young and tends to only obey his commands."

"It is quite alright, Mrs Keppel," I giggle, just as the young dog falls completely against me, "I am not feared of him. You are a very handsome boy aren't you, Monty? And you were only coming to say hello."

The poor dog waggles around so much he ends up falling onto his hide and twisting his body around to try and get back up to me. He reminds me of a beetle I once saw in my back garden, a large beast of a bug, that had fallen on its back and couldn't right itself no matter how hard it wriggled its stumpy little legs about in the air. I cannot help but laugh even harder which only serves to make the dog more excited while dear Mrs Keppel gets herself into more of a fluster.

"Monty!" a low, stern-sounding male voice calls out from the side of us before he emits a quick whistle which he manages to emit through his teeth.

The dog quickly and obediently gets to his feet and paces over to his master, the same one who is also mine. He sits without any command necessary but seems content when Tobias rewards him with a quick rub behind his ear. Just like the dog, I immediately bow my head, keeping my eyes to the ground, just waiting for when I am spoken to.

"Your Grace," Mrs Keppel speaks out loudly and confidently. She is clearly not a fan of the duke's pet, and given the smirk on his face, he is more than aware of the fact. "I do apologise. Monty escaped through the kitchen door when I was occupied with a delivery."

"No need to apologise, Mrs Keppel," he replies with a friendliness he has never once afforded to me. "Will you see to Lord Brown in the entrance hall, he is waiting for me. Tell him I will be there shortly."

"Of course, Your Grace," she replies with relief in her voice. "I'll offer him some refreshments. Mary, do come and help me, will you? Your Grace," she says as she nods to Lord Hardy, then me, before taking Mary with her, thus leaving me completely alone with my husband.

I stay rooted in my seat, trying to get a hold of my nerves while I listen to his boots pacing up to the table upon the paving slabs. Each click makes me jump a little with anxiety, anticipating something unpleasant to come out of his mouth the moment he reaches me. Eventually, he sits in the chair beside me, sighing heavily as though he has just taken the same tour of his monstrous estate.

"Emily," he says by way of greeting. I momentarily look up to nod in acknowledgement, with a small smile upon my face. "Did you enjoy looking around the estate yet again this morning?"

"Very," I reply, "though it is so large I fear I will still disappoint you when you finally decide to question me on it later."

He smiles tightly, as though it pains him to show any kind of emotion other than disdain for me. I wonder if he would act this way with any woman he chose to marry or is it just me who causes him so much vexation.

"One cannot be disappointed if one expected nothing less," he replies with a condescending shrug, and I close my eyes to yet another insult so easily thrown my way. "No need to worry, darling, there will be no questions from me."

"Will you always regard me so harshly?" I ask with a weary sigh. I may as well be forthright for he does not appreciate any of my efforts to at least try and be a lady he would find less wearisome. Alas, my boldness does not prevent my hands from trembling when in his presence; they more than give away how feared I am of my new husband. I try to tell them to stop, to not make me look so foolish in front of him, but they pay no heed to my instruction.

"Will you always tremble in my presence?" he retorts.

"What else would you have me do, Tobias?" I say his name with a shudder. "Your need to frequently insult me causes me to tremble whenever you are near. My body naturally braces itself for your obvious disdain towards me. To be honest, My Lord, I still cannot understand why you chose to marry me. You clearly do not like me."

"I rarely enjoy anyone's company," he says almost bitterly, "though sometimes it is something one has to endure. This afternoon you will join me to learn the waltz without stepping on my toes."

"A request or a command, husband?" I find the courage to ask.

"I will let you come to your own conclusion," he replies before turning to give me a wicked smile. "However, you will have to bear the consequences should you come to the incorrect one."

"I see," I utter with a sad sigh and with tears already building upon my lower lashes.

"Mont-" he begins to call out, but I cut him off before the dog can even get to his feet.

"Please, may I keep him with me?" I ask with pleading eyes which rival those belonging to the dog in question. "I could use a friend and he seems content to be near me."

He eyes me and the dog for a few long moments, as though debating which way to go with his answer. Eventually, he nods stiffly before addressing the dog again, "Monty, stay!" The dog seems to look at him for added confirmation before lying back down and relaxing. I am given the same stiff nod before he about turns and marches away. His confident stature soon turns off, back into the house, and completely out of view. Only then do I begin to let the tears cascade silently down my cheeks. I have never considered myself a particularly emotional creature. I did not cry when those brambles had ripped through my skin, neither when I was told I could not play with Edmund anymore, nor when I had watched my family growing smaller and smaller as the carriage had led me away to my new home. However, it would seem my husband brings out the worst qualities in me.

Tobias

For the first time since I set my eyes on Emily, I am beginning to have doubts over whether I made the right decision. Life would be simpler if I disliked the girl, hated her even, but I strangely find myself not *not* liking her. Her appearance certainly attracts my baser needs, but her subtle nuances are beginning to grow on me too. She maintains her emotions as well as she can, even when I am an out and out cad towards her. I can certainly see the desperation to release those tears whenever I have insulted her, but she always manages to maintain her decorum. I am almost certain this is an added act of defiance towards me; a resistance I find endearing. Though, it will only have me trying harder to break it, as wicked as that sounds. I refuse to simply undo years of training myself to form my own resistance. Resistance against attaching myself to anyone who might have me feeling as desperate as I had when I lost my mother, and then later, my sister, Genevieve. Feeling like that again is simply unacceptable.

My new wife is clearly more interested in the world around her instead of the grandeur of my home and its commodities. My priceless heirlooms and wall to wall works of art do not grab her attention as much as the natural beauty of my gardens. And her reaction towards Monty, a ridiculous dog who has somehow gotten under my skin, is somewhat appealing. I cannot tell you how many insipid ladies have squealed and flustered when faced with a dog that is bigger than a pug. Emily, however, shows no fear or apprehension when faced with any sort of adversity. Apart from when she in the presence of her husband. She physically trembles under my touch, though, I am still unsure as to whether this is to do with my general being or what she understands of being intimate with a person.

"Hardy!" Frederick booms from the parlour where I have already caught him flirting with one of the prettier maids. She blushes the instant she sees me coming. The smile she had just put on for his pleasure, now turns into a look of horror, and with a hint of humiliation. I glare back at her, dismissing her with just a raise of my brow. My imbecile of a friend, who has the willpower of Monty when it comes to women, simply chuckles when the poor girl scurries away.

"Frederick," I mutter before taking the seat opposite to him, still looking through various letters that have been sent to me from some of my other estates. "To what do I owe the pleasure? Did you not hear? I married a mere week ago and shouldn't be accepting visitors this early on."

"Ah, yes, I think I was there," he teases, "brute of a groom, terrified bride. Yes, it's all coming back to me now!"

"The point, Frederick, get to it a little faster," I mumble from behind one of my letters.

"Why? So you can go and whisper sweet nothings to your pretty, new wife?"

His comment has me slamming down my papers in frustration before glaring at him again, which only serves to make him laugh all the harder.

"Do not refer to the way my wife looks," I warn him, "it is for no man other than myself to look at her as if she is something to be ogled."

"Well, now, this is a surprise!" he gasps with what looks like utter glee all over his face. "Could it be the Duke of Kent, the brooding Tobias Hardy, has found a girl he could possibly feel something for?!"

"Careful, Brown." I smile darkly and with menace in my voice.

"Tell me, have you and she consummated the marriage yet?" He leans in a little closer and had it not been for our twenty years of friendship, I would have smacked him between the eyes for asking such a thing. My expression tells him as such. "How very honourable of you, Tobias, so very honourable and unlike you!"

"She is more like a child than a woman I would desire, one who shudders under my touch," I reply before picking up my papers again.

"She is older than others who have been married to men far more advanced in their years than you, Tobias," he says thoughtfully.

I simply scoff over his observation; even I know that is not reason enough to force myself upon a girl who is so obviously not ready for such a thing. I may well be a cold man, a seemingly uncaring husband, but I was raised by a woman who taught me how to be a gentleman.

"Perhaps she is enamoured by you which is why she trembles so. Have you ever considered that, my friend?"

I shake my head over his romantic notion, for I have made it virtually impossible for her to like me. I do not wish for her to like me; she is a commodity with a later purpose, nothing more. Should she get notions of anything else it could lead to emotion between us, and I already decided upon the eve of my sister's death, I would not get close to another human being, not when they can be so cruelly ripped away from me. Indifference is better than being heartbroken through loss and grief.

"Well, as much as I like to see you deny any feelings you may or may not have, I am here to plead my case to stay with you over the next couple of days. You see, I have grown rather fond of a Lady from Whitstable, which is but a short hop, skip, and a jump from here, as you well know. In fact, there is to be a ball in the next two days, over at her father's house-"

"I am well aware of the event, especially being that my new bride and I have been formally invited," I reply whilst still casting my bored eyes over the papers in front of me. "Not that I have any intention of attending. I already have a wife; such events will be purposefully avoided if at all possible."

"Oh, but Tobias, you must go, I *need* you to go," he begs like the damn dog was doing with Emily just now. "I believe the family would look rather fondly on me if I were to turn up with you in tow, *Your Grace!*"

"And still for the life of me, I cannot see why you think this would interest me?" I look at him with sarcasm practically spilling out from my pores.

"For starters, I feel you owe me for the many years I have supported you as a close friend!" Once again, I scoff over such an assumption. "Though, mainly because I heard a little bird tell me that your wife's former *friend* will be in attendance. Young

Edmund Barton has been spreading some rather vicious rumours about you."

"Oh?" I ask, suddenly sounding much more interested. I even throw the papers onto the table beside me so I can give him my full attention.

"According to Mr Barton, you practically threatened to have Emily's family ruined if her father did not agree to the marriage!" He takes a moment to smirk at me because this is only mildly true. "You only wanted her hand so she will give you handsome babies, but otherwise, you broke up a loving relationship for the sake of your own ego."

"I cannot completely deny his accusations, though it is highly disrespectful of him to voice such things in good society," I mutter bitterly, "and they were never in a *loving relationship*. She told me as much herself. She thought more of him as a brother than any sort of a lover."

"True, he has made himself look rather foolish, but it still has tongues wagging back in London," Frederick counters, "still puts you under a bad spot. And with some of those loyal to his family talking about cutting ties with some of your business ventures."

"They would be pretty foolish to do so," I reply, now getting to my feet to march out and check on the girl in question. "But I suppose it doesn't put one out too much to show my face with Emily for at least one societal event."

We reach the double set of doors to the terrace where my wife is walking around the flower garden with Monty at her heels. The dog is already besotted with her, gifting her with a pathetic, sloppy smile whenever she pats his head. He may be just a beast of lower intelligence, but when I look at him, he shows me exactly what could happen to me should I allow myself to feel any affection towards her. I shudder over the thought of being that dependent on the love of a woman again. Unfortunately, it is an action that Frederick immediately picks up on.

"You know, it is a pity you refuse to let anyone in," he mumbles with a silly grin on his face, "being that you have no family, I would have thought you would be putting all of your efforts into properly wooing that pretty, young thing. It was more than obvious that many a man would have given anything to have captured her affections."

"I do not need her affections," I reply coldly, "I already own her; she is mine. No matter what her idiot *friend* says about how I got my ring on her finger, it is clearly there for all to see. What is more, no one more than Emily understands that fact, and therefore, I have nothing to worry about."

"You never did like sharing your toys did you, Tobias? Nor your horse," he says with a now serious expression. "But most of all, you have never liked sharing your heart. She is more than a toy, Tobias, and could be a lot more to you, if only you allowed yourself to feel happiness again."

I simply look at him, carefully considering my next words before I voice something that could lead us to blows. His eyes glance back over at Emily who is now bent low, cuddling the silly hound with his tail wagging into oblivion. She offers him smiles, infinite pats to the head, and words of affection I have not heard since my mother died when I was only eight years old.

"I know you're going to break hearts one day, my handsome son."

I haven't broken anyone's heart, for I have never given myself the opportunity to do so.

"I shall tell Lord Gray that Emily and I will be attending," I reply rather formally. My ridiculous friend smiles, knowing he has vexed me. Sporting a stiff upper lip and clenched jaw, is my usual response when feeling highly irritated, especially when he has managed to trick me into submission. "You may stay in the usual suite. Please excuse me, some of us have business to attend to."

"Your Grace," he smiles with a taunting smirk, which I would so dearly love to wipe from his face. Instead, however, I whistle for Monty to come and march back to his bed in my study. If I am to feel this wearisome over unwanted houseguests, then so too, can my wife.

Chapter 7

Emily

I barely touched my afternoon tea; I was feeling much too nervous over my impending dance lesson with Tobias. I fear I could be the most elegant and skilled dancer in all of England and yet he would still find fault. Fault he would then use to belittle me without any kind of thought for my feelings. I half wonder if I should purposefully stand on his feet so I might at least inflict a little of my own pain. It would do no good, however, for I am sure he would show but a slight grimace, or perhaps a tightening of his lips, but nothing to give me any true satisfaction.

Mrs Keppel had come to fetch me so I would be sure to arrive punctually for His Grace, though I am sure this was for my benefit as much as it was for his. I feel I am most fortunate to have Mrs Keppel as our housekeeper; she really is a kind lady. The same sort my mother would have kept as close company, for she knows all, and treats me with the dignity my husband refuses to bestow upon me. Mary has also become essential to my wellbeing in my new role as duchess, mostly because she sees me as Emily, a person, and lets me rabbit away about everything and nothing; she always knows what to say to keep my mind from wandering into dark thoughts that might seek to bring me down in mood and temperament. She is more a friend than a servant.

As usual, I have let my thoughts run off at a tangent so that when I find myself being led into yet another unfamiliar room, I am quite unaware of how I got here. Not that I have long to ponder on this mystery, for once inside, I cannot help but take in my surroundings with astonishment. The airy room is full to the brim with landscape paintings and antique statues which, although expensive, make me feel eerily like I am being watched from every angle. However, I do enjoy looking at the paintings; they remind me of trips to the countryside when I was younger, of climbing trees with Edmund, and rambling through the woods with my father so very long ago. A time when the notion of being a proper lady had seemed so far away, it was almost like taking a glimpse at an entirely different world.

The sun shines through the windows and I take a moment to bask in its warmth, closing my eyes to the brightness whilst thinking about running freely through the trees as a child. Even when I hear the click clack of his heels, I do not turn or alter my stance; I'm much too comforted by the nostalgia of my thoughts. He thinks so little of me, what reason do I have to try and persuade him otherwise.

"Emily," he says by way of greeting with his usual low, authoritarian voice that contrasts so vividly with my free-flowing daydreams. We are like chalk and cheese, the sun and the moon, laughter and silence; it is little wonder we do not exist well together.

After a moment or two of ignoring his presence, a difficult feat given the intensity of his general being, I eventually emit a small sigh. It is so tiny he surely cannot have heard it for it was not my intention for him to do so. Yet when I finally turn to face him, his deep-set frown tells me he might well have. However, for the first time since being in this house, which is so obviously his and not a fraction of mine, I do not find myself caring what he thinks. In fact, I rather hope I might laugh the next time he chooses to insult me. My trembling hands, however, do not appear to agree with my desire; they are quite out of my control.

"Tobias," I reply, ignoring my hands as I shuffle them in front of my skirt, and instead, attempt to sound just as confident as he does. "I am ready for my lesson."

"Good," he snaps as he removes his jacket and places it upon a chair in one elegant motion. This one act in itself was beautiful enough to put my dancing skills to shame. "Though, my feet might not altogether agree with that sentiment. Please, at least try to be graceful so I might be able to leave this room without the need for a crutch."

"I shall do my best," I reply with a small smirk upon my face, completely ignoring the thunderous scowl upon his.

We walk towards one another, with my eyes looking right into his with an element of defiance, which if I am not mistaken, has surprised him somewhat. When we are but a few feet apart, he lifts his arms up before me, takes hold of my waist, and pulls me in closer. With his other hand, he takes hold of mine, so I place my free one onto his shoulder. All appears well, but my trembling beneath his touch continues involuntarily; I could almost curse myself for it.

Once we begin to move around the room, first slow, then a little quicker when my feet choose to behave themselves, he opens his mouth to speak. I brace myself for what is about to come, reminding myself that this is nothing unusual and to not let myself get upset over it.

"You are doing better today, Emily," he says, strangely complimenting me for the first time since…well, ever.

"Thank you," I reply, keeping my eyes firmly fixed upon our clasped hands so as not to look into those icy eyes of his, the ones that will freeze me and cause me to blunder my footwork.

"Though, we should be looking at one another," he says, as though he has a direct line to my thoughts. "We are married after all. We should be madly in love, should we not?"

"Not necessarily," I reply, still keeping my focus on our hands. "My sister used to tell me that marriages are often built on convenience rather than love. If nothing else, Your Grace, I did learn that."

"Very wise," he smirks. "However, these societal balls are all about appearances, so we must at least look as though we are in love. Look at me, Emily."

Reluctantly, and only because he added a hint of warning to his voice when giving me his instruction, I look up into his eyes. His cold stare looks right back at me with the power to freeze me to this very spot. His face, though handsome, inflicts fear into my very soul. Even though I can try not to fall prey to his malicious insults, I know this man has the power to bring me down to naught but dirt upon the ground.

"You do not like looking at your husband, Emily?" he asks with a cruel smile. "Do you find me so terribly ugly?"

"Not at all!" I barely manage to say much louder than a whisper at the same time as I feel a heated blush spreading over my cheeks and around my neck. He pauses to smile even wider; no doubt having spotted the crimson glow he has inflicted through words alone. The man is a master of being able to humiliate and belittle and executes his skill with a devilish smile upon his handsome face.

"Then tell me, what do you think of my face, my stature, my 'appearance'?" he asks with that cruel smile revealing his even, white teeth and a set of dimples in his cheeks.

"I-" I falter before he cuts in.

"And do be honest, my darling wife, for I shall know if you are lying to me."

"Honestly?" I ask with a quirk of my brow, to which he slowly nods, the motion of which appears menacing. "Well, it is true you are as handsome as they say you are, breath-taking for some. But..."

"But..." he leans in and whispers inside of my ear, unnerving me with his body now being ever so close to mine. So close, I feel quite giddy.

"But..." I whisper, losing all breath when he suddenly places his lips to a patch of sensitive skin beneath my earlobe.

"But?" he whispers again, but this time brings his hand to rest gently around my neck, all while beginning to kiss me along the curve of my jaw. Such wickedness by teasing me with tantalising softness, as well as an unfamiliar pleasure igniting beneath his cruel lips, has me closing my eyes in reverence. I silently pray for the strength I need to resist his false affections. Even with my lack of experience, I know this can only end badly for me.

"But, I...hmmm...I fear you," I finally manage to push out between my already parted lips.

Whatever spell he had been trying to cast over me, and possibly himself too, is suddenly broken, prompting him to draw back. Initially, I feel strangely frustrated, though when I finally come too, I am thankful for his distance. Tobias, on the other hand, looks indescribable. He is wearing an expression from which I cannot fathom what his true emotions are. I immediately look away from it, to save myself from its intensity.

"You seem to take pleasure in being hurtful towards me, after which I am often left feeling confused," I explain with a strange sort of shame floating around inside of my chest.

We stand so still in those initial few moments, that I feel like I should start running about the room just to dispense of the uncomfortable atmosphere. Tobias maintains an expression that could so easily break into any number of emotions - grief, rage, laughter. Eventually, after saying nothing, he turns around, picks up his coat, puts it on, and leaves without another word. This time, confusion is not a strong enough word to convey what I am feeling after this strange occurrence. I only know that it doesn't feel good, in fact, it has left me feeling thoroughly wretched. A frustrating revelation has come to pass, one that shows I am no happier after having seemingly upset him, than I am when he upsets me. I am lost to a battle I cannot win.

Day turns into night with dinner only being but a short time away. After our strange dance lesson, Mrs Keppel had appeared to escort me back to my room where I was instructed to dress accordingly for guests. A nauseated feeling overcame me for I have never been good at presenting myself before unfamiliar people. The last time I had done such a thing, I had been left insulted and engaged to a duke. However, my mind was put at ease when Mary informed me that it was only Tobias' friend attending, and from her experience, Lord Brown isn't one to stand to attention. Neither does he concern himself with the usual social niceties of upper crust London.

However, now that I am dressed and almost ready to join Tobias and his guest, I am suddenly feeling overwhelmed with nerves again. For even though Lord Brown sounds very much more relaxed than my husband, it is obvious by his instruction to dress accordingly, that Tobias wishes to show me off to this man. Failure to achieve the desired effect will no doubt mean a brash and cruel onslaught of words from my husband. My mother had taught me that men like to present their wives for others to admire and be impressed by, particularly business associates. She always giggled about it afterwards, telling me what ridiculous creatures men are. Though now, it does not seem so funny to be in the same position. My father was always proud of his family, so long as Elsie and I kept our sisterly bickering away from the dinner table. He never felt ashamed of how we looked or how we talked before his guests, but I have a feeling Tobias will be more than critical if my performance does not meet his high standards.

Mrs Keppel soon arrives to accompany me to dinner, which is highly unnecessary and not something she has done before this night. However, I have to admit I am grateful for her company. The thought of walking into that dining room with Tobias and Lord Brown alone was having an adverse effect on my stomach, and I was very much dreading it. No one seems to argue with Mrs Keppel, not even my husband.

The moment I set foot inside of the dining room, one of the few rooms with which I am familiar, both the Duke and Lord Brown stand to formally greet me. The usual bow and curtseys are adhered to whilst one of the butlers pulls a chair away from the table to have me seated. It has been more or less the same protocol since I arrived here. I long for the day when it might be less formal, and when talk will be free, friendly, and without the fear of being chastised or undermined. I wonder if this day will ever come.

"Good evening, Emily," Tobias says with a straight face, showing nothing of his reaction from our dance lesson. "You remember my best man, Lord Frederick Brown."

"Just Frederick, please," his fair-haired friend smiles at me with his teeth; he looks so much more jovial and approachable than my stern-faced husband.

"Of course," I murmur, trying to smile but finding the company so stifling and intimidating, I am afraid to do or say anything at all. "G-good evening."

I watch my husband roll his eyes over my timidity and stuttering whilst his friend merely frowns for a moment or two. He sees my cheeks turn red under a blush of embarrassment for my faltering and offers me another warm smile. Already, I feel more at ease in this man's company and cannot help wishing he was my husband instead of the man still glaring at me from the other end of the table.

"Please, be yourself with me, Lady Hardy." Frederick smiles with his glass hovering about near his lips. "Act as you would have back in your London home."

"You forget your place, Frederick," Tobias intervenes with a casual tone of voice, but then turns his icy blue eyes on me as if in warning to not do as his friend has just requested. "This is my house and my wife. Please do not presume to instruct her as to how to act."

My mouth parts in shock over the way he has just spoken to not only a guest, but a close friend of his, and at the dinner table of all places. The way people had spoken about Tobias had always seemed to have been greatly over-exaggerated, painting him as a cold, calculating, unfeeling monster, who did not possess a heart or a soul. However, the more closely I am acquainted with my husband, the more I am beginning to believe they were seriously underestimating his villainous tongue.

Whilst my thoughts spin inside of my head, his friend simply chuckles over Tobias' threatening words.

"Tis true, Tobias, though I fear your wife does not know how she should act, for you do not give anything away other than contempt. Please, Emily, you must forgive Tobias, he lost his heart a long time ago. And do not take his cold exterior to heart, for he is the same with everybody, even his long-suffering friend who has stood by his side since we were children."

I simply smile and nod, just as dinner is served before us. It is a concoction of fresh vegetables and meat from one of the local farms on the estate. Under normal circumstances, I would be diving in with my mouth drooling for more, however, I cannot even begin to stomach what is sitting before me on my plate. Instead, I sit still, just staring and willing it to get smaller so that it might vanish altogether.

"Something wrong with your food, Emily?" Tobias asks without even looking at me or ceasing in his own eating.

"Nothing at all," I reply before forcing myself to place a small morsel inside of my mouth, the act of which has me feeling instantly sick.

"Do you or do you not wish to eat your food?" he asks me like I am still in pinafores and simply choosing to misbehave at the dinner table. "And may I remind you to be always honest with me. I can always see when someone is lying."

He stares at me so intensely that I begin to tremble and tears trail along the bottom of my lashes. A huge lump in my throat forms a painful ache that I force to keep inside of me. I cannot still the tremble of my hands, for they are lost to their own consciousness, but I do manage to hold back my tears. A small success, and one I hold onto all the while he now stares at me with intent. After a moment or two being held captive under those icy cold eyes, and with Frederick now figuratively boring a hole in the side of my head, the humiliation gets to me. My trembling hands eventually drop my fork to my plate with such a loud clatter, I am forced to close my eyes to it.

"Leave," he orders, "there is no point to you being here if you do not intend to eat. You are excused!"

"I…" I open my mouth to explain, to argue, or to scream; I am not yet sure of which one I wish to release.

"Tobias, please, do not-" Frederick begins, but is quickly cut off from his attempts to defend my dignity.

"If she doesn't eat, she doesn't stay!" Tobias snaps, then returns to his own dinner plate where he continues to cut the food into little, chewable pieces. "Goodnight, Emily."

Feeling lower than that poor beetle I had seen struggling on his back, I slowly push away from the table to stand, nod my head to Frederick who looks on me with such pity, it allows a stray tear to escape. My husband does not pay me anymore attention as I walk towards the door, but I still mutter a quiet 'goodnight' before leaving. Mary is already on the other side of the door, offering me her arm whilst I silently fall apart from humiliation, all the way back to my room.

Tobias

"That," Frederick positively growls at me, "was totally uncalled for, Tobias!"

"I disagree," I reply, shrugging my shoulders with a smug jerk. "And seeing as we are in my house, I believe what I say goes."

"As you wish, Your Grace," he mutters angrily. I know how much I have vexed him, for he does not offer me his usual teasing. "Please excuse me, but I suddenly do not feel like I want to eat and seeing as you only allow those who wish to eat at your table, I fear I must retreat to my own quarters. Enjoy your meal, Your Grace, and your own, solitary company."

I continue eating the whole time he storms noisily away from the room. Once the door slams shut, I look up and notice one of the butlers staring directly at me with a horrified expression. I quirk an eyebrow at him, causing him to immediately remember his position and to adjust himself. On the outside, I am the calm, villainous monster who tore the princess from her family, only to treat her with less respect and care than my dog. My insides, however, look like an artist's palette of mixed-up colours, all mingling together into one dark mess.

Chapter 8

Tobias

The hour is late when I finally decide to leave Monty in front of the dying fire, and only because the flames no longer burn at my eyes when I stare into them. I embrace the pain of it, the burn that reminds me of who I've become, of what little I deserve after I had left Gennie to pass on without me. After I had broken the only promise I had given my mother before, she too, left me all too soon. The rest of the house has grown cold, for it is a clear night and offers no blanket of cloud to insulate the earth below. I welcome the change of temperature, for it makes me feel uncomfortable, as I should do being the monster that I am. Moments like these keep me grounded, preventing me from freefalling into notions of love and affection towards the girl who I continually belittle on a daily basis.

Before I retire to my own bed, I do as I have done every other night since arriving back from London last week. I go into Emily's room, pull up one of the hard, uncomfortable chairs, and sit beside her bed. Watching, only ever watching, as she sleeps soundly under her pure white covers. Her lips are slightly parted, her lashes fanning her cheeks, and her hair tightly tucked behind her shoulder which is only partly covered by a lace nightgown.

I sit and stare at her for I don't know how long, lost in thoughts, not all of them about her, but most of them. She baffles me with her looking every part the beautiful lady, her trying to act like one, even though it almost pains her. Having no idea what her calf of a *friend* really thought of her; having no idea of what she looks like; her trembling every time I am near. And yet, she does not cry. No matter how hard I push, she does not let me break her. I am both drawn to, and exasperated by her defiance

Whilst my head begins to ache over too much liquor and too many bewildering thoughts, I notice her begin to shiver under the dropping temperatures of early morning. I watch as her body tries to fold in on itself, looking desperate to keep any warmth it can clasp hold of. For a wicked moment, I smile while resting my face upon my fist, slumped in the discomfort of the hard chair, just thinking how I would enjoy warming her up with my own source of heat. In the end, however, I sigh to myself in frustration, get up, and retrieve another comforter to provide an extra layer. It does not take her long to settle, for the shivering to pass, and for me to resist any urges I might have had.

"I am not that much of a monster," I whisper to myself, and if I'm not mistaken, she gives me the faintest grace of a smile. It taunts me enough to leave her be, to force myself to bed where I will pass out, far away from all of these conflicting thoughts.

Emily

"Mm, good morning, Mary," I emit as I yawn, noticing her

drawing open the heavy curtains. I take an indulgent moment to stretch with my arms reaching high into the air. "Did you put an extra cover on me, Mary?"

"No," she replies as she begins getting my clothes out ready.

"That's funny." I frown over the presence of an extra comforter; one I have never seen before. In fact, I would not even have had any idea as to where to find such a thing inside of this house.

Before I can question its presence any further, there is a small knock on my door, causing Mary and I to look at one another with matching furrowed brows. Mary shakes hers away first, then marches herself over to the door to open it. Her curtsey tells me my husband has decided to grace me with his presence this morning. The only other person she would bow to so immediately, is Frederick, and I highly doubt he would be coming to visit his host's wife so early in the morning.

"Your Grace," she says, clear as day, while I strangely let out a relieved breath. Why his being here should bring any form of comfort, I have no idea. He not only humiliated me last night, but he also had me feeling so homesick, so in need of familiar affection, I had cried until I was indeed sick.

My momentary relief is replaced by my usual trembling when Mary leaves me to face Tobias by myself. If I had had more of an engagement with him, I may have had the chance to get used to his company with a chaperone in attendance. The trembling in my hands might not have been such an affliction had this happened. Alas, he did not afford me such a luxury.

Trembling aside, he walks into my room while I remain seated in a pool of sheets, quilts and comforters, whose apparition is still a complete mystery to me. I wait patiently as he nears my bed, with his eyes burning into the side of my head, so much so, I feel the need to take in a deep breath to steady my nerves.

"Good morning, Emily," he says calmly and proceeds to perch on the edge of my bed, which dips beneath his frame. "I trust you slept well. That you were warm enough?"

I look at the comforter, then back to him, watching him watching me as it finally dawns on me where my extra cover had come from. I cannot fathom how I actually feel about it. Fearful over the fact he obviously comes in to visit me in my sleep, or bewilderment over the idea of him actually showing any sort of concern for my comfort. In the end, I decide to show him nothing; to give him the same indifference he so frequently bestows upon me.

"As well as I can," I reply, "after I was publicly banished to bed."

His immediate response is to smile at me, adding a smugness to his features that reveals just how much he enjoys making me feel inadequate.

"Does my humiliation amuse you, Your Grace?" I ask him rather coldly, even if my trembling hands are now having to grip at the extra comforter to try and still them.

"Not your humiliation, no." He shrugs from his position on the bed. "The obvious disdain in your voice is what amuses me this morning." He pauses in his reply to take hold of one of my white knuckled hands and study it before telling my fist to, "Still!"

"I cannot help it," I whisper ashamedly. "You never gave me the opportunity to get used to your company, nor your contempt for me."

"*Contempt*?! That's a strong word, Emily," he says, still with that insufferable smirk on his face. "Besides, I thought you were a girl who enjoyed the liberty of being a child, of being able to do all those things that were halted the moment you became a lady of age. I bet you argued with your sister frequently. I bet you even fought with your ridiculous friend, Edmund. Not to mention, climbed trees, rode horses with each leg over the saddle, snuck into places one shouldn't in your position, bantered with your father because you were his favourite, the babe he never wanted to grow up. You, Emily, were the only girl to look me in the eye that night without blushing. And yet, now you are here, you are nothing but a trembling shadow of that girl."

I stare at him with incredulity over his description of me, of his disappointment for not being the wild girl who defied social convention without even meaning to. I am so stunned; I have no words with which to answer him with.

"Pity," he says softly whilst looking at me with another unreadable expression, "I thought I could like that girl. I thought she might be able to hold my interest for longer than the duration of a rather clumsy waltz. But now that I have you here, I realise you are not her."

"I am sorry to disappoint you, My Lord," I mutter towards the bed sheets again. "Perhaps you killed her spirit when you decided to bring me here and offer me nothing but your cruel words and obvious distain for me."

"Perhaps," he simply shrugs as he finally releases my hand and gets back up to his feet. "We are to attend a ball this evening at the Greyson estate. You will need to dress accordingly and attempt to act the part of a proper duchess. I shall require you to at least pretend to like me, even if that is a hardship for you."

He pauses for my reaction, waiting for me to respond to his suggestion that I despise him, but I give him nothing. I do not know how to respond to such a statement without incurring his wrath and his usual derision.

"Good," he says almost decidedly, then walks to the door to leave. "And Emily?"

I look up at him and brace myself for what is about to fall from his wicked lips.

"Do try not to tremble," he growls with a deep-set frown upon his face. "We are supposed to be happy-in-love newlyweds."

He slams my door shut before I even have a chance to respond to such an unthinkable notion.

Emily

"Monty!" I shout out for the ridiculous dog who is all ears, giant paws, and wiggly bottom. I swear he falls over himself more times than he actually manages to walk around. I can see why Tobias has made him his companion; the lovable hound just oozes warmth and affection while expecting nothing in return. He's just what I need in this place, living with a man like my husband. In fact, had it not been for Monty, I do not think I would have managed to tear myself out of bed after Tobias' meeting with me this morning.

I try not to tremble, I really do, but I am not used to men

like Tobias. My father and Edmund are worlds' apart from him. They offered warmth, love, and friendship, whereas Tobias offers nothing but coldness. Put that together with my life being turned upside down in such a short period of time, what does he expect?

The girl he talks of from back home, is very much lost at the moment. I have no idea who I am here, or who I am expected to be. I was the way I was because I felt safe and free to be who I wanted to be; a girl who was held in her family's affection no matter what she did. Here, I fear what will happen if I put so much as one foot wrong. I had been banished before an audience for simply dropping my fork onto my plate, so who knows what I would have to endure if I truly spoke my mind. I do not wish to find out.

Then, there is the other side of the duke. The one who is a man who likes to touch, to taste, and to remind me that I am his wife, legally, spiritually, and…physically. My knowledge of such things is deeply lacking, which only serves to make the whole concept of love between a man and a woman all the more terrifying. I fear what he alludes to, yet I do not know what it is. What is it that a man has from a woman when they are joined in matrimony? Why was my mother insistent that I forget what I had seen the day we had travelled to Hampshire to stay with Edmund and his brother? And why had my governess refused to tell me anything about it?

The night before we were wed, Mother had come into my room to talk to me, to have that conversation all girls who are about to be married have with their mama. But instead of passing on her wisdom, we had ended up crying together. By the time she was able to once again broach the subject, I had covered my ears like a stubborn child and refused to listen to hear a single word about it. Eventually, the maid had brought me some hot milk just to calm me down enough to go to sleep. It was as much my fault as it was hers. I cannot tell you if I feel regret about it, for I am starting to believe that perhaps it is better to remain ignorant until the time is upon me.

"Monty, stop doing that!" I giggle when he begins licking at his unmentionables, right before my very eyes.

"Oh, come now," a male voice calls over from not too far away, "I'm sure he cannot help it."

When I look up to find the owner of such a masculine voice, I see Tobias's best man and friend, Lord Brown, or Frederick as I've been instructed to call him. He's smiling and looking very much the antithesis to my husband. He is fair, where Tobias is dark; relaxed where my husband is stiff; kind, where the duke is wicked.

"Good afternoon, Lord Brown," I smile and nod before him, to which he does the same. "Come to join us in the afternoon sunshine?"

"How could one deny such a glorious scene," he says with a smile and pats Monty's head. "I left your brooding husband to scowl away the day in his study. I must say, Lady Hardy, you look very beautiful when you are able to smile."

I instantly blush and feel guilty for receiving such a compliment, especially when my husband is very much absent.

"You should not say such things," I smile awkwardly, "even I know that."

"No one is here to tell on us, Emily." He smiles, and not at all in a lascivious way, but in a genuinely friendly manner. "And I merely meant it is nice to see you acting your natural self instead of looking terrified before your brute of a husband."

"I thought he was your friend, Frederick?" I ask him with a curious expression.

"Not at the moment," he says, though still with a warm smile on his face. "I did not approve of the way he spoke to you last night and I said as much when you left."

Without realising it, we've fallen into a comfortable walk beside one another, along with Monty trotting closely at our heels. Mary is polishing some silverware at a nearby bench, enjoying the sun herself. I am glad for her watchful eyes, not because I do not trust Lord Brown, but because I do not wish my husband to have more reason to be angry with me.

"That wasn't necessary," I reply dutifully, even though Tobias did deserve to be told off for his awful behaviour last night.

"I disagree," he says firmly, "it was not honourable of him to humiliate you in such a way. I have to say you have got him quite tied up in knots. Tobias has always been…prone to sulking, but never have I seen him so vexed by somebody."

"Oh," I answer sadly, "I do not mean to cause him such stress. I do not mean to cause him anything. I think I would be quite content to remain unnoticed if I'm being truly honest."

"Alas, Emily, your fortunate features meant that was never going to occur." He smiles when I blush again. "I rather think, deep down, under all of that hostility, he likes you."

"Forgive me for laughing, Frederick," I giggle, "but I think you are sorely mistaken."

"It frustrates him when you are fearful around him, which makes him angry, which makes you frightened and act unnaturally," he sighs. "It's a vicious cycle. Someone should break it."

"I'm afraid my reaction to him is quite out of my hands." We both take a moment to laugh over my unintentional pun. "I am not used to men who intimidate me."

"No," he says as though lost in thought. "I am glad that *I* do not intimidate you."

He pushes his chin out towards my still hands when I look at him in for further explanation. I cannot help but smile in recognition of their natural motionless state. We then begin to walk back towards the house, just in time to see Tobias watching us from his study window with a fixed scowl upon his face, one that is not impressed with seeing his friend walking so casually alongside his wife.

Tobias

Angry does not even come close to how I am feeling when I see my wife and friend laughing and joking with one another, and without a tremor in sight. Of course, I only have myself to blame, but where's the fun in that. Instead, I do what I always do, I scowl, mutter bitterly to myself, and generally make everyone else feel uncomfortable. To admit that I feel jealous is simply unacceptable. It would suggest I have feelings for my wife, when in fact, she is a means to an end, and perhaps something to gaze upon when the mood so takes me.

To satisfy my baser urges, I am sure to take on a different mistress at least every three months, ensuring I do not stay with the same woman for any longer. My rather simple strategy ensures I can safely say I have never felt remorse or regret over letting any one of them go. My affections have not had the chance to develop any further than enjoying her body with some inconsequential conversation. My wife will provide me with the same, except she will also bear my offspring to continue my heritage. They will be gifted with her beauty, her nurturing, and my instruction as to how to compose oneself as a Lady or Gentleman baring the Hardy name.

And yet…

"Frederick, I see you are taking liberties with my hospitality," I huff at him when he enters my study with a ridiculous grin. It is so wide and genuine; it would even rival that of Monty's.

"Are you alluding to me taking a turnabout the garden with your delightful wife?" he asks whilst slumping inside of the chair across from my desk. I merely raise my eyes to peer over his boots that are now crossed over one another on top of my workspace.

"That is exactly what I am accusing you of," I reply, looking back down to a letter which is only fit for the bin. I still look at it as though it is one of the most vitally important pieces of paper for my eyes to have ever borne witness to. "Do not even consider the idea of making her fall in love with you, *friend*!"

"I wouldn't dream of such a thing, Tobias," he scoffs, and I do believe he is being quite serious. "Have you really sunk so low into the depths of bitterness that you would believe me, your oldest friend, would try and make a move on your wife?"

I take a moment to look up at him, with my expression remaining neutral, and my elbows now perched on top of the illegible letter. He looks affronted, if not horrified over what I have just suggested, and for a moment, I feel guilty. However, I soon shake it away again when I remember the image of them laughing together only moments ago.

"Just so we're clear, Frederick," I mutter as I theatrically pick up the letter again.

"Do you know, Tobias, one of the many reasons I would rather walk through fire than make a move on your beautiful wife, is the fact that I truly believe she would be good for you. She is warm, caring, full of good humour, and intelligent, even by your impossible standards."

I merely hook up an eyebrow to show I am far from convinced by his description of a young girl who knows very little of the world, other than the one in which she grew up.

"If only you'd let her in, Tobias," he says with a grace of a smile before leaping back up to his feet. "But you always have stood in your own way."

He leaves the room before I am able to reply, not that I was planning to gift him with anything at all meaningful. His words turn over in my head for a few minutes, with a picture of my young bride smiling and laughing the way she had just now, like a beautiful portrait come to life for but a few moments. Before I let any of those thoughts sink further into something close to affection for her, I shake them away and finally throw the wretched letter into the fireplace behind me.

Emily

What a perplexing thing to consider. Here I stand, dressed in one of the most beautiful gowns I have ever placed upon my body, and with my hair styled into something so indescribably elegant, ready to attend Lord and Lady Greyson's ball, as a duchess, and yet it is only my second formal outing as a grown woman. Most married ladies have had plenty of practice for these sorts of events, having attended many of them to find a husband. I doubt many of them found their betrothed on their very first one, and not after having turned eighteen but a few months before. But then, I had truly believed I was going to have at least another year or two before Papa would have been open to agreeing to a match. What a pity the duke decided he wanted a wife when I so happened to be attending my first ball.

"I think it is time for you to go, Emily," Mary says sympathetically from the side of me. She knows I am petrified of upsetting my husband tonight, especially with my trembling hands that I seem unable to control whenever I am near him. "Would you like me to accompany you to the Duke and Lord Brown?"

"Please," I barely manage to say out loud. "I feel I might need your arm to steady me, Mary."

"Of course."

She smiles before helping me to my feet and offering me her arm. Once I thread mine through hers, I take in a deep breath and let her lead the way. She's become both my friend and a mother figure of sorts, even if she is only but a few years older than I am.

As we make our way down the main staircase, our feet seem to echo much louder than usual, and the lights flicker in my eyes with an almost painful effect. With each step towards my husband, who is no doubt waiting for me in the entrance hall, I feel my hands begin to shudder with nerves. Mary tries to smile encouragingly, but it does nothing to soothe them. I am sure nothing could.

Once led downstairs, where my male chaperones are waiting for me in their grandeur - one smiling, the other painfully neutral in his expression - I take in an audible gulp of air. All the while we walk, I silently tell myself to calm down, to be brave and to not upset or embarrass my husband. A significantly difficult undertaking, seeing as he is frequently upset with me without me even having to try.

Mary leads me over to Tobias, who offers me his arm expectantly and without a smile. I offer Mary my silent thanks, to which she nods and places my arm through his. He looks me up and down as if assessing my efforts and whether they meet his lofty standards. His friend eventually intervenes with a warm smile and a nod of his head.

"May I say, Tobias, your wife looks flawless," he says in a friendly manner, one which I cannot help smiling and blushing over. "You will be the belle of the ball, Duchess, and will no doubt have all the gentlemen cursing your husband for having whipped you up so quickly. Tobias, you always did have impeccable taste!"

"Quite," Tobias says with what looks like a sneer.

"Thank you," are all the words I manage to release before taking in a deep breath to avoid the threat of tears over my husband's coldness.

If I really think about it, I never wanted a husband. In fact, I never even thought about having one. But now that I am here, married to a man who holds me in such low esteem, together with his friend who reminds me of Edmund and his warmth, I am beginning to feel regretful that I didn't have the opportunity to marry for love instead of status. Not that such a thing was ever truly in my hands. But I like to think that if the duke had never asked for my hand, my father would have taken my feelings into account when choosing a husband for me. Alas, there was no saying no to someone as revered as Tobias Hardy. Neither of us saw him coming, nor could we refuse him when he had decided I was going to be his wife.

"Frederick, will you go ahead of us and inform the driver that we are to leave in two minutes. I wish to have a word with Emily," Tobias instructs him like he is one of the servants. Fredrick rolls his eyes before marching away with a bounce in his step.

"He appears to be full of cheer," I say to Tobias with the hopes of avoiding a stern talking to, one that will be scathing and no doubt leaving me feeling even more uncomfortable than I already am.

"He has his eyes set on a young lady tonight; you should know the man is a rake. In fact, you should be pleased you avoided such a gentleman during your coming out," he says before looking at my hand which is noticeably trembling against his arm. I almost shout at it, for I know it will be making him feel angry.

"I'm sorry," I whisper, "I cannot help it."

"Try harder, Emily," he snaps. "Do not embarrass me by shivering like a dog whilst in the same vicinity as your husband. You are a duchess now, act as such!"

"Of course," I murmur and look to my feet in shame. His finger finds my chin and pulls it up to looking at him so I can see nothing other than but those icy blue orbs of his.

"Look up!" he snaps. "Always."

Chapter 9

Emily

I spend the journey holding my tongue whilst only half-listening to Frederick and Tobias discussing matters of business. They talk of subjects I try to make sense of, though the facts and figures of it all leave me uninterested and thinking of other things. I think of my parents, of Elsie and Edmund, and wonder how they are all getting along without me. In fact, I am so lost in my thoughts about them, Tobias has to clutch hold of my hand to alert me to our arrival. I smile shyly just as Fredrick gives me a secretive wink.

Tobias helps me to exit the carriage and holds onto me like I am the most precious thing in the world to him. It surprises me at first, but when I see him nodding smugly at a few other people we meet along the way, I fast come to realise why he is being so suddenly attentive. I cannot help but slump a little with disappointment, knowing that he is only showing a hint of care for me for appearance's sake. Remembering his words from earlier, I try to keep my head up as much as possible, though I still cannot help the tremble in my hands. Tobias attempts to remedy this by squeezing hold of me more tightly so no one else can see what effect he has on me.

Once inside the Greyson estate, I cannot help but take in

the extremely grand interior. Every nook and cranny has been decorated with flowers, feathers, and other beautiful trinkets. This home isn't as striking as the Hardy estate; however, I can feel a warmth that is missing in my new home. A warmth I am trying to find from Mary, Mrs Keppel, and Monty, seeing as my husband appears to be incapable of offering such a thing.

I try to mask my inexperience to attending such events by sticking close to my husband, as well as keeping my greetings short. Tobias doesn't say anything to me. In fact, he doesn't give any indication that I should say anything to anyone, so to avoid any further unpleasantness from him, I decide to remain as tight lipped as much as possible.

Not before long, I find myself being presented before a couple, who I assume are Lord and Lady Greyson, together with their daughter, Victoria, and their son, Thomas. The usual rigmarole of curtseying and saying 'how do you do' are exchanged; a protocol that even has Tobias having to sport a smile. The sight of which has me taking a glance at Frederick; he is deeply amused by his usually stern-faced friend having to make an effort. He notices me watching and has to place his fingers to his lips to cover his mirth.

"Your Grace, we are most humbled to have you attend our ball this evening, especially with the new Duchess of Kent!" Lord Greyson beams at my husband before turning his attentions to me. "Please let me introduce my daughter, Victoria, and my eldest, Thomas."

Both children look to be of a similar age, somewhere between mine and my husband's years. His son, Thomas, takes me in with a disturbingly smug expression before offering Tobias the usual social niceties. Once he has finished saying all the required compliments one is expected to give a duke, he turns to give me a sly wink, an action that has me feeling uncomfortable and slightly nauseated, if I am being perfectly honest. Victoria, on the other hand, blushes, curtseys, then looks at Frederick with obvious attraction to him.

"Of course. May I formally introduce to you my new wife, Emily Hardy," Tobias replies, pulling me forward and patting my hand with pretend affection. "We are honoured to be here with you this evening. In fact, it is our very first outing together as man and wife."

"How lovely!" Lady Greyson smiles before looking at me with a motherly expression, one I have been missing, so take it in for all it is worth. "You look simply exquisite, Your Grace. Thomas, wasn't I saying what a beautiful wife the duke had, just the other day in fact?"

"Indeed, you were, Mother," Thomas replies as he steps in to kiss my hand, just before Tobias subtly pulls me back and away from him. "Your Grace is most fortunate."

"Might I also introduce my good friend, Lord Frederick Brown," Tobias says though his teeth, still glaring at Thomas. He manages to gesture towards Frederick who steps forward to bow and kiss Victoria's elegant hand. She smiles shyly and with a crimson blush spreading over her cheeks. It is interesting to watch how a normal couple who are attracted to one another should interact. I suppose it is something I shall never experience.

"Might I be honoured enough to have a dance with you, Miss Greyson," Fredrick asks Victoria with expert charm; so much so, I have to stifle a smile.

"I would be delighted," she replies in such a way, he smiles, and she blushes an even deeper shade of red.

Tobias nods at our hosts before eventually pulling us away to reside alongside the dancefloor where young couples are already moving energetically across the room. Tobias keeps a tight hold on me whilst Frederick eyes some of the eligible ladies dancing about with their gentleman partners. They look like they are having fun, engaging in conversation and laughter with one another. It reminds me of Elsie and Edmund, and a deep pang of sadness hits me.

"Frederick," Tobias says without looking at him, to which Frederick turns his way with a knowing smile, "behave yourself. You are here with me. Do not embarrass me by becoming embroiled in a dual because you are unable to help yourself with a certain Miss Greyson."

"I wouldn't dream of it," Frederick replies with an obvious tone of sarcasm before smiling at me with a menacing wink. It is enough to lift my melancholy a little.

"And Emily," he says before turning to face me, thus blocking my entire view of the room so I can only look into his icy blue eyes. "You are to keep away from Thomas Greyson. Do you understand?"

Fredrick's jovial expression turns serious all of a sudden, but I waste no time in nodding my head so rapidly, his friend's concerned face soon becomes a blur. Not only do I not want to upset my husband, but I must confess, I want to engage with that man even less so. He reminds me of a snake, one who could bite at any given opportunity. Tobias averts his eyes to Frederick before walking away, thus leaving me under his friend's protection. His tall, broad back wanders across the room with a slow confidence I have not seen on any other man before. People automatically move out of his path, and without him even having to say a single word. Eyes remain on him in his wake, often with a few whispered words behind his back.

Just before I see him exit the room altogether, a familiar face catches my eye, right at the exact same time their eyes notice me too. When the realisation of who the other is finally sinks in, I cannot keep the wide smile from my face, though neither can he.

Edmund, a warm and familiar face from home and childhood, is stood beside the very same man I've been told to keep away from. They are chatting together like old friends; it unnerves me a little. Frederick remains oblivious to the scene before me, so I decide in that moment, to keep him that way. I think it is for the best, especially when Tobias has been so adamant about me keeping away from both gentlemen.

"Frederick, might I go to the powder room?" I ask him sweetly while he continues to stare at all the beautiful ladies on show. "I'll be back before you know it."

"Of course, Emily," he says with a cheerful smile, "you are a married woman now, and I'm sure there will be plenty of eyes and ears on you. Keep out of trouble, Your Grace."

I nervously laugh over his playfulness before crossing the room to go to the powder room, hoping to be fortunate enough to catch Edmund in the hallway. I know I have promised not to talk to him, or the man who has spotted me and is now subtly gesturing to my presence, but I am so homesick, I feel like I will die if I do not get the chance to speak with him, even if it is only to say hello.

Once inside of the lady's private room, I find somewhere to hide away so I can try and calm my emotions. A long, heavy curtain provides a cover and I manage to shield myself from view whilst using the stillness of the dark outdoors to soothe my over exposed senses. I just about manage to feel a little more relaxed when I hear two loud ladies enter the room with lots of laughing and cackling between one another. They soon fall into gossip, and I instantly conjure up a picture of the ladies who would frequent my mother's many tea afternoons. I used to giggle with Elsie over their ridiculousness, however, now it doesn't seem so funny to be within earshot of them. So much so, I find myself retreating further into the heavy fabric of the curtains to ensure my whereabouts remain unknown.

They begin talking about who is courting who, then move onto discussing scandals that have occurred back in London. All stuff and nonsense I have never much been interested in. That is until I hear names I recognise; names I do not want to hear about but have very little choice in the matter.

"And did you see the duke?" one of them says as if conspiring with the other. "So handsome, don't you think?"

"Oh, yes, but the man is contemptable," the other replies, "his eyes could turn you to ice, he's so cold."

"True," the first sighs. "What about his new wife, the now Duchess of Kent?"

"I know very little about her, seems awfully young though…poor girl."

"I wonder if they shall produce an heir any time soon," the original says in a dreamy kind of way, "between them they would have such beautiful children."

"Come, Amy," the other one says with air of amusement, "I doubt he even sleeps in the same bed as her. She still looks as innocent as the day she came out of pinafores!"

"Do you think?" the first one laughs, then lowers her voice to nearly a whisper. "Do you think the marriage is unconsummated?"

"Amy, I am sure the poor girl doesn't even know what the word means, let alone to have been privy to such an act!"

I wait with bated breath until I am sure they have vacated the room altogether, giggling away as they do so. For some reason, I have a desperate urge to cry, though I cannot begin to figure out why. Perhaps it is because I feel small, humiliated, and jaded by something I do not even know or understand. In the end, I wipe away at my wet eyes, check myself in the mirror, all before exiting the stifling little room. I need to leave before anyone else can come in to cast aspersions my way.

I check the hallway for the gossipy women, and when I see the coast is clear, I walk away in hurried steps, completely forgetting my original intention to find Edmund alone. I am too upset and angry to think clearly, so when I run slap bang into his warm chest, I cannot help but forget that we are in company, or that I am married, so throw my arms around his shoulders, just like I would have back home. My *real* home.

He is quick to take hold of my arms and glance around to ensure no one has seen my suspicious-looking outburst. Once safe in the knowledge that we are alone, he pulls me out onto the terrace where there are a few other gentlemen smoking cigars and drinking whiskey out of their crystal glass tumblers. I take in greedy gulps of air as I begin pacing up and down, trying anything to stop myself from crying.

"Em?" he says with such pity in his voice, I have to sniff back and swallow a whimper. I feel myself having to physically shaking away the urge to hug him again. "It's not that bad, is it?"

"Oh, Edmund," I whisper, "it's worse!"

"Em, tell me he doesn't hurt you, tell me you are safe!" he pleads as he takes a few steps towards me. I notice his hands balling into fists in an attempt to stop himself from touching me, especially now that one of the men from the other end of the terrace has begun to watch our interaction with a thoroughly furrowed brow.

"No," I reply truthfully while shaking my head. "But he's so cruel, Edmund. I do not even know why he wanted me; he seems to hate me that much. It is much like having to walk over eggshells whenever I am in his presence."

"From what I hear, Em, that isn't personal to you," he sighs sadly. "It is his flaw, not yours."

"Perhaps," I mutter, knowing it makes no difference to his treatment of me, nor of my hurt when he says such awful things. "But I miss you all so terribly! How are my family? How is father?"

"They are missing you deeply, Em, you have left a hole they cannot fill," he says with his warm smile and soft eyes. "I feel it too…everyday."

"But they are well, yes?" I ask with desperation in my voice.

"Yes, you need not fear for their wellbeing," he reassures me and begins to rub his hand against my upper arm. "I miss you too, Em, so much."

"Me too," I say with a smile, then notice that his hand has remained firmly on top of my naked arm. I begin to feel awkward over it. "You are my best friend, Edmund, even if you are better at sword fighting than I am."

"Remember when I fell and sprained my ankle?" He smiles and I laugh over his clumsiness as a child. "Em, that's when I knew I-"

"Emily!" a bark of a voice calls over to me, sounding beyond angry and ready to cause a scene. Edmund hears it too and immediately withdraws his hand from my arm whilst I simultaneously jump back. Within seconds, my husband is before me, snarling and clenching every muscle in his body. My trembling hands return almost instantly, which Edmund notices. Concern spreads over his entire face, and I silently beg him to not say anything.

"Your Grace," Edmund says confidently, trying to sweep over the whole heavy atmosphere. "Emily and I were just saying hello and I was just telling her about her fam-"

"She is Lady Hardy to you," Tobias snaps, "and my wife!"

"Of course," Edmund answers him, dipping his chin into his neck as if in submission. "My apologies, Lord and Lady Hardy."

At this point, I notice we have now attracted a small audience, including Fredrick, Thomas, and lots of whispering ladies who seem to be finding my public ordeal fascinating to watch. Tobias looks at them with a tight upper lip and a desperation to shout at all of them. I watch him silently counting to ten before taking hold of my hand and leading me towards the house again. I smile apologetically to Edmund before following my husband through the main hallway and out the other side of the house where the carriages are waiting. We cannot have been here long, and already I have managed to shame my husband, who has then publicly disgraced me. As if the skies above have sensed my mounting fear, it begins to rain with rumbles of thunder sounding off in the distance.

"Tobias!" Fredrick begins shouting out from behind us, all the while Tobias pulls at my arm to reach the carriage before it's even been brought over to the front doors of the house. "Tobias, what in God's name are you doing?!"

Tobias turns on him with such anger, Frederick takes a step back and eyes me with concern. It is more than obvious how upset I am, as well as how furious my husband is. Even if I am trying to maintain what little bit of dignity that I have left by holding my tears inside.

"We are leaving before my wife can disgrace our name anymore," he says so calmly, it only sounds all the more terrifying than if he had begun shouting at the top of his voice. "You are welcome to join us but if you choose to, we are leaving this instant."

Fredrick looks between Tobias and me, before sighing and nodding his head in defeat.

"Then I shall come with you," he declares, and looks at me with the grace of a comforting smile. Tobias doesn't say another word, instead, he turns on his heel to violently pull open the carriage door. I am pushed inside and made to sit so close to him, I can feel the heat of his anger rolling off into the atmosphere all around us. No words are spoken, no looks exchanged, just the sniffing back of my fear and the trembling of my hands against my skirts. Halfway home, the storm breaks in a spectacular display of thunder, lightning, and heavy sheets of unrelenting rain. It is so noisy, my shuddering worsens, and I have to grip hold of the leather of the seat to try and steady myself.

Once we arrive back at the estate, Tobias practically leaps out of the carriage before holding his hand out for mine. I take it only to try and keep his anger at bay, which feels like a futile feat, but one I will try and grab onto, for I am feeling that afraid of him. The rain continues to beat down, practically soaking us within the few feet between the carriage and the front door. I am sure I would have gotten wetter if hadn't been for the fact that I am forced to run to keep up with Tobias' large, determined footsteps. Even George, my husband's personal butler, withers when he sees the fury on his face. He soon moves out of the way as we approach the door, where I brace myself for Tobias' impending explosion.

"Tobias, calm yourself!" Frederick tries to soothe him when we get into the entrance hall, where he practically pushes me away from him. Mary is soon at my side, taking my wet cloak whilst George removes those from Frederick and Tobias. My husband says nothing, just places his hands on his hips and begins pacing with rage-filled stomps of his boots.

"Tobias, what on earth has you so riled up, man?"

"My wife, not only talking to a man I told her not to," he snaps at the same time as suddenly looking up at me with his stormy eyes, "but also allowing him to have his hand on her!"

Frederick looks at me for some sort of affirmation, but all I can do is continue to look ashamedly towards the floor.

"I was unaware I had married a harlot!"

"Tobias!" Frederick snaps at him as I look up at him with such anger, I do not think I have ever felt like this before. I even take a step towards him, ready to defend my honour, even if he has none. He hooks up his eyebrow with a grimace of a taunting smile and I don't know if he wants me to say something, or if he wants me to step down again. In the end, I decide to only offer a defiant sigh and return to looking at the floor. I refuse to engage with his form of torture or game playing.

"I notice you didn't tremble under his touch, my darling wife!" he snarls at me. "Get.Out.Of.My.Sight!"

His voice is low, eerily level, though definitely close to the edge of losing his temper and self-control. I have never been struck before; my father was never the sort of man to lose his temper with a woman. I know he would rather hit himself before he lay his hands on my mother, but I know it happens. I am not naïve enough to think such things do not occur in our circles. Perhaps it will happen now, with me, here, tonight.

To my surprise, he remains rigid, far out of reach of me, so I take the opportunity to about turn and walk slowly up the stairs. My hands remained clasped together tightly in front of me, and with my breathing slow and deep to try and keep my mouth from opening to argue with him, to tell him exactly what I think of him. I know better than to let everything out, so I bite my lips together, almost to the point of drawing blood. Even when I hear him stomp away into his study, followed by the tip tapping of Frederick's shoes, even when I hear a glass being obliterated against a wall, I keep my lips closed and make my way slowly up to my room.

Just before I close my door on this horrid night, Mary comes rushing up to me, looking concerned and sorry for me.

"Emily," she says on a rush of air escaping from her lips, then reaches for my arm, but I hold up my hand to halt her, a small smile upon my face.

"Please, Mary, do not be nice to me," I reply calmly and evenly. "I do not want to cry for him, and if you are nice to me, I am not sure I will succeed in that feat."

She smiles, even though she is not entirely convinced by my words, then nods her head and leaves me be. I close the door softly for but a moment, pausing to make sure she is gone, and then…then I run.

Chapter 10

Tobias

"Tobias!" Frederick shouts angrily just before I reach for my glass and haul it across the room, which smashes on impact against the study wall. I wanted to feel a release from it, to enjoy the sound of its destruction, but I still feel nothing but rage coursing through my veins. When it fails to soothe me, even just a fraction, I clench my teeth together, brace my fists against my desk and drop my head down to try and stop the dizziness that is threatening me to pass out altogether.

"Leave!" I growl at him, knowing he is about to try and talk his own form of sense into me.

"No!" he retorts in such a way, I know my usual jovial friend is no longer here with me. Instead, I have angry Frederick, a man who always knows how to make me feel small. "You know I will not stand for your arrogance when you've severely fucked up, Tobias, and you, my friend, have fucked up so much, I'm not even sure how to get you out of it."

"Do not use your brash language with me when I am in such a foul mood, Frederick," I mutter before standing up tall against him, my raging eyes staring right into his own. "I am liable to take my temper out on you when we all know it is my wife who has caused me to feel so vexed."

"Your *wife*?! Is that what you call her?" he snaps as he crosses his arms, all the while feigning confusion.

"Yes, my wife, that is what Emily is, though the way she was simpering around that young fool of a man, I can see why you might have trouble understanding that."

"I think it is you who has trouble seeing that, Tobias!" He sighs heavily before pacing back and forth, now rivalling me with his wrath. "And you know that what you saw was completely innocent. Not that I would blame the poor girl for seeking any kind of comfort when you offer her nothing but your vitriol!"

"She does not need comfort; she needs drawstrings and her mother's teat!" I spit out bitterly. "I thought she was far removed from all the insufferable ladies of society, frilly girls like her sister, but she is just as meek as the rest of them! I should have left her to have had a thoroughly uninteresting life with that pup, that fool, Edmund Barton!"

A silence falls over the room with only the heat of our fury to fill the atmosphere that's gathering all around us. It is only when Frederick begins to laugh that I look up at him again. His sudden outburst causes me to feel only the angrier towards him, Emily, all of this.

"You think she is meek?!" He continues to laugh with his arms still folded in contempt. His question causes me to falter, to look at him with confusion falling over me like an unwanted cloud on an otherwise sunny day. "Your wife, Emily, is anything but weak, Tobias! Why, I don't think I have ever met a more courageous woman, not since-"

"Don't say it!" I positively growl at him.

"Genevieve," he says anyway, completely ignoring the threat in my voice.

I walk right up to him, mere inches from his face and with steam positively billowing out through my nostrils like an angry bull. He looks right back at me without flinching; to be fair, he never has done.

"And just like your sister, Tobias, she refuses to cry in the face of a man who is determined to make her. Or do you forget so quickly, Tobias; do you forget how your father tormented her? Blaming her for your mother's death?"

His words gut me, to the point whereby I have to turn away. I cannot look at him while he accuses me of being no better than the man who routinely bullied my sweet, innocent, little sister. The girl who my mother had begged me to look after and protect. And now, here I stand, being no better than him.

"You were the only one to stand up for Genevieve, to fight against him when he was at his worst. You were her saviour and now," he says, walking over so I can feel him at my back, "you are no better than him; you have become the villain!"

"Don't..." I whisper.

"Your wife? Your *meek* and *frilly* wife is alone here. She doesn't have a saviour, you made sure of that!" he says with disappointment dripping from each of his words. "You conduct yourself with dishonour, and you should be ashamed." I close my eyes to his accusation, to his words of truth. "I know Genevieve would be. Hell, even your mother would be. *I* am ashamed of you, Tobias!"

"I know," I mutter before bracing myself to turn and face him. "What would you have me do, Frederick?"

"Go," he says, "go and tell her you are sorry and that you will stop acting like a spoilt prince who does not know how to treat a woman with respect or honour. And do it now, Tobias!"

I smile tightly, knowing he is right before nodding my head and looking towards the doorway. The storm is still raging outside, and it has me pulling my jacket back on so I can make my way upstairs. Frederick begins walking first, setting the wheels into motion before my stubbornness and pride can get in my way again. However, no sooner do we step out into the hallway, than we notice the front door swinging back and forth with the sound of the wind continuing to howl away outside.

"Tobias, why is the door open?" Frederick turns back to face me with a concerned frown.

"George!" I shout as I stride over to look outside into the pitch blackness. My butler soon comes pacing into the hall with his tapping shoes upon the stone tiles. "George, why is the door open? Did you not close it after we returned?"

"But of course, Your Grace, I locked it myself," he says, now looking just as lost over it as Frederick.

"Would anyone else open it for any other reason, George?" I ask, now beginning to panic, for I may well have driven Emily into doing something foolish, something that could cause her harm. My heart begins beating rapidly when the poor butler shakes his head, still looking confused over the whole matter.

"Frederick," I call out, turning to face him to see that he has now come to the same conclusion as I have, "will you go and check my wife's chambers? George, please fetch my horse."

"Of course," Frederick replies at the same time as George nods.

When they both leave, I begin pacing and pushing back my hair in frustration. If Emily has come to any harm, I will never forgive myself. With such painful thoughts threatening to push me to the brink of insanity, I quickly go to retrieve my coats, Frederick's too. If she is out there, I will not stop until I find her.

"Her room is empty," Frederick shouts from the top of the staircase, confirming my fears, "her cloak is gone too."

I make no attempt to answer him, just put on my cloak and begin walking out into the night so I can try and find her. I have no idea where to start, so whistle for Monty, hoping he might be able to put his nose to good use.

"I will come with you," Frederick shouts, "through the woods on foot. You can take the fields with your horse."

"If you do not find her in the woods, you are to return back here," I tell him before getting onto my horse's back. "We do not need two missing people."

Tobias

The rain is unrelenting, and the wind is strong enough to take my horse off course. The storm is loud enough to mask my shouting, but none of it will stop me in my quest to find Emily. I would call her my wife, but right now, I do not feel like I deserve to. My only saving grace is Monty, who remains dead ahead in my line of vision. He keeps ahead, sniffing out the ground for what I hope is Emily, and only stops to come back and make sure I am still behind him. I would hazard a guess that we have already covered a number of acres, though I shouldn't be surprised to learn that we have been going around in circles. The loss of feeling in my extremities is telling me to return to the house, and to see if Fredrick has had any more luck. It is something I almost decide to do, and even go as far as to pull on the reins, but Monty instantly stops me with his sudden whimpering and barking, just ahead of us. It looks as if he has found something by the side of the stream that runs along the bottom of a small valley.

With hope beginning to build inside of me, I pull my horse to the side so I can carefully navigate the hill without the risk of us falling. Monty remains whimpering by the side of whatever it is he has found. It is only when he moves but a fraction that I see the whites of her petticoats, laying in stark contrast against the thick, muddy grass. Without even thinking about it, I jump from my horse and hastily run over to where Monty is resting against her arm, looking up at me with those big, brown eyes of his.

"Emily," I gasp as I look at her shut eyes, her bloodied temple, and soaking wet body. Monty begins to bark at the same time as I shout out her name and attempt to get her to wake up, but she remains rigidly still. Realising my efforts are proving futile, I begin to move my hands underneath her legs and back before lifting her motionless body into my arms. Monty is quick to get up and follow me, only stopping when I push her up and onto the horse. When I haul myself up to join her, to hold her in a more comfortable position, I waste no time in getting us going, back in the direction of the house. With Monty running beside us, I mentally tell myself to reward his efforts with a juicy bone, one from the farm on the estate. He has more than earnt it.

When I carry Emily into the hallway, both of us being

dripping wet and likely riddled with influenza, Frederick is already there, looking wet himself, but ready to take Emily from me. Mary and Mrs Keppel are also at the ready, even though they are flustering and looking fearful for my wife.

"Fredrick, take Emily to my room; Mrs Keppel, will you please send a messenger for the doctor," I pant whilst trying to rid myself of my cloak and water sodden boots.

"Of course," she gasps. "Mary, follow Lord Brown and make sure there are plenty of robes and blankets for Lady Hardy."

I am soon left alone in the hallway, soaked to the bone but feeling nothing but guilt and self-loathing. How could I have let myself become the very man whom I despised. When I think back to the way Genevieve had always looked following each and every interaction with our father, I feel sick. When I leave Emily after I have released my venom on her, does she look just as destroyed as she had? She trembles over the mere sound of my presence. I remember Genevieve would do that too, violently.

I should go up and see her, make sure she is being cared for properly. But what right do I have to do that when it is I who has caused this tragedy to occur. Instead, I pour myself a stiff drink and settle into my chair, listening to the sounds of people rushing around to tend to her. In fact, I sit there for so long I hear Frederick welcoming the doctor inside of the house, then marching up to see to her needs, and finally my friend seeing the man out again. After which, I brace myself for his oncoming footsteps.

"Tobias," he announces, "hiding, are we?"

"Before you attempt to make me feel even worse than I already do, please, tell me how she is." I watch as he walks in with a smile on his face, obviously enjoying the fact that he was right, and I was wrong. So very wrong. "Please?"

"She is a little battered and bruised, susceptible to catching a cold, but ultimately, she'll be fine. How about you, Your Grace?"

"Do not call me that," I huff as I drink back the last of my drink. "I have been anything but graceful with her."

"No, I guess not," he admits when he finally takes the seat opposite me. "What are you going to do?"

"Besides tell you that you were right?" I reply, to which he emits a small laugh because he knows how much admitting that would have pained me. "Perhaps I should let her return home. Keep up the pretence of this marriage but let her be with her family."

"Hmmm," he mumbles before pouring his own drink, "I think it is a little late for that, my friend. You know as well as I do, she cannot return to London without tongues wagging. No," he declares as he gulps back the drink all in one mouthful, "you are actually going to have to put the work into this one, Tobias, go and make things right with her."

I do not reply to his suggestion, merely lean onto the desk in front of me and nod my head in agreement. Moments later, I will myself to get up and head towards the door so I can go and begin to make things right with my wife.

"You never know, Tobias," Frederick halts me before I manage to step through the door, "this could be the push you needed to finally put you on the path to happiness. After all, you like her, don't you?"

I pause for a moment or two, and even though I have my back to him, I can hear the smile he is directing my way. A torrent of comebacks enters my head, each one begging to be let loose and win this battle of words. However, in the end, I have to concede that he already has.

By the time I reach Emily, lying in my bed, she is already sleeping off her traumatic evening. The sun is beginning to make its ascent into the sky that is still grey with cloud, but at least absent of any rain. The storm only relinquished its punishing onslaught an hour or so ago but has left behind a heavy silence which only makes me feel all the more anxious for Emily whilst she sleeps on. In between checking her breathing, I try to lie across the uncomfortable chair that sits in front of my window. I know I cannot sleep, so I do not even bother to try, just remain staring at her, wondering what caused me to go so far off track.

"Mmm…" I hear her whimper from the bed, causing me to pull my chair up beside her so I can be closer to her if she needs me. When her eyes open wide, showing her green irises that remind me of the treetops outside in the woods, the same one she is so desperate to explore, I take in a deep breath and wait for her to speak first. It is the very least I can do.

"Tobias?" she asks with a voice that sounds so hoarse, it hardly sounds like her. She brings her hand to her throat while looking at me for an explanation I do not even know how to begin.

At first, I say and do nothing but emit a long, heavy, and guilty sigh. Once I feel able to, I reach out and take hold of her hand, clasping it between my much warmer ones, then offer a smile. Something I should have done long before now. Understandably, she eyes me with suspicion, as though expecting me to say something scathing so that I might bring her to tears again.

"Emily," I reply on yet another sigh.

"What happened last night?" she asks before putting her hand to her temple and rubbing against the bandaged wound. I gently pull it away before she can undo what the doctor did last night.

"You ran into the storm," I reply, feeling incredibly guilty all over again. "I found you lying unconscious, by the stream," I explain before emitting a soft laugh, "actually, it was Monty who found you."

"It was?" She graces a smile before frowning as if in deep thought again. "I slipped on the mud…I think."

"Emily, I want to beg for your forgiveness," I finally admit, swallowing hard for I cannot even remember the last time I apologised to anyone. "I think I lost my way a long time ago and you were just another person to blame for it. When I saw you with Edmund, when I saw that you did not flinch like you do with me, my bitterness came out in all its ugliness."

"Tobias," she croaks, "I did not mean to dishonour you, I just wanted so desperately to know about my family, to know that they are well. I miss them-"

"I know, Emily, and you do not need to explain it to me," I tell her, squeezing her hand that more tightly so she understands. "I want you…I mean, I'm hoping you will give me the opportunity to make things better for you here. We hardly even know each other."

"I know a little," she says with a smile, one I have never seen her use with me before. It is soothing and I cannot help already missing it when it leaves her face again. "You have a bad temper, Tobias."

"That is true," I reply and hang my head low in shame.

"You do not like beans," she smirks, causing me to look up at her with a half-smile, "and you love that silly dog of yours."

"*Love* is such a strong word," I interrupt, feigning a perplexed frown.

"One that is warranted in this case," she smiles, and I cannot help enjoying it all over again. "You…you don't think a lot of me, Tobias."

"I do not like a lot of people, Emily," I tell her truthfully, "but you are not people, you are my wife. And when you are better, I would like to get to know you. Perhaps even get to a point whereby you no longer tremble in my presence." I point to her free hand which is still shuddering against her thigh. She watches as it quivers inside of her lap, then looks back to me with a shameful expression. "It is my fault, Emily, not yours."

We remain in silence for a few awkward moments, both looking nervous and unsure as to what to say to one another. I then open my mouth to say something, though I cannot tell you what it is, but thankfully, I am stopped by a knock at the door.

"Come in," I call out, but with my eyes still fixed on Emily.

"Oh, do excuse me, Your Grace, but I thought I might bring some breakfast up for Em…I mean, Her Grace," Mary, her maid, corrects herself, and I have to smirk at Emily over her slip of the tongue. My wife blushes at me before fidgeting with her sheets beneath her fingertips.

"Of course," I reply as I get to my feet, "I shall leave you in peace."

Before I go, I make the decision to lean in and kiss her on

her still blushing cheek. The action causes her to gasp, though I pretend to ignore it, and make my way over to the door.

"Oh, and Emily," I call out just as Mary reaches Emily's bedside. When she looks up at me, I stare into her eyes for a moment before I continue. "When you are well enough, I thought I might finally take you for that walk in the woods?"

"I would like that," she replies with a warm and genuine smile. "I shall let you know as soon as I am able."

Chapter 11

Emily

It is a few days before I feel myself again. I have seen Tobias on a few occasions; he helped to move me back into my own room and has dined with me every evening. His conversation is limited but his smiles appear genuine, so much so, Mary has been teasing me. It is a strange place in which we are residing, one between friend and stranger, though at least he is no longer angry or finding fault in everything I say or do. I like this version of him, even if we are still not altogether comfortable when left alone in each other's company. But, for the first time since moving into this house, I am beginning to feel safe.

Frederick only returned to London yesterday in the hopes of courting the lovely Victoria Greyson. We have taken many turns about the garden, discussing his time growing up with my husband and how he hopes to settle down in the near future. It would seem his days of being a bachelor are becoming lonely and empty. Our friendship has grown into something that feels a lot like what Edmund and I once shared. Tobias joined us for tea on a few occasions, however I often found myself remaining quiet during these times, and instead, listened to them banter away to each other. It was most amusing to listen to them poking fun at one another.

From what my husband had said during these informal chats, I fear poor Frederick might have some stark competition for Victoria Greyson's affections, for she seemed to catch the eye of many young gentlemen on the evening of her parent's ball. She also has a rather large dowery from what Fredrick has told us, though he swears it is not the driving force behind his own attraction.

Now that he has gone, I cannot decide whether his departure is a good thing, or something to be worried over; it leaves me very much in the solitary company of my husband.

"Emily," Tobias says across the dining table. I look up to see him sitting comfortably within his own skin, leaning back against his chair, and lazily clasping at his glass of wine. I cannot help but offer him a shy smile, for I still brace myself for him saying something innocuous; unfortunately, it will take time to believe he has truly changed his opinion of me. But I will admit, we are on the right path to friendship. "I have decided to take a few days off from work, so we may spend some more time together, just like we discussed. I was thinking I might take you into the village tomorrow, to meet some of the tenants. Would this be agreeable with you?"

"Very much," I reply with what I hope is a smile, because I can see he is trying, and the last thing I wish to do is break his resolve to do so. "Will Monty be joining us?"

"Would you like Monty to accompany us?" he asks with a small laugh, for he knows I love that dog just as much as he does.

"Well, he did save me, it seems only fair," I reply as I return the smile before taking a sip of my own wine.

"If I didn't know any better, I would believe I have reason to feel jealous," he teases, though I blush because he has never hinted to having strong enough feelings to be jealous before. He doesn't comment on my obvious crimson glow, simply smiles again. "It is agreed then, we shall take the lovable beast."

The following morning, I meet Tobias by the front door, ready to walk across the fields and into the village. He had asked if I wanted to take a carriage, but I can think of nothing better than taking a jaunt across the countryside. I have always loved the outdoors and being in such a beautiful area of the country is only adding to the appeal. Besides, we do have Monty to take into consideration, and what dog wants to stay couped up inside of a carriage when he has the option of wide-open space to in which to run wild.

To begin with, the walk is an awkward affair with both of us looking towards the daisies instead of each other, bar the odd tight-lipped smile. He was speaking the truth when he told me we hardly knew one another, but I have already learnt that Tobias is not as worldly wise with women as he is portrayed to be. If he were, this would be far easier for him. By the time we're at the end of the first field, I feel like I have to say something, much like I would have done with Edmund by now.

"Did you grow up here, Tobias?" I ask him, and he smiles, as though glad for the fact that someone has broken the stony silence. "It's so beautiful."

"Yes, until I was sent away to school," he replies. "I was always outside, getting into mischief, even after my mother died."

"I heard she died shortly after having your sister; I'm sorry, Tobias," I say to him, hoping that I sound genuine. "I cannot imagine having to go through something like that at such a young age."

"Thank you, but it was a long time ago," he says, effectively shutting down the conversation. "I would place money on you being an outdoorsy girl."

"And you would win big," I laugh, as does he. "I never quite grew out of it either. My sister, on the other hand, has always been the proper lady with her embroidery and singing. Though I can play the piano if the mood so takes me."

"Really?" he asks, looking at me with surprise. "I never would have thought so."

"My father taught me when I turned twelve. My mother worried she would never get me indoors; I think she thought he would chastise me into submission," I explain, giggling over the memory of it, "but he was much more sly in his manipulation of me. I think he knew it would do him no good to try and bark his orders at me."

"Quite," he says with an amused smile. "I would love to hear you play sometime."

I grin, forgetting myself with him over my carefree talking, and shake my head in answer.

"I am much too shy to play. I have only done so a handful of times, and those were in front of my father when he was teaching me."

"I will take that as a challenge, Lady Hardy," he replies with a mischievous smile. Before I can argue, he stops dead and looks ahead to where a small stream of water is rushing across the bottom of the second field. He eyes it with deep thought before turning to face me. "The storm must have caused the stream to overflow; I shall have to carry you over."

"No need, Your Grace," I reply with a cheeky smile, one that always caused my mother to roll her eyes. "Watch and learn!"

I proceed to take a small run up to the edge of the stream before leaping over it, clearing the water completely before landing with an ungraceful thud back onto the muddy ground. I turn to him with a triumphant smile, smug you might say, only to see him staring back at me with an undecipherable expression. The sight of which causes me to drop my smile, for I fear he might return to throwing his contempt back at me. However, I am pleasantly surprised when he suddenly breaks into a run and leaps over the water himself. Only he doesn't clear the water as I did, instead, he lands in the stream and makes such a splash it sprays up his trousers. When he rights himself, I notice how wet he is and cannot help but point and laugh at him.

"I was merely trying to make you feel good about yourself, My Lady," he says with a ridiculous look of hurt pride on his face, just before he breaks into laughing with me. "Tell anyone of this and I shall keep Monty away from you all week."

Once clear of the water, he wonders up beside me and offers me his arm, which I take before emitting a small burst of laughter from my lips. It is the most comfortable I have ever felt with him.

Tobias

"Today, we venture into the woods!" I announce to Emily, who is sitting across the table, where Monty is sat by her side. It would seem that after building a friendship of sorts over the last few days, she has managed to forgo my rule of not having him in the room whilst we dine. My words have her looking up at me mid-chew, with the dog now snaffling her half-eaten piece of bread from her hand. She remains staring at me just as I frown at Monty for being so disobedient.

"You swear?" she asks, looking about ready to explode with excitement. "Do not tell me you are teasing me."

"Would I do such a thing?" I smirk at her, for this is exactly what my wife and I have fallen into doing since I admitted to behaving so abysmally towards her. She looks back at me as if to say as much, which only makes my smile spread even wider. "No, I am not teasing."

Her smile is so full, so genuine, I want to kiss it before it disappears altogether. Not that I would ever say such a thing, for she still trembles at my touch, and I know she fears any intimacy from me, that she simply isn't ready for any of that. But I am more than willing to wait; it is only what I deserve after the way I treated her.

"Then I must go and get ready," she beams and immediately jumps up from her chair. "Shall I ask Mrs Keppel to pack a picnic? It is such a lovely day…and can Monty come…and-"

"The picnic is already ordered, Monty is indeed invited, and yes to whatever you want," I reply, looking at her so intensely, she swallows hard and lets her breathing betray her fear; or could it be something else?

"I shall be down as soon as possible," she says softly, then walks over to where I am still sitting and covers my hand with her own. It is the very first time she has offered her touch without me giving it to her first. We both look to where our hands are joined, hers shuddering, mine remaining still for her to hold onto. She looks at her quivering and blushes with a shameful, sorrowful look.

"Thank you, Tobias."

"It is my pleasure," I reply, all the while she continues to look at her shivering hand. She opens her mouth as if to say something, but I cut her off before she can make a single sound. "Do not apologise for it, Emily, it will stop when you are ready. Until then, it does not bother me."

She looks back into my eyes, trying to find the sincerity in my words, but eventually nods with one of her warming smiles. She then turns towards the door and makes her way out with the ridiculous dog following after her. I fear my hound has suddenly become my wife's dog; if I cannot win him over with food, what hope do I really have?

My wife's joy over taking a turn around a few trees and a small stream is so mesmerizing, I forget what I am talking about no less than three times during our adventure. I believe she is even more excited than Monty, who is always running around in a frenzy to chase squirrels, rabbits and whatever else he can find, sometimes nothing at all. Emily soon begins collecting small sticks, seeds, and flowers along the way, putting them inside of a small bag hanging down from her skirts. I do not even ask her the reason as to why she is picking these things up, I just take pleasure in her looking so happy.

Her hair catches on various branches, but she pays no heed to it. She simply continues on her path without a care in the world. Watching her bounding along after Monty, it occurs to me that she has not pinned her hair up even a single time since our walk to the village a few days ago, but I find I like it. It makes Emily exactly who she is.

"Tobias!" she squeals. "Look, there is a bridge!" She points and runs towards it with the same enthusiasm as the dog. "Oh gosh, the water is fast, look!"

"I do believe my grandfather built this thing many years ago," I comment as I saunter over to join her. She leans far over the side to watch Monty paddling in the fast-running water below. Her hair falls over her shoulder, making it look like a golden waterfall.

"Shall we race sticks?" she asks with a huge smile when she finally comes back up to face me.

"I have not done such a thing since I was a boy, and even then, it was only to appease Genevieve," I laugh as I take in her ridiculous goofy smile.

"Oh, come on!" she groans, then goes off to hunt for the perfect stick with which to play. "Why, I played only last month!"

"I well believe it," I mutter drily, "very well!"

I pick up the nearest stick within my grasp and hold it before her. Looking like a detective inspecting an item for clues, she takes a small while to study my offering to make sure it is no bigger than her own. Only when she is happy with her findings do we walk to the edge and hold them out over the water.

"One, two, three!" she calls before we drop them into the flowing water below. "Monty, no!"

I cannot help but laugh when the dog picks up her stick and begins chewing on it just as mine sails through to the other side.

"That wasn't fair! Your dog ate my stick!"

"Oh, so he's *my* dog again?" I scoff. "Besides, all is fair in stick races." She pouts while I continue to smirk at her. When she finally relents to give me a small smile, I take a look at the time on my pocket watch. "I do believe it is time for our picnic, Duchess. Our rematch will have to wait until we are fed."

"Oh, ok," she sulks before smiling again. A real smile with her teeth on show, the most beautiful one she has in her remit.

We amble through the woods until we hit a clearing on the other side. A meadow with tall growing grasses and poppies is providing the perfect backdrop for our sunny picnic. We march over to where the tree is casting some shade and begin to set up a blanket in comfortable silence. Monty sniffs around the basket of cold meats and other delicacies he would no doubt like to dive headfirst into, causing Emily to giggle and offer him lots of pats to his smooth head. She opens up the picnic and starts serving up the food from inside. Her growing confidence is putting me more at ease and feeling less guilty for being the cold-hearted bully that I was when I first brought her here. I admire her ability to forgive me, for I cannot say I would be so generous.

We laze in the sunshine for at least an hour, talking about everything and nothing to do with each other, including her desire to one day visit France. I already mentally make the decision to grant her that wish one day, I owe her that much at least. I tell her a little about Genevieve, though nothing of note, for I do not wish to dampen our time together with sad tales. Not today, not when she is beginning to want to be in my company.

"I bet you I can climb that tree," she says all of a sudden, pointing at the old oak just behind us. "And I'll do so in these ridiculous skirts!"

"I've no doubt you could," I reply with a small smirk on my face, "but I fail to see why I would want you to. You've already been laid up in bed for a few days whilst in my care, why would I also risk you breaking your neck?"

"I'll have you know I am a champion tree climber," she declares with a look of immense pride on her face. "There would be no 'breaking my neck'."

"No!" I say sternly, to which she arches her delicate brow and smiles tauntingly at me.

"*No*?! What do you mean *no*?" she asks, already getting to her feet in defiance. Monty comes trotting over, being suddenly interested in this new game between us.

"Precisely that, no!" I shrug. "I am your husband, after all, mine to do with as I please."

"I never thought of that," she says, beginning to frown whilst putting her finger to her lips, which only has me remembering what it was like to place mine to them. "Though, you would have to catch me first."

"Emily…" I warn her, but she's already about turned and is now running towards it. In fact, by the time I get to my own feet, she's already climbing at such a speed, I would not have thought it possible in all of her skirts. Being that she's already positioning herself along a thick branch, I decide to pace over at my own leisure before crossing my arms and looking at her with disapproval.

"Are you impressed, Your Grace?" She grins cheekily and with her legs now hanging down from the branch she has sat herself upon. Monty is now barking up at her with worry.

"Now look what you have done," I reply calmly, "you've

upset poor Monty, which is particularly cruel on your part. After all, he did save you the other night."

"Cruelty that I must have learnt from my husband," she teases. "He'll be fine, won't you boy?"

"Well, then, you've upset me. How will you make up for such a crime?"

"Laugh smugly," she says and does exactly that. "There is room enough for both of us up here," she says as she gestures to the space beside her, "and you should see the view!"

"I am not climbing a tree," I say point blankly, "and you *will* come down!"

"Uh-uh," she giggles, a delicious sound I didn't realise was so intoxicating. "Trust me, Tobias, I am the second child, I can be far more stubborn than you!"

"Then how about a wager, Lady Hardy?" I smile to myself. "If I climb that tree, you have to…kiss me," I tell her as I point to my left cheek, "right here."

"I was taught never to kiss boys; it is most unbecoming of a lady to kiss a boy, even if it is only on the cheek!"

"I am no boy, Emily, I am your husband," I argue, "and ladies are meant to kiss their husbands."

She looks at me suspiciously, though I can tell she's finding the whole proposal amusing, and her frowning is just an act to tease me with. I merely wait patiently for her reply, hiding the anticipation of her answer, with my arms folded and a smug smirk upon my face.

"Alright," she says softly, causing my breath to

momentarily stop, though I try not to show that her one worded answer has had any effect on me. "If you can climb to this branch and sit here with me, then I will kiss you."

I widen my smile, so my teeth are showing, and give a quick nod before walking over to the very tree that is standing between me and her kiss. Only when I get to it, I notice there are no knots, holes or even branches on which to place my foot upon. I circle the whole damn thing to try and find some way of stepping up, but there's nothing, just a solid trunk.

"How in God's name did you get up there, Emily? Are you some form of monkey?" I scoff at her as I place my hands on my hips.

She simply laughs at me, making me want that kiss even more, so I reach up high to try and haul myself up using a weedy looking branch. It works to some extent, but no sooner have I reached up and placed my foot against the trunk, the damn entire thing breaks off and sends me flying to the ground on my back. I let out a long groan of pain at the same time as the sweet sound of her girlish laughter floats around in the background. To add insult to injury, Monty comes bounding across to me and presses his paws into my stomach before licking my entire face.

"Tobias Hardy, did you never climb trees when you were young?" Emily asks as she makes her way down from her branch.

"No," I answer truthfully.

"Why, that is sacrilege given where you grew up. Why ever not?" she questions me, now being suddenly in front me and studying for my head for injury. She is but a few inches away from my face; every detail of her is making me feel heady and lustful.

"Because I always fell out of them," I eventually manage to reply, which has her bursting into fits of laughter. "I was not meant for climbing."

"Then why did you agree to my challenge?" she giggles as she pushes back some of my hair, which is no doubt sticking up in a most unflattering manner.

"Because…" I begin, turning serious for a moment and looking deep inside of her eyes, "I wanted that kiss."

My words have her freezing in her crouched position, but with her breathing suddenly shallow and quick. I take in her delicate mouth that is posing a small o shape, telling me that she was not expecting such an answer. I remain staring at her beautiful face; a face that had made me pick her out from the dozens of girls in that ballroom in the first place. Though, in all honesty, it was her defiant and courageous expression that had sealed her fate to me.

Eventually she closes her mouth, swallows, and completely shocks me by placing her soft lips to my cheek, and delivering me the most beautiful of kisses.

"I did not climb the tree," I barely manage to whisper.

"That was for trying," she replies, and smiles with a distinct blush to her cheeks.

I want to grab her and bring her in for a proper kiss, one full of passion, lust, and all the things I would so dearly love to do to her, even in the middle of an open meadow. I wonder, given the look of fear on her face, if she is confusing my shock for anger. I cannot help it, however, for I am literally having to tighten every muscle to stop myself from burying myself inside of those rosy, pink lips of hers.

"Tobias?" she whispers, just before Monty comes leaping in between us. It is enough to break whatever spell she just cast over me.

"Yes," I cry out much too loudly, "time to go, I think."

"Of course," she replies quietly, though still looks utterly muddled over my strange behaviour.

How sheltered my little wife has been.

Chapter 12

Emily

The sun is beginning to lower in the sky by the time we walk back to the rear of Tobias' massive house, with shadows lengthening in the gardens before us. A warm glow is being cast against each and every flower, the sight of which puts a bounce in my step. I have to admit, Tobias' gardener is a true artist in the way he has managed to create such a beautiful picture with wild, unyielding flowers, grasses and trees. I love that it isn't ordered, neat and rigid in its design. The plants look free, content, and are blooming without the usual stuffiness most of these country estates often prefer.

Monty comes bounding up between us, nearly sending my husband flying with his whipping tail and wiggly bottom going at such a speed, I doubt he even saw us. I laugh, only to cover my mouth with my hand so as not to appear wicked with my mirth. To my pleasant surprise, he simply smirks and shakes his head in the direction of the clumsy hound.

"I do believe he is even more of a beloved friend to you than Lord Brown," I observe with a smile for him.

"Of course he is," he replies without any thought over the

matter and with a shrug of his shoulders. "He never answers back and is always in agreement with me."

"Ah, so is that how to get on your good side, Tobias?" I tease.

"If you are a man, yes," he says cryptically, "if you are a lady, my wife for example, there are other things you can do."

"Oh?" I ask as we approach the wall running alongside the house, the same one that leads around to the front entrance. "You must elaborate, Your Grace."

"I would dearly love to," he smiles, looking to the ground as we walk side by side, "though, I am not convinced-"

Before he can finish his sentence, he suddenly pulls me behind his back, taking hold of my hands and pushing us flat against the wall. I emit a breathy giggle; one I cannot help because his sudden anxiety is both surprising and amusing given how usually confident he is. He squeezes my hands tightly between his and quietly tells me to cease with my laughter.

"Emily, shh!"

Before I can even ask him why is behaving so unnaturally, I hear other voices coming from around the corner. One sounds older, flustered, and is clearly giving the other one, George, from the sound of the timbre of his voice, a difficult time.

"Well, where the devil is he?!" she snaps at the poor man.

"I do apologise, Lady Haysom," George replies, "your nephew took his wife out this morning. We are expecting him back sometime this afternoon."

"A most unhelpful response, George," she huffs, and I have

to stifle another laugh. "As always, your ability to enlighten me with the most useless of information truly astounds me!"

"Yes, apologies, Lady Haysom," the poor man says rather stoically, "perhaps some tea?"

"I do not need any more damn tea, George," she replies sternly, "I shall never leave the chamber pot if I have any more of the ridiculous beverage. It was surely invented by a man to keep ladies quiet or confined to their bedrooms."

"Who is that?" I whisper to Tobias, only to end up giggling when he shushes me again.

"My Aunt Elizabeth," he finally replies with a whisper of his own, "we must remain quiet! With any luck, she will tire and leave before she is aware of our return."

"She sounds fun," I laugh at him, "perhaps I should call out to say hello."

He turns to give me a taunting smirk, one that tells me not to dare do such a thing. I arch my brow as if to tell him that I might, but then he looks at me so intensely, I lose all ability to continue with my laughter. In fact, I feel as though I have lost all breath, just in the waiting for something I am not even sure of. Memories of his rubbing and kissing my ankle on our wedding night flit in and out of my head with such clarity, it feels as if something strange is dancing around inside of my stomach.

He looks to my chest, rising and falling with deep movements, ones that betray just how strange I am feeling within his close proximity. His eyes move back to mine for just a moment before they drop all the way down to where our hands are clasped. His mouth suddenly parts, as if in surprise, and with his brow furrowed in such a way, I have to look at them too. The normality of what I see has me looking at him for answers.

"Your hands," he whispers, as if by way of explanation, but when I remain looking dumbfounded, he releases a small laugh. "They are still."

For a moment, I do not fully understand what his words mean, but as soon as I do, I look at him with a smile so wide, I want to jump up and down like a child on her birthday. He beams back at me with those dimples, and it suddenly feels like something is melting inside of me. He continues to play with my hands and my fingers for a while, just marvelling over the fact that they no longer tremble inside of his. I watch them too, just before he leans in close, the whole time staring at my lips, and with him now looking intensely serious.

"There you are you wicked boy!" the older voice from before grumbles from behind him. He instantly closes his eyes and appears to brace himself for this meeting which he was so desperate to avoid. "You may well be an adult, Tobias Hardy, but I will still take my cane to your backside!"

Her words have me bursting with laughter before quickly bringing my hand up to cover my mouth so I might silence it. The older lady instantly looks at me with an expression that does not immediately tell me if she is amused by what she sees, or unimpressed. I try to compose myself, all the while she seems to silently assess me. My heart feels like it might give out, but then she smiles and looks very much like she approves.

"Well, Tobias, now is this her?" she begins, and I notice Tobias straightening up to his full height.

"Aunty," he says in a formal tone of voice. I stifle back another giggle; the title he just afforded her does not seem to match the sudden stiffness in his frame. "So nice to see you, as always.

This…" he says, now pulling me forward, "…is my wife, Emily."

He keeps hold of my hand, clasping it tightly, as though letting go will break the spell and have me trembling before him once again.

"Good afternoon, my dear," she says as I nod my head in greeting. "I am Tobias' Aunty Elizabeth, which you may also call me."

"Thank you, Aunty Elizabeth, "I reply, giving her a genuine smile, "it is lovely to meet you. I must confess, my husband failed to mention he had an aunt."

"Is that so?" she says with an unimpressed tone of voice. "Well, do not take it personally; I was unaware he had a new wife until last week!"

"It was a short engagement," Tobias explains away his faux pas with a small shrug. "And we are still getting to know one another. I would have invited you soon enough."

"You are a wicked liar, Tobias," she says bluntly. "But not to worry, I have made the necessary arrangements myself."

"*Arrangements*?" Tobias repeats abruptly, suddenly relinquishing his grip on my hand. "What *arrangements*?"

"Why, your first ball as the Duke and Duchess of Kent!" she replies with a smug smile, one that resembles that of her nephew.

"Aunt Elizabeth!" he snaps.

"No need to thank me, dear," she says before heading out towards the garden and taking hold of my hand in the process. "Now, excuse us, Tobias, but I need to speak with your wife, to introduce myself properly, seeing as you lack the manners to do so."

I watch every muscle in his face clench up in frustration, but merely smile sympathetically whilst being led away by his aunt. The dog follows us with acceptance over it all, leaving Tobias to stand brooding beside the building. The last thing I see is him shaking his head and then looking to the sky. He looks as if he is questioning as to why he has been sent such a feat to bear.

Now that I am here, by myself with this lady who is even older than my mother, in fact, even older than Mrs Keppel, I suddenly feel a little unsure of myself. This lady is undeniably bold and very sure of herself, two things I have not felt since I became somebody else's property. Though, in truth, I no longer feel like this with my husband. Things have shifted since we decided to bury the hatchet and build a friendship. I now feel differently; not equal as such, but less like a pet.

"Tell me, dear," Elizabeth says to me in a tone of voice that tells me she means no harm, "how are you finding married life? Particularly with my nephew."

"Er, well, I…" I fluster, trying to think of the right thing to say.

"Be frank with me, Emily, for I am more than aware of what a brute my nephew can be," she says with a smile before we take up a couple of seats where I often have my afternoon tea. "It is a pity really; he was such a sweet child. Between you and I, Tobias used to love having cuddles with his mother. His loss was hard for him to bear. Then, when Genevieve passed so suddenly, well, I think it was the final straw for him."

"I admit, he has not shared much with me about his family," I reply with a shy smile. "In fact, we haven't talked much at all."

"Oh," she says, drawing the word out with a sly expression, "the honeymoon has been that good has it. It does not surprise me. I have heard the rumours about my nephew, most of which an aunt does not need to know."

"I'm sorry, I do not follow," I reply with a look of bewilderment on my face.

"Between the sheets?" she murmurs, still wearing a sly smirk, but also offers a mischievous wink. "You need not be coy with me, my dear. I will be as silent as the grave!"

"Between the sheets?" I question her, for I have very little clue as to what she is talking about. "Tobias and I sleep in separate rooms, if that is what you mean."

"Oh…oh dear!" she gasps, looking deeply baffled. "Emily, my dear, do you mean to tell me your marriage has not yet been consummated?"

"I don't know," I whisper ashamedly, "I am not entirely sure of what the word means. Our engagement was quick, and the night before had been full of emotions. I believe my mother had meant to tell me what was expected from a wife, but after a lot of crying, from both of us, I had been given hot milk to calm me into sleep. Tobias has mentioned that word to me before but has never elaborated on its meaning."

"Oh, oh I say," she laughs awkwardly, "I had no idea Tobias had given you so little consideration when he took you for a wife. I shall be having some choice words with him!"

"No, please don't!" I push out before she can get anymore worked up. "It has taken us a long while to get to the point of friendship. You see, things weren't entirely good when he first brought me here. In fact, up until you arrived, I would tremble in his presence. I fear if you confront him, it might destroy whatever progress we have made."

After this admission, she sighs and takes a moment or two to think, as if silently battling against her urge to go and give Tobias a stern talking to. I have a feeling Aunt Elizabeth specialises in such talks, especially with her nephew. Eventually, however, when the tea arrives, she smiles at me, as though relinquishing her anger so she can adhere to my wishes.

"Elizabeth," I say quietly, and only when Mary has returned indoors, "you could do something for me."

"Sounds ominous," she says but leans in a little closer, looking very intrigued.

"Can *you* tell me what it means? What it is that a man and a woman are meant to do on their wedding night?"

"Oh," she gasps and laughs awkwardly, just as Monty comes trotting up to ask for some more head pats. His face looks goofy with his tongue hanging out the side of his mouth, being beyond content to have any form of attention. "You know, I never had children of my own. I've been a spinster all of my life. I cannot say I am much of an expert on such matters-"

"Please?" I place my hands on top of her frail ones and give her the same pleading eyes Monty offers when he is watching me eating at the table. "I feel like I need to know, that I am somehow inadequate without that knowledge."

She looks at me in such a way, I know she is still not overly sure of doing what I am so clearly begging for, which only sets my nerves alight even more so than they were before. What is it that I am so in the dark about?

"Ok, Emily, you are right," she says, now rubbing my hand with reassurance. "I clearly know more than you and it is only fair that I share such information that is going to be far more beneficial to you than it is to me."

"Thank you," I all but whisper, then brace myself to finally learn what it is we are supposed to have done on the night of our wedding.

"Right, well, where to begin?" she says whilst taking special note of Monty who has now rolled onto his back to bare all. "There, right there," she says pointing to the dog, so I look at him, only to feel even more confused than I was before.

"Monty?" I ask her, probably sounding like I think she has gone quite insane.

"Yes, Monty is a male dog and acts much the same as any other male creature when it comes to what happens between the sheets. His face pretty much shows what every other man does when he is in the throes of…consummating one's marriage.

"Elizabeth, are you telling me I am supposed to pat my husband's head?" I question her, not sounding at all convinced. She shoots her eyes back to mine and bursts out laughing.

"Oh, child, if only it were that simple! Oh, Emily, I do like you."

"I take it that is a no?" I smile at her, for she has such a wicked laugh it is hard not to join in with her mirth.

"No, what I mean is, look at what Monty has riding along his belly," she says and the poor woman blushes. I look to see he has something that resembles what I had seen between Edmund's legs, when he was a child swimming in the river, what my mother has told me to never mention again. I slump a little in disappointment, for I already knew men had these appendages; this tells me very little.

"Take that tree over there," she says, now pointing to one of the wild apple trees, so I look in its direction. "What did that grow from, Emily?"

"A seed," I reply, having helped our gardener back at home many times as a child. I had learnt about how plants grow when I was still in pinafores.

"Precisely, a seed," she says with a smile, as though I should know everything from her rather disjointed explanation. "Men have their own seed, inside of them. But to make that seed grow into something, it has to be put inside of a woman."

"Ok," I reply slowly as I nod along.

"And to get that seed into a woman, he must come together with her," she says, "they must fit together. Do you understand?"

"So far, but how do they fit together?" I ask and she seems to sigh with awkwardness, as though she was hoping this would have been explanation enough.

"Well, if it were Monty, with a bitch, he would put his…" she says as she moves her hand around in the air, gesturing towards his appendage, "…inside of what rests between her legs."

"Oh!" I say in sudden recognition of what she has been trying to tell me. "That sounds…intrusive."

"Yes, well, Mother Nature obviously didn't have any better ideas at the time," she says with an awkward laugh.

"And do men like doing this?"

"Very much so," she replies with a wink. "I hear some

ladies like it to, though not on one's first time. Tobias's mother, my sister, once told me about it, how she had bled…though it is perfectly natural, Emily. You mustn't fear it," she tries to reassure me, as she quickly grabs hold of my hands, probably noticing that my eyes have now widened over the mention of bleeding. "His mother also told me how it had made her fall in love with his father that little bit more. That it became better, more pleasurable for her over time. Besides, it is the only way to have children of your own."

"Hmmm," I smile tightly, now fearing it all the more. "Tobias told me he was not interested in doing such a thing with me until he decides he wants children."

"Well, given the way he just looked at you, I am more than sure he was lying," she states, "you are a pretty girl and his wife. Believe me, men like to claim their pretty wives as their own, and as far as they are concerned, this is how they cement their claim."

"Tobias doesn't like me in that way…" I muse before remembering how he had wanted to kiss me at the tree, how he had looked at me, how he had tried to touch me, even before the night I had run away from him. "At least, I don't think he does."

"Tobias lost the two most important women in his life, one he swore to the other he would protect," she explains. "And when men get scared, they try to stop it by cutting themselves off, thus avoiding it altogether."

"Perhaps," I reply with a sad smile, "though I cannot help him if he does not share with me."

"He will, in time," she says, "but for now, keep being his friend. He could always do with more of those; everyone can."

"Thank you, Elizabeth," I say with real sincerity behind my

words, "truly, I am glad you are going to be staying for a while."

"Give it a few more days, child, you may well change your mind!" she teases and we have a good giggle together.

Chapter 13

Tobias

I struggled to keep myself busy after Elizabeth had taken my wife away from me this afternoon. I could have stayed and joined in with tea and gossip, but after nearly kissing her this afternoon, coming so close to showing her all that I could be to her, I couldn't simply sit there and keep up social niceties without losing my head over it. Instead, I took to my study and fooled myself into believing that I was making any headway with the estate accounts. In truth, I had sat before my desk and simply fallen into daydreams. Dreams about Emily and my growing feelings for her. Dreams that turned into my mother, and then Genevieve. Guilt grows from guilt; how I have behaved towards my wife has had me thinking how I might have saved Genevieve if only I had been there. I know her governess was with her when she passed on, but I cannot help but wonder if it had been me instead, could I have saved her where her governess could not.

And so, with the night only just beginning to fall, I purposefully decide to arrive early for dinner. I strangely wanted a few moments alone with my dog before a fire, so I might shake away this melancholy. My aunt managed to commandeer his time as well as that of my wife. It is a funny thing to crave someone else's time, but being without Emily this afternoon has made me decidedly more tetchy than usual. Though I love my aunt, for she reminds me of my mother, I cannot help wishing she wasn't here to monopolise Emily's attention. Is it wrong of me to want to be selfish during this time when my wife and I are truly beginning to get to know one another? Perhaps. And I can admit, the fact that Aunt Elizabeth has immediately taken to Emily comforts me.

"You fool," I laugh to myself, even though I am pretending to be saying these words to Monty. For it suddenly occurs to me that having Elizabeth's acceptance of Emily is like having my own mother accept her.

"I do hope you weren't calling me a fool, Nephew," my aunt calls out from across the room, where she has just entered like she is the queen. "Though, it wouldn't surprise me; your beastly manners need some much-needed attention, young man."

I purse my lips before standing to officially greet her with a soft kiss to her cheek. I am gifted with the smell of lavender, the same scent my mother used to wear. She tuts before tapping me on the cheek with her hand. The old woman loves me really, for I am the son she never had, as well as a reminder of the sister she lost. We are all each other have left, though maybe Emily will help to change that. If we were to have children, it would be like a small part of my mother and sister being passed on. It is whilst I'm musing about such things that I notice her watching me, smiling slyly as she does so.

"Speak," I instruct with a sigh.

"Well, if you are going to bark out orders to me like I am no more worthy than your dog…" she replies rather huffily, and I roll my eyes over her need to drag these sorts of conversations out for longer than is necessary.

"Please, Aunty, say whatever it is you wish to tell me," I

say to her with just a touch more patience. "Your opinion has always mattered to me Elizabeth."

"Of course it does," she replies with what looks like an air of superiority. "I am a font of knowledge; you know that, Tobias."

"And, as always, so modest, Aunty." I smile at her, to which she relents and returns the sentiment.

"Tobias," she says in a much smaller voice, causing me to brace myself because I know things are about to turn more serious. "I love you like you are my own; in fact, in my mind, you are mine. But please, stop being such a fool when it comes to your own happiness!"

"I can guess as to what you are alluding to, Aunty, and if I am right, I can assure you that I am trying my upmost to remedy my previous actions," I reply truthfully. "You have my word."

"And be patient," she says with a knowing wink. "Emily knows very little in the way of men and women coming together…you know…" I watch her fluster with both her words and hands running completely away from her.

"Yes, Aunty," I finally reply, holding up my hands defensively so as to cut her off before she can cause herself an injury, or far worse, manage to finish that sentence. "Haven't I shown enough restraint? Most husbands would not have been so patient."

"That is not reason enough to behave less than is gentlemanly," she pipes up. "I remember your mother teaching you better, even if it was for such a short length of time, God rest her soul."

"I have no intention of pushing Emily beyond what she is ready for," I reassure her. "Though I can admit to being less than honourable in the past, I have never forced myself upon her."

"Good boy," she replies with one of her superior expressions. "The same cannot be said for that beast of yours!"

I look at the dog before me and smile at his being so content to rest by my feet. Though, as soon as Emily comes in to join us, he will be on her without shame.

Emily

Brushing my hair in front of my dressing table, already dressed for bed, and readying myself for a long read, I find myself smiling at my reflection. It suddenly dawns on me, that for the first time since arriving here, I feel content, relaxed, and like this could be my home. I no longer feel like an intruder in my husband's house, nor his life. He is my friend, as is his friend, Frederick, and his dog my dog. And now, Aunty Elizabeth is also my aunty. I still miss my family to the extent that I feel a daily pain in my heart, but I no longer have a need to run back to them; to run into the darkness if only to catch a glimpse of them.

The comforting feeling in which I am indulging is suddenly interrupted by someone thudding on my door. It is so unexpected, it has me jumping in fright. I just about manage to turn to answer it when the thudding returns, but this time, with a lot more urgency behind each knock. It sounds so insistent; I hurry my footsteps for fear something awful is happening. The thought of which suddenly fills me with gut wrenching fear over something bad having happened to Monty, Elizabeth, but perhaps more importantly, Tobias.

No sooner have I opened the door than Tobias is pushing at

it with such insistence, my nerves only grow with intensity. I step back to let him pass, just before he gently closes the door so as to stop it from making any sound. Once he hears the click of the catch, he braces his hands against the wooden panels, then places his ear to it, as if trying to eaves drop on a conversation that is happening out in the hallway. I walk up to him in utter bewilderment, looking at him in such a way, I hope he is going to offer some sort of explanation for his rather erratic behaviour.

"Tobi-" I begin, but he cuts me off by turning and placing his forefinger to my lips, quietly shushing me as he does so. He looks so unnatural to his usual countenance right now, that I end up smiling against his finger. He takes a brief moment to look back at the door, but soon returns his eyes to mine and with his stern expression now breaking into a wide grin.

"My apologies, Emily," he whispers as he grips hold of my shoulders and turns me to face him. "I cannot talk about balls, guest lists, and music for dancing, for one more minute. The woman is on a mission, and I am no longer able to bear her intolerable ability to gab for hours about such things!"

"Tobias," I giggle, "are you hiding?"

"No," he replies, acting all affronted, "I am merely inspecting my wife's bed chamber to make sure it is up to standard."

"Oh, I see," I nod along, acting with him because this game is much too fun not to. "Well, as you can see, it is more than adequate, so feel free to return to your own bed chamber. Though, be careful as you go, I have heard there might be some terrifying old ladies prowling about the corridors!"

"It may be up to your standards, Duchess," he smirks smugly, "but is it up to a duke's standards?"

With a smile on my face, I fold my arms in front of me, if only to let him know that he is being more than a little ridiculous. In return, he merely arches one of those eyebrows of his, smirks, and begins walking about the room, as if inspecting for inadequacies. First the windows, then the armoire, a few of my clothes, which he tuts at me for them being left lying about, my dressing table, and then finally, the bed. He begins to press his hand to the mattress, testing it for comfort whilst furrowing his brow with concern.

"Something wrong, husband?" I ask, enjoying this little play of his.

"Something is very wrong," he replies, "this will not do at all!"

I watch as he walks up to me, rubbing his hands together before him, and all the while looking at me with a wicked grin upon his face. It is only when he is up before me, his smile drops, and he now looks a little serious. It is the most serious he has looked in days. My heart picks up with speed, and I find myself trying to swallow back a large lump of fear that is sitting firmly inside of my throat.

"Emily," he whispers as he takes hold of my hands, the ones that no longer tremble inside of his. I momentarily check for their stillness before looking back up into his eyes that are so close, I can see the pattern within his icy blue irises.

"Yes?" I reply with a strange feeling stirring deep inside of me, one I have felt but a few times in my life, all of them with this man.

"I want you-" he begins but is swiftly cut off by the sound of Elizabeth calling out my name through the door, along with a gentle knocking. Upon which, our eyes turn comically wide, with mine soon narrowing in amusement.

"Emily, do not make a sound!" he whispers with urgency.

"I cannot ignore her," I whisper back, "she is sure to know I am in here."

He darts his frightened eyes around the room, looking for somewhere he can stay hidden. With nowhere obvious to hand, he pulls us towards the door where he uses me as a shield to his aunt's eyes. It also ensures he remains hidden behind the door when I finally come to open it.

"Ok," he whispers, "you may open it."

I take a moment or two to try and compose myself, feeling as though I may burst with laughter if I do not take in a few deep breaths beforehand.

"Elizabeth," I beam at her when I finally open the door, "is something wrong?"

"Have you seen that husband of yours?" She tuts. "I was halfway through the guest list when he told me he had to ask George about the fire, then failed to return."

"Oh, how strange, that does not sound like something Tobias would do!" I reply whilst feigning shock.

"It is precisely what that boy would do!" she huffs.

"I am afraid I have not heard a thing since coming to bed," I lie and feel a little wicked for it. "Though, I have been a little engrossed in my latest book."

"Blast it all!" She frowns, then looks up at me with a completely different expression, one that almost looks mischievous. "Whilst you are here, I have decided I would like you and Tobias to begin a family as soon as possible, so I might see them before I depart this mortal coil."

"Oh…er…" I fluster whilst I feel his head fall onto the back of mine with a soft, exasperated sigh. "I will be sure to let Tobias know."

"Yes, do, I am sure he'll be over the moon," she says, grinning a little more deviously. "You remember what I told you in the garden?"

"Yes," I reply, only to take in deep breath when I suddenly feel his finger running through my hair, right down the length of it, all the way to the small of my back. It is so light, but it still feels extremely intimate, especially when I hear him inhaling its floral scent.

"Best to get that first time over with, then you can really start trying," she continues, "every other day should do it!"

"Every…" I gasp at the same time as I hear a soft chuckle from behind me.

"Yes, wouldn't you agree, Tobias?" she calls out around my shoulder, forcing him to freeze in his touch, and eventually shuffle out from behind me. Meanwhile, the wicked lady is winking at me over her teasing.

"Aunty," he tries to say proudly, "I hope you are not leading my wife astray with these lessons of yours."

"Someone has to tell the poor girl if her mother and husband are content to leave her in the dark," she argues. "Now, shall we leave Emily to ponder on that whilst we go and complete the plans for next week's ball?"

"Must we?" he grumbles, almost sounding childlike.

"Elizabeth, might I go in his place?" I cut in. "My mother told me this sort of thing usually falls to the lady of the house, and I might prove more willing than poor Tobias. Besides, he works so very hard already."

"Excellent suggestion!" Elizabeth beams. "Tobias you are excused."

"Let me just get my robe," I tell them before wandering off to retrieve it.

Tobias

"What is wrong, boy? You should be pleased; your wife has just got you out of an evening of having to discuss all those inconsequential things you so hate!"

"You are commandeering my wife yet again, Aunty," I pout, "I was about to tell her that I should like her to move into my bedroom. As ever, Aunt Elizabeth, you have impeccable timing!"

"My apologies, Tobias," she says, though she is grinning like she is far from feeling such a sentiment, "but there will be plenty of time for all that. Remember to exercise a little more patience, Tobias!"

"I hope you sleep well, Tobias," Emily says to me before affording me one of her fluttery kisses to my cheek; one that has me closing my eyes to indulge in it without allowing my other senses to take away from the deliciousness of it.

"My eternal gratitude, Emily," I murmur, fisting my hands to stop myself from grabbing her and pulling her into me.

Tobias

Three days after my wife saved me from having to plan some insufferable ball, and I am in a thoroughly bad mood; I have barely seen her. The house is in a constant state of disarray and full of people I do not even recognise. All of whom are running around trying to fill in every single nook and cranny with frilly bits of decor. One fool even made his way into my study. He was quickly 'reminded' that this area is out of bounds, to which he physically whimpered and ran off to seek solace from one of the other strangers who are currently residing inside of my house. Even dear old Monty has grown tired of all the people invading his territory and has now taken to hiding away with me in what feels like the only tolerable place within the entire house. He frequently sighs and flops about the place; he is probably missing my wife just as much as I am.

At least this ball is only two days away, after which, all can return to as it should be. I silently make this promise to Monty before continuing to try and work, even though I am frequently disturbed by the sound of distant crashing and banging. After the fifth disturbance to break my concentration, I finally give in and drop my pen to throw my head against my fists. I then force myself to count to ten to try and steady my nerves and calm my mounting temper. Just as I reach number eight, someone thumps upon my door, causing me to emit a low and rumbly groan, just as Monty releases a long sigh of despair.

"What!" I shout out, making it clear to whoever it is, they are not welcome.

"Morning, Tobias," a familiar voice calls over to me with his usual joviality, "Monty."

"Fredrick, I should have known you'd be here for an

opportunity to get involved with an event that is bound to summon the eligible ladies of the area."

"And London," he smirks, "I was put in charge of that area. They are going to be flocking this way in no less than forty-eight hours!"

"Oh, deep joy," I reply sarcastically. "And yet all I want to do is spend time with my new wife…alone!"

"Things are going well in that department then?" he asks with a smug look upon his face.

"We are friendly with one another, if that is what you are asking," I reply as I get up to settle Monty, who has taken to sniffing Fredrick in the most inappropriate of places. "It is a pity my aunt Elizabeth arrived to rile everything up with all of this silly ball business."

"Well, it just so happens, I overheard your wife telling her maid that she was escaping to take a short break from all of the excitement," he informs me. "I rather think she feels the exact same way as you from what Elizabeth just told me. Going somewhere, Tobias?"

He laughs when I walk straight past him, getting ready to go in search of Emily whilst she is alone.

"The drawing room," he calls out before I even ask as to where she might be.

Minutes later, far away from the hustle and bustle of the staff making never-ending arrangements for a party I do not want, I hear the sound of someone playing the piano. I immediately slow my steps, trying to keep as quiet as possible for fear of her catching me. Though, when I reach the door to the drawing room, where a grand piano sits by the light of the sun in the window, I can tell from Emily's expression that she is too lost in the music to even notice me.

As her fingers dance across the keys, I lean up against the doorframe and watch with avid fascination. She isn't playing any of the normal melodies that ladies choose to show off their talents with. Instead, she plays a piece which is both dramatic and soothing, fast, then slow, and so incredibly beautiful, I am in complete awe of her. It peaks and troughs with delicate scales of notes, just like her.

Her face remains focused on the keys as they dip and rise beneath her graceful fingers, looking as though she is completely oblivious to everything else. The sun hits her porcelain skin and lights her entire face. Every shade of colour sparkles in that midday sun, and I find myself getting lost in her. My wife is truly beautiful.

When her eyes close and her fingers remain dancing over those keys, I take the opportunity to walk slowly up to where she sits. When I perch upon the stall beside her, still she plays. When I lean in to inhale the scent of her hair, still she plays, and when I run my finger down her naked arm, still she plays. She plays until her melody has ended, when she is finally released from whatever hypnotic state of mind she was just lost to. Then…then she looks at me with those wide eyes and lips that are just begging to be kissed. I could kiss them if it wasn't for the fact that tears are now falling over her cheeks.

"You are sad, Emily?" I whisper as I reach in to chase away those tears with my finger. "You play so beautifully, so passionately."

"My father taught me that piece," she explains with a smile, though it is one of sadness and full of grief. I nod in understanding.

"You miss them?" I ask, to which she nods, looking as if she is ashamed of it.

"Frederick informed me that he had invited them, but Elise is sick with flu," she informs me with a heavy sigh, "so they are unable to attend."

"Then," I begin before kissing the last tear away from her cheek, "we shall go to them; as soon as your sister is well again."

"Really?" she asks with a smile of hope beginning to break through.

"Of course," I reply as I place my hand to her cheek, "I want you to be happy, Emily."

"Thank you."

"Play for me again," I ask, and she does without question, timidity, or fear.

Chapter 14

Emily

It feels like the guests have been arriving for so long, I begin to wonder if it is the next day already. Elizabeth has done an exquisite job with the decorations; there are so many of them, I hardly recognise the place. Lords and Ladies, all of whom seem to know my husband, flock in from their carriages and put on a show of introducing themselves to me, so much so, I begin to feel a little overwhelmed. I do not know half the people here and those of whom I do, are quickly whisked away before I even have a chance to converse with them. Besides, when I remember that the people who are most important to me will not be attending, I suddenly feel sad again. I try not to, try to push it away for another day, but it is hard.

Before I can dwell on the disappointment of not seeing Mother, Father, or Elise, we are greeted by Lord and Lady Greyson, the lovely Victoria, and their less than affable son, Thomas. The latter of which still looks as untrustworthy as he had the last time that I saw him. His smile is a little too smug, his confidence too much for someone who doesn't know me, and his eyes are looking too lascivious for comfort. When I take a glance at Tobias, I can tell he feels the same way, and when he places his arm tightly around my waist, I am sure of it.

"Your Grace," Lord Greyson greets my husband before bowing his head. "Your Grace," they then say to me, and I curtsey as I am expected to.

"Your Grace, I never had a chance to ask your new wife to dance with me," Thomas says to Tobias before gifting me with a crooked smile. "Might I this evening?"

"You will have to see if I let go of her for long enough," Tobias replies with a tight smile. "Though, I do not like your chances."

The family laugh awkwardly in the wake of Tobias' possessiveness, all the while I try not to show my relief too openly. Thomas nods my way before walking over to a group of young ladies, most likely to ask them to dance. Fredrick is quick to ask Victoria for a waltz whilst their parents take their leave out onto the terrace where some of the other older couples have retired to chat. There are plenty of eyes and ears on their children, especially Victoria, who has a number of gentlemen already looking her way.

"You are not to go anywhere near that cad," Tobias mutters to me, though this time he has a small smirk upon his face. "The thought of his hands on you has my insides itching."

"Behave, Your Grace, he is still one of our guests," I whisper with a small laugh.

"Come with me," he says with a rather cryptic look on his face, one that says he knows something that I am not yet privy to. He proceeds to lead me out onto the terrace, which is warm and glowing under candlelight. The music from inside can still be heard, but it is still a relief to embrace the quiet after being in the throngs of everything.

"Dance with me."

"W-what?" I laugh when he swings me around to hold me as if ready to waltz. He cocks his head to the side with that bossy eyebrow of his arching, as if silently daring me to refuse. I giggle one more time before relenting, even if some of the other guests are now turning to watch us. Most of them smile, knowing we are newlyweds, and this looks incredibly romantic of my husband, a man with a stony reputation, no less.

"May I cut in?" a voice I haven't heard for a long time says from behind me, making my husband grin with his teeth on show and dimples in his cheeks.

"Father!" I positively shriek. He laughs before I literally throw myself into his arms, where he holds me so tightly, I feel like he'll never let me go. "I thought you were unable to come?"

"Your mother is taking care of Elsie," he replies before pulling me back to study me more carefully. "When I received a letter from your husband, telling me how sad you were, I knew had to come."

"You did that for me?" I turn to ask Tobias, who stands sheepishly to the side and nods. "Thank you," I cry before throwing my arms around his neck, taking him in just as much as I had done with my father.

"For you, always," he whispers. "I think I will leave you both to catch up. After all, I know my wife is in safe hands with her father."

My father eyes him with the same apprehension as before, but his smile is genuine. Tobias gives me one last small kiss on the cheek before about turning and walking back towards the foray of inside.

"Oh, Emily, I have missed you!" Father whispers to me as

he gifts me another one of his warm hugs. "Is he treating you well? Edmund told me how awful he was at Lord and Lady Greyson's ball, and it took every piece of will power not to come here and rescue you."

"Yes. I'll admit, it was not smooth sailing to begin with," I replay as we begin walking across the terrace. "I feared Tobias and he was easily frustrated by me."

"And now?" he asks, looking as if he knows things cannot be as bad as they once were.

"We are friends," I confirm with a smile, "good friends."

"And if I said you could leave all of this behind and come home with me?" he asks with a look of triumph on his face.

"I think…I think I would choose to stay," I reply as I return his warm smile, only to then giggle a little when he sighs in what looks like relief.

"I think marriage might suit you, my darling girl," he says, "you look so grown up, but happy."

"We have a way to go, Father," I tell him. "For one thing, the man can't even climb a tree!"

"Oh, well, that simply will not do!" he declares as he plays along with me. "If anyone can teach him, though, it is my daughter."

He kisses my forehead before we descend into gossip about home, Monty, and Tobias' aunt Elizabeth.

Tobias

I give my heart permission to beat again, knowing that I have made Emily happy. Hearing that she would choose to stay with me is an added bonus, one I shall treasure while I am forced from her side. After losing her to Elizabeth this week, I am itching to have her close to me. But, for once, I feel like I need to put my own needs behind those of hers. She needs this night with her father, and I shall do all that I can to make up for my past transgressions. The way I had forced her into marriage without taking the proper time to court her as a gentleman should, was inexcusable. And as for the way I had treated her afterwards, I cannot even put into words how regretful I feel for forcing that kind of hurt on her. I will make it right; I will be who she needs me to be.

Feeling light footed, I make my way over to one of the private rooms that has been filled with men and their cigars, tumblers of whiskey, and tedious talk of politics and business. I notice Frederick straight away and make my way over. Alas, my endeavour soon has me coming face to face with that cur, Thomas Greyson. I wouldn't trust the man as far as I could throw him, so I have to question as to why my best friend has chosen to engage in conversation with him. When I am but a few feet away, Frederick can see how unimpressed I am by just the look on my face.

"Ah, Tobias," he calls out, ignoring my look of disdain for the man standing beside him, "we were just talking about your trip to London next week."

"I had no idea it would be of any interest to anyone," I reply tightly, "least of all Lord Greyson here."

"On the contrary, I was just saying how lovely your wife makes a room look," he grins with his teeth. Teeth I would like to knock out with one of my fists if he continues to talk about Emily in such a manner.

"My wife is not an ornament," I growl, "and certainly not

one for your eyes."

"Of course not," Thomas replies, feigning all innocence, "I was merely giving a compliment."

"Perhaps you should offer them to ladies who are not already taken!" I snap.

The scoundrel and I stare at one another as if in a silent battle of wills, him with that ridiculously smirk that makes me want to obliterate it, and me, no doubt resembling Monty when he thinks there is an intruder in the house. Eventually, I cease my stare off, for it occurs to me that he is beneath me. To show him as such, I walk away for the purpose of refilling my drink. I am soon joined by Frederick, baring a soft smile; one that is meant to reassure me.

"Tobias," he says cautiously, "remember to keep your temper. Not only would it make you look like a fool in front of all your guests, but your aunt Elizabeth would literally dismember you if you were to start a fray."

"I must insist you do not discuss my wife with that man, Fredrick," I mutter between my teeth. "It insults me to see you talking with him so casually."

"He is Victoria's brother, and he came to talk to me," he says with an exasperated sigh. "Even you can agree that it would be rather foolish of me to ignore him."

"Well, perhaps he is reason enough to pursue another," I scoff, to which he laughs at me. "I cannot think of anything worse than having to see his face on a regular basis."

"Some of us aren't quite so tightly wound up as you, Tobias," he smiles. "Speaking of which, have you thought of what you will do when you come across Edmund Barton when you visit

London next week?"

"No," I reply honestly, "hopefully the pup will know his place and keep his distance."

"It amuses me to hear you refer to him as a dog," he chuckles, "when you are the one marking your territory."

"How very drole," I reply with sarcasm.

We stand in comfortable silence for a little while longer, watching the comings and goings of various guests, most of whom I cannot say I am all that familiar with. Thomas, thank goodness, has left the room entirely. As such, I am finally able to relax enough to fall into casual conversation with a few other gentlemen inside of the room. I play my part of the welcoming host, though only because my aunt had warned me on pain of death, to behave myself. It isn't so bad, but soon my thoughts are brought back to Emily and the fact that I am missing her greatly.

An hour later and I decide I can no longer keep away from her, so make my excuses to Lord Cabot, who has been talking about the price of cheese for the last twenty minutes or so. I then wander out onto the terrace where I see, to my utter horror, Emily, her father, and Thomas Greyson, all engaged in conversation.

Emily

Thomas Greyson has been talking non-stop drivel since the moment he approached my father and I, which was a little over half an hour ago. It irks me that he is impinging on my time with Papa, but for Elizabeth's sake, I ignore the niggling feeling within my chest, and decide to keep up a polite façade. It is only when my father turns to speak to another gentlemen, that Mr Greyson reveals just how vile he really is.

"How are you, Duchess? And I mean really?" he asks with

a wink that causes me to frown.

"I am well, thank you, Lord Greyson," I reply and hope to leave it at that.

"Your husband was quite the brute on the last occasion we saw one another," he says before leaning in a little closer, so close, I can smell the liquor on his breath. "Edmund was quite concerned afterwards."

"I can imagine, but I have reassured my father that I am quite alright. You can be sure he will pass this message onto Edmund as soon as he returns home," I reply in a formal tone before trying to step away. However, as soon as my shoulder is turned away from him, his hand reaches out for my upper arm and pulls me back with such force, I emit a small, shocked gasp. Even the heated stare I give doesn't loosen his grip.

"I told him I would make sure you were ok, Emily," he mutters beside my ear, "and I always keep my promises. Tell me, are you still a maid?"

"Lord-" I begin to snap at him, when all of a sudden, Tobias appears to the side of us and is soon lunging at Thomas with so much rage, they tumble to the ground. With the sound of their scuffling, the other guests all turn to watch them fighting, all the while I yelp out with horror. I am lost as to how on earth all of this has come to pass so quickly and so suddenly.

"You dare to touch my wife!" Tobias growls at him through clenched teeth like a rabid dog, and with him throwing his fists into Thomas Greyson's face, chest, neck, wherever else he can land them. I call out for him to stop, to reassure him that I am fine, but he is much too lost to his anger. "You are not worthy enough to even look at her, let alone touch her!"

"Tobias!" Frederick shouts as he runs over to try and separate the brawling men.

"Emily?" The sound of my father's anxious voice has me turning to see him looking at me in such a way, I cannot even try to stop the tears of shock from falling. The humiliation of it all, together with so many pairs of eyes staring at me, have me feeling ashamed and unclean. It is so overwhelming, I have an urge to run and hide, which is exactly what I do.

Chapter 15

Emily

By the time I have reached my bedroom, my tears have thankfully dried up, but my breathing is rapid, and my heart is still thumping wildly about inside my chest. I have never been a witness to men behaving in such a way before, and I have never had so many pairs of eyes on me. They all looked at me as though they were judging me for causing such a fray. But more worrying than that was seeing my husband's temper. It was frightening, for there was no talking to him when his eyes had darkened, and his skin had turned red with rage. I did not know how to stop him; I did not know how to help him.

Once my breathing returns to somewhere near normal, I slowly walk over to my bed. I brush my hand across the soft, satin sheets before allowing myself to bend and sit upon the edge. The sensuous touch helps to soothe my nerves, and removing my tight-fitting shoes forces me to emit a thankful sigh. I can still hear the muffled sound of music coming from downstairs, as well as the chatter of guests, but thankfully, no hint of a fight. I can only hope Frederick managed to haul Tobias away from Thomas; to calm the storm that I cannot.

Before I have the chance to fall into more thoughts of what might be happening in my absence, about what people might be saying, the door bursts open and in walks my husband. His jacket is dishevelled, his tie missing, and his face full of concern. I look at him with my breath catching in my throat, and I no longer feel sure of what he's going to say or do. Will he be mad at me for Thomas' actions? Will he return to being scornful and full of contempt?

"Emily," he says breathily before crossing the room to reach me. To my utter surprise, he drops to his knees and takes hold of my hands with the softest of touches. "Forgive me, Emily, please?"

When I make no sound, not even a gasp or intake of breath, he tightens his clasp around my hands and drops his forehead to my knees. I brace myself for him to speak again, but he does not. In fact, neither one of us make a single move to speak, so we remain as statues, contemplating on the situation before us.

"Perhaps you should return with your father, Emily," he eventually utters against my skirts before looking into my eyes which now feel dry from being so wide open. "I will not force you to stay, but I will remain. I release you, to keep my name but to live your own life."

He moves to get to his feet, then begins to walk over to the door, only stopping when he hears me sniff back on a sob I didn't even know was there until it had escaped from my lips. At first, he keeps his back to me, but turns his head to look to the side of where he now stands frozen. It as though he is not quite sure of what he has just heard. It is enough for me, however, to hide my shame and the sight of my tears behind my hands.

"Emily?" he whispers with a bewildered tone of voice. "You are sad?"

"Of course, I am sad," I whimper as I finally feel my feet

enough to stand. I do not know if I am feeling outraged or distraught, but I know it is not a good emotion. "You finally had me believing you felt something for me and now you are sending me away? Why? What did I do wrong?!"

"No, no, no, Emily," he rushes out whilst he paces at speed towards me, reaching for my hands and kissing them with an urgency to reassure my doubts. "I am doing this for you! I want more than anything for you to be happy, and if that means you leaving me, then so be it."

"Have you even asked me what will make me happy, Tobias? Have you ever?" I snap with frustration reigning supreme in my current mix of emotions. "You forced my father to have me marry you; you gave me no time to get to know you; took me away from my family; bullied me with your vicious, bitter words; drove me away, only to now say I can leave when I finally realise that I am undeniably in love you!"

"You love me?" he questions with his eyes now looking wider than mine, and with obvious shock written all over his face. His words break me from my ranting and leave me with only the ability to sulkily slap away at my tears. On a heavy sigh, I notice his face slowly breaking into the silliest of smiles I have ever seen on him, even rivalling that of Monty when I rub at his special spot behind his ear. "You love me, Emily?"

"It is as much of a shock to me too," I pout, just as he reaches for my hands and pulls me against his chest.

"My wife loves me," he whispers as he brushes my hair away from my face. "What more could a man ask for than that?"

"A wife who can dance without fear of bruising her partner's feet? A wife who doesn't climb trees? A wife-"

Before I can finish a list of my own flaws, he places his lips to mine and kisses me; a kiss that encompasses all of me; a kiss that cements my love for him. It's intimate, it's passionate, it's without a doubt, the most terrifying moment of my life. I have never kissed someone like this before, and when his hands move to my back and pull me up against him, I know I will never want to stop kissing him like this. My lips seem to act of their own accord when they part for his tongue to find mine, and with it, he seems to stroke, control, claim, and make silent promises to me. Its intensity has me reaching up for him, only so I might be able to cling on for dear life. I fear if I do not, I will fall to into a puddle on the floor.

"I want you," he whispers in between kissing my lips, as though separating from them will cause him to lose them forever.

"You want me?" I ask as if for clarification, the whole time feeling both nervous and curious. He pulls back and plants the smallest of kisses to the top of my nose before trailing a finger down my neck and over the swell of my breast.

"Want…you!" he says in the strangest of ways, and with his eyes turning dark. Though, they look as if there is a different storm brewing behind them, not one of anger, but one of something else.

"You will have to show me," I whisper with all the courage I have inside of me, "show me how a man and a woman fit together."

My words cause him to lean back but with his eyes remaining firmly fixed upon mine. They hold me prisoner whilst he removes his jacket, his waistcoat, and finally his shirt. As I stand frozen before him, I take all of him in with awe and wonder, marvelling at his body that calls to me in an intimate way. He lets me, knowing that I need to have this opportunity to study what I never have done before. He then reaches out for my hands and places them to his chest, to where his skin is stretched taught across the indents of his muscles.

"Keep looking at me, Emily," he instructs, "tonight we show each other everything."

Swallowing back my fear, I slowly trail my eyes along every detail of his naked flesh, which is a little darker than mine. I notice a few curls of dark hair speckled across his chest, then again underneath his bellybutton, and then all the way into his trousers. He smiles when I look up to seek permission to explore with my fingers, which I do with quiet fascination. Whilst I enjoy the feeling of his soft skin, his delicate hair, I notice his eyes closing and his breathing becoming a little laboured, as if he is in rapture. When I reach the waistband of his dress trousers, his hands quickly catch hold of mine, stopping them before I can go any further.

"I want to see you," he whispers as he reaches for the back of my dress.

As he begins to unclasp the back of my dress, his fingers work steadily, so as to not lose control of his desires. It feels like much too long to be left in nervous anticipation, but I try not to show him as such. Instead, I watch as he carefully pulls down at my sleeves. Time then speeds up, and my dress is soon falling to the floor in a puddle of silk and lace. The sight of which has me involuntarily emitting a nervous, breathy laugh, especially now that I am standing before him in my stay.

"Turn around, Emily," he murmurs with what sounds like strain in his voice.

Turning around slowly, I place my back before him so he

may begin loosening up the ties of my undergarments. As it is every night, the release feels euphoric, only on this night, I can feel his fingers gently trailing against my skin where the fastenings have been so tightly stuck to my body.

"You are bruised," he observes, and begins kissing each of them one by one, until eventually, he is kneeling upon the floor, pulling at my last pieces of clothing. When I am fully naked, I feel his hands covering my hips, using them to turn me so that I am facing him still kneeling upon the floor. I watch his eyes gazing over every piece of me, his expression telling me that he is enjoying what he sees.

"You are beautiful…so beautiful," he whispers and begins placing soft kisses to my inside thighs, just before he places a hand to my soft curls below. The feeling of which has me emitting an audible gasp, one that tells him I am enjoying the sensation of something that I have been taught to feel shameful of. A finger trails along what feels like my insides, and I moan without having any control over it. "Do not feel ashamed, Emily, this is what a man and a woman do when they are married, when she belongs to him."

"Can I see you?" I ask bravely.

He smiles against my naked skin before rising to his full height, whereby I am having to crane my neck to see his darkened eyes. He places a chaste kiss to my lips before picking me up like a baby inside of his arms.

"All in good time," he says.

Whilst kissing me, he walks us over to the side of the bed and lays me down upon the satin sheets that had soothed me only moments ago. His body moves to cover mine, though in such a way his weight does not feel uncomfortable. Indeed, it feels nice, intimate, right. His hands begin to move around my naked body, reaching for me everywhere, all the while we continue kissing like we've wanted to since that moment beneath the tree. Soon, our bodies are moving against one another, with mine writhing underneath of his, seeking something more intimate. In fact, our moves become so frantic, so wanting, I do not stop, even when he is moving his mouth over my neck, down my chest and onto my breast.

"Emily," he groans against my hardened nipple, which instantly reacts to his open mouth. At the same time, his hand is moving down, down, and into my curls which sound wet and slick with want for him. His fingers move back and forth, causing me to clasp at his hair, feeling as though I need more of something I am not even sure of.

"Tell me how that feels!" he pleads between his touching and kissing.

"Mm...strange, good," I gasp, "like I am chasing something."

His laugh is low but fleeting, before he moves further down to replace his hand with his mouth. He kisses me there, just like he was kissing my mouth, and it feels like something else entirely. It has me clutching at the sheets at the same time as gasping for air I do not seem to have. It feels as if I am running towards a precipice that I need to leap from. When I finally do, I gasp with a scream like moan and my muscles tense up so tightly, Tobias is having to hold me down with his hands firmly planted upon my hips.

"How do you feel?" he smiles as he comes back up to kiss me.

"Like I've never felt before," I answer with a smile for him, "but still like there is more to discover."

"There is," he whispers before kissing me again. "I will show you."

With that promise, he gets up to sit on the side of the bed, all the while looking at me with a mischievous smile on his face. He then bends to pull away at his boots, showing strain when they finally come away. After which, I watch as he stands before me, holding my gaze as he reaches up to pull away at the last piece of his clothing. When he finally shows me his full nudity, he remains still, waiting for me to study his body without shame. Between his legs hangs a long, smooth, and hard appendage, something that I realise has to go inside of me. The thought of which causes me to tense up a little in trepidation.

He sees my fear, but simply smiles while crawling between my legs once again. His hand reaches to stroke my cheek as I take a deep inhale of breath. His eyes soften in such a way, I instantly feel comforted and safe within his arms.

"Do not fear me, Emily," he whispers, "we are in this together, you and I, always."

"It will hurt," I murmur, and he kisses me gently.

"It will," he replies with honesty. "But not forever, not always. And then it will be good; in fact, it will be amazing for it will bring us so much closer together. Ok?"

I cannot find the voice to answer him, so instead, I nod. I try to release my nerves and let him take hold of my hands so he may help me through what is about to happen. With his lips, he reaches for the crook of my neck, and begins to kiss me with his open mouth against my skin. It feels nice, soothing, and intimate, and I indulge in every movement. I feel myself falling into a completely relaxed state just before he pushes inwards. My eyes suddenly burst open at the intrusion, at the sting of him stretching me open.

"Do you want me to stop?" he asks, genuinely seeking my permission to keep going.

"No," I reply, and clasp hold of his hands so tightly, I hope he knows how much I need him to *not* stop. "Keep going."

He drives forward and I fight the urge to cry out, to gasp with pain over the intense sting inside of me. For a while, I do not believe a man and a woman truly do fit together, but when he kisses me, I soon begin to relax into his touch again.

"Ok?" he asks though his heavy panting, and when I nod, he begins to move against me once more. Drawing out and back in again, he repeats these motions until he is going at such a pace, it soon turns into something more natural, more like we do fit, just him and I. As he feels my body turn softer beneath his, he pulls my legs up around him. It is better, deeper, and has me wanting more.

The whole time we look at one another; the intensity of which has me feeling emotional and filled with something I cannot even describe. He cups my face before moving faster against me, his breathing becoming almost erratic before, eventually, he seems to find his own precipice. At such a point, he sounds as if he is growling, low and wanting. Suddenly, he stills, and I feel a throbbing sensation below that has me gasping with him.

"Emily," he whispers before leaning down to kiss me, as though thanking me for giving this to him. I kiss him too, thanking him back.

Tobias

It sounds as though everyone has finally left. To be truthful, I couldn't care either way, not while I am lying naked upon this bed across from my beautiful wife. The room is dark save the moonlight that is streaming in through the windows. Her body is bathed in darkness, but with white luminosity touching every dip and curve of her perfect body. We have not spoken in a while, just laid here looking at one another with ridiculously silly, but contented expressions. The sight of which has me reaching out for her hand; she gives it to me freely, and without a tremble in sight.

"Tell me what you are thinking, wife," I ask with a grin so wide with happiness, it has her laughing at me.

"In truth, I cannot put into words how I am feeling, except..." she begins before pausing to think for a moment, "happy."

"In love?" I venture.

"So in love," she replies, and my heart somersaults. "And you? You have never told me how you feel, husband. Do you love me?"

"Love is such a strong word," I tease, only to laugh when I watch her mouth drop open with a gasp, as if I have deeply wounded her. Before she can even allow a single doubt of my affections enter her beautiful head, I lean in and kiss her with a whisper of, "But one that is warranted. I love you, Emily Hardy."

"As much as you do Monty?"

Her teasing smile has me pulling her into me again, where I look right into her wide eyes, which are forever searching for truth.

"More," I reply, before holding onto her.

Even in this contented bliss, my demons rear their heads, and I find myself silently begging her not to leave me. To not leave me alone like my mother and sister did all those years ago.

Chapter 16

Tobias

We both wake at the same time, but only because there are two voices practically shouting at one another in the corridor outside of Emily's room. A room which is soon to be empty, for I have already decided my wife will be moving in with me, her husband. She is everything I have ever wanted, everything I have ever needed, but also everything I have been running away from for fear of losing it. To feel like this once again, and to have her ripped away from me, is not something I think I can endure. Losing my mother and sister almost destroyed me, losing Emily would only finish the job. But when she smiles shyly at me, and with a crimson hue to her cheeks, it reassures my fears, if only for this moment in time.

I reach out for her hand to pull her close to me, however, my intentions are immediately and suddenly halted. Our worried eyes find one another when one of the voices from the corridor outside, one that sounds decidedly like Fredrick, calls out, "Please, Lady Elizabeth, I am sure Tobias and Emily are fine!"

"Oh no!" Emily gasps before pulling the covers up and over her head to hide.

She only just about manages to settle the sheet upon her

hidden body when the door swings open to reveal my aunt and the man himself. The older lady waltzes in with an expression that tells me she is about ready to give me one of her infamous lectures over my appalling behaviour. I make no such attempt to hide myself; in fact, I simply lie back against the ornate headboard and gift my aunt with a smile that can only be described as smug. I have to swallow back my laughter when her mouth drops open in delighted shock.

"Morning, Tobias," Frederick greets me with one of his mischievous grins, no doubt having guessed as to what my wife and I have been up to. "Lady Hardy."

My attempts to hide my laughter are made all the harder when her small hand slowly reaches above the sheet to give our uninvited guests a slight wave. Even Frederick has taken to covering his mouth to hide his mirth, all the while my poor aunt Elizabeth sports a healthy blush across her cheeks. However, it does not take her long before she is grinning at Frederick with an expression of sheer delight.

"I did not realise my wife's bed chamber was to become a venue for a gathering," I muse, "had I known, I would have dressed a little more appropriately."

"You, Nephew, should learn to lock a door!" Elizabeth declares whilst trying to feign indignity.

"My mind was a little preoccupied, caught up in the moment!" I reply with a grin when I hear Emily emit a squeak of embarrassment from beneath the sheets. "Was there something you needed, Aunty?"

"Well, I had come to whip your hide for making such a spectacle of yourself last night," she says with a small tut, "though, given what I am seeing, I suppose I can let it slide. Well done,

Tobias!"

I give her a quick nod with a proud smile upon my face. Frederick raises a playful brow whilst he helps to shuffle Elizabeth out of the door. It is a relief to hear the click of it finally shutting, knowing that I can finally have Emily all to myself. At the sound, Emily pulls back the sheet, gasping for air, looks at me, then proceeds to laugh over yet more of my appalling behaviour. I try to keep up the pretence of looking nonchalant about it, but her infectious giggling has me joining in with her before kissing those delicious lips.

"Good morning," I whisper between kisses, "how are you feeling?"

"I am well," she replies, "and you?"

"Very well," I declare, "though I do believe we should have a hearty breakfast."

"You do?" she asks, with a curious frown upon her face.

"Of course," I tell her as I finally break into a smile, "once we have moved you into my bedroom, we have a lot of consummating to make up for."

She drops her mouth open in shock over my blunt declaration, but also with a clear smile breaking through, just before I smother it with my lips, wrapping my arms around her to pull her in even closer. I cannot help myself any longer; breakfast can wait until after I have made love to my beautiful wife.

Emily

My husband kept me prisoner inside of his room for two

days straight, but I had a smile on my face for the entire time. His worshipping of me became easier, less painful, more…intense. Every time, we seemed to lose ourselves a little more. We laughed frequently and talked of things we have never admitted to anyone else. Other times, we'd lie in silence, just staring at one another, and when we finally found our voices again, it was to tell one another of how we felt. It is a strange thing to feel this way for another, to be totally dependent on him for a happiness I have never felt before. A happiness that is consuming and dangerously addictive. I fear it on some level, and I worry about a time when I might not have him. I can tell he feels it too, by the way he looks at me, the way he brushes his fingers against my skin, or inhales the scent of my hair. I feel his all-encompassing love for me by the way he sinks inside of me, and when we both gasp in those first few moments of connection.

"Are you happy, Emily?" he whispers.

I couldn't even tell you what time of day it is, for I am so lost to him, to us.

"Very," I tell him, smiling and reaching up to cup his face with my hand. The feeling of his bristly jaw has me giggling, for it forces me to acknowledge the fact that we need to attend to our personal hygiene, if nothing else. "I fear we will have to leave this room today, husband."

"We will," he agrees, but only pulls me in closer against him, with his kissing keeping me prisoner all over again. "I love you, Emily."

"I love you too, Tobias."

"What is this?" he asks as his fingers brush over the scar left by those bramble bushes from over six years ago.

"It is the one time I managed to fall from a tree," I explain, causing him to widen his eyes in playful shock over my admission. "Right through a bramble bush that not only ripped my dress, but also my skin. I had to have stitches, though not before my mother had given me a stern talking to for ruining my dress."

"How old were you?" he asks, running his forefinger up and down the raised patch of skin with a sort of quiet fascination.

"It was on my twelfth birthday," I mutter with a soft smile as he kisses the marred skin. "Do you think I am damaged?"

He looks at me from where his mouth remains clasped to my scar, and I lose track of where, and even who I am. With my heart in my throat, it is as though I am having to remain suspended, waiting for him to reply with those large, blue eyes of his.

"You are perfectly imperfect, my darling," he whispers with those eyes softening with comforting reassurance. "It is one of the main reasons I love you, Emily Hardy."

I smile with my teeth over his flawless answer, one that tells me I am beautiful but without the pressure to be anything other than what I already am. I also know that I am to be lost to him for at least another half a day, to his kissing, his body, his warmth.

Tobias

Monty's reaction to seeing Emily after I have commandeered her for the last three days, almost has me feeling guilty. I have never seen him shake his body so vibrantly or without control when he first sets eyes on my wife. He almost takes her completely off her feet, that is before he proceeds to slobber her face with that ridiculous tongue of his. Under normal circumstances, I would chastise him, but in this instance, I cannot blame the poor fool. He is as lost to her as I am.

"Mary, will you accompany me to take Monty for a walk across the fields?" Emily asks her maid with a new confidence; one I hope has something to do with me. "Tobias needs to work this afternoon. I fear I have kept him...er, busy, for far too long."

She blushes over her admission with my smirk doing nothing to ease the sudden heat in her cheeks.

"Of course, Your Grace," Mary dutifully replies with a nod and a wink when she thinks I am not looking. "You say the word, and I'll make sure I am ready."

"Emily, do remember that we depart for London the day after next," I say to her, peering over the paper. She is eating her breakfast, which she shares with the dog, all the while reading a letter that she received from her sister this morning. "You shall need to pack at some point, my dear. And I shall be expecting frequent visits to my study to make sure you do not forget me."

I take another peek over my paper to look at her with a mischievous smile, to which she freezes with her toast hovering half-way between her plate and her mouth, along with a crimson hue to her cheeks. We have been greedily feasting upon each other nonstop for the past few days; why should I not expect a few opportunities to make love to her throughout the day? My wife has undoubtedly awoken a baser desire within me after going so long without.

"Of course," she eventually replies with a grace of her own menacing smile. "I am here but to serve you, my husband."

"And I you," I reply with a wicked arch of my brow. She covers her mouth to try and hide a small giggle, though the staff are more than aware as to what we are alluding to. However, Emily is still young and naïve; she does not need to know such things.

"Will Monty be joining us on our trip to London?" she asks as she passes the drooling hound her last piece of her toast.

"Do *you* want Monty to come with us?" I ask, for I am officially dedicated to making her happy.

She gifts me one of her delicious grins and nods her head at a rapid pace, all the while patting the dog as he chomps down on his treat. I merely roll my eyes before looking at my paper again, the whole time trying to hide the fact that I too, am smiling with giddiness.

"Very well, Emily," I reply and continue reading, only to be momentarily surprised when she comes up and places a kiss on my cheek. When she tries to move away again, I pull her back to kiss her properly; a kiss that will have to keep me satisfied until she feels the need to afford me one of those long-awaited visits.

A day and many delicious visits to my office later, ones that had me making love to Emily over my desk, we arrive at my London house with Mary and Monty accompanying us in the carriage behind. Even the ride in our carriage was a rather steamy affair. In fact, I have to wonder if our path to parenthood might be brought forward by our frequent and passionate embraces. Not that I am worried about the notion. Instead, I find myself smiling over the thought of Emily being a mother to my children, of becoming a family with the woman who I am hopelessly in love with. But then, it is followed by deep rooted fear of losing her, like my father lost my mother. Would I also turn into a bitter old man who took out his grief on his children? I would like to think not.

Emily has not seen this house before, but given the wide eyes and smile on her face, I can tell she more than approves. As does Monty who has ignited the staff into a small frenzy with his rushing around and causing a vase to go flying with his ridiculous tail wagging.

"Monty!" I call sternly. He drops his head and obediently comes skulking over to my side.

"Oh, poor boy," Emily coos, to which the hound gives his widest and most pathetic eyes. "Did he shout at you?"

"Dogs need discipline, Emily," I argue when she finally looks at me again, "as do children when we have them."

"Oh, hush, I shall spoil any children we may have rotten, just like I do with Monty!"

She gifts me with a chaste kiss upon my lips before offering me an innocent smile. It's enough to have me pick her up in my arms, ignoring the small yelp she emits over the shock of it, and begin marching us towards the staircase.

"Well, if we are going to have these children, darling, we had best get to work making them!"

My desire for her becomes primal, and by the time we reach the master bedroom, I am literally ripping at her clothes. She grips hold of my arms and kisses me back with just as much want as I have for her. In fact, removing her clothing soon comes second to wanting to be inside of her. With that being said, I place her onto the floor, push her towards the bed and begin to pull up her skirts so I can enter her from behind. She is ready for me, wet and wanting, as well as moaning before I have even filled her up.

"Tobias…" she gasps when I finally thrust all the way inside of her, "more!"

"I have created quite the temptress," I tease as I begin moving in and out of her warmth.

She laughs softly but when I reach for her shoulder and begin moving at a much harder and faster pace, her mirth turns to heavy panting. She clenches her muscles so tightly around me, I fear I won't be able to pleasure her first. I reach around to run my fingers through her wet lips below, then begin to circle where I know she likes it. Her gasping tells me she is as close as I am.

Just before I explode with a force I cannot hold back, she screams and clutches tightly at the bedsheets, blanching her knuckles white and making the mattress wrinkled. One more hard thrust and I release, deep inside of her. We hold still, trying to get our breath back, feeling content in this moment of closeness with one another.

"I want more of you," I whisper, pulling her up to rest against me.

"Tobias Hardy, will you ever grow tired of me?" she says with a soft laugh, with her eyes still closed and her clothing dishevelled.

"Never," I reply against her ear, "I shall-"

Our moment of euphoria is cut short by someone knocking awkwardly at the door. It has me growling in frustration and Emily gasping with embarrassment over having just been caught in the act.

"What?!" I snap angrily whilst tucking myself away. I then turn to help to straighten Emily's skirts. She begins to giggle over my stern, irritated expression, which soon softens me into a stupor again.

"Apologies, Your Grace, but Lord Brown has just arrived," one of the butlers calls through the door, the thickness of which muffles his already anxious voice. "Sh-should I send him away?"

"No," Emily manages to call out before I have even opened my mouth to say the complete opposite. "Tell him we shall be down presently."

"Of course," he replies before shuffling away as quickly as possible.

"I was not anywhere near finished with you yet," I chastise her, "I told you *I* want more."

"Later, Tobias," she grins smugly, "there is always later."

Chapter 17

Emily

A few days after our arrival in London, I finally get to spend some time with my sister in the form of a good jaunt around the park. We are accompanied by the most highly esteemed of chaperones, in the form of her rat like dogs and our handsome beast of a hound, Monty. I have to laugh to myself when I consider I am now my sister's watchful eyes, seeing as I am a married woman, and she is still a maid. Not that I would say such a thing to Elsie, she remains to be a little out of sorts over the whole affair. Though she does seem to be exceptionally pleased to see me; happier than she's ever been in fact.

After an initial chaotic meeting of dogs and people, Monty soon settles down into walking proudly alongside the river with me. Poor Elsie's dogs have to maintain a quick pace just to keep up with him. Elsie now looks the picture of health, no longer showing any hint of having suffered from flu, even though it had kept her bed ridden for almost a week.

I ask her about Mother and how she really feels about me not being at home anymore. Initially she had cried, frequently. However, since my father's visit, she is unsure as to what to feel about my marriage to Tobias. Unfortunately, my father witnessed Tobias' temper at its worst. My reassurances had helped, but not enough to put their fears to rest. Edmund, on the other hand, is even more withdrawn than he was before. He is in a constant state of anxiety for my wellbeing, and visits my family house daily, if only to see if they have heard anything new. Her words have me feeling guilty for Edmund, so much so, that when I see him right ahead of us, it takes my breath away.

He does not see us straight away, which gives me a moment or two to study the boy who I remember as always laughing with during my childhood. Such good times we shared together, but never to be repeated again. A pang of guilt hits me when I remember the warning that I had given him on my twelfth birthday. I knew back then that the joys of innocence were coming to an end; he did not believe me. And now, he looks a shadow of the man I used to know. He is stood with a hunch in his back, his fingers fiddling with his hat between his hands, only now looking at me with a ghost like expression. His eyes are dark, his complexion pale, and it would not surprise me to learn that he isn't sleeping properly.

"You should go to him," Elsie says as she halts us by taking hold of my hand in support, "if only to let him know you are truly ok."

"I cannot, Elsie, I promised my husband I would not," I reply, sounding guilty for the fact. "If he found out I went against his wishes, it would hurt him."

"Emily, is your life long best friend not hurting? Does he not deserve your comfort?" she says to me with a longing look in her eye, one that makes me feel small, conflicted, and unsure as to what to do for the best. "Besides, Tobias is not here, so how would he know? I am not asking you to say anything untoward, or to touch him in anyway. Just talk to him, please?"

"Alright," I reply quietly before emitting a long breath of air, readying myself to talk to another man behind my husband's back.

Ever my loyal hound, Monty trots happily alongside me, content to be at my heel and being completely unaware as to how I am going behind his master's back. He wags his tail at the new stranger, cowering before him in the hopes he'll receive a head pat and some words of affection from this new man. Edmund bends down to greet the dog, smiling and rubbing at his ears in exchange for moans of appreciation from Monty.

"Hello, Edmund," I say meekly, stopping him from loving the dog so he can stand up to look at me properly.

"Hello, Emily," he returns shyly, before cracking an awkward smile. "How are you?"

"I am well, and you?" I ask with a small wince of my features, for I already know he has been suffering. "Edmund, you look like you are not sleeping."

"I have been worried about you, Em," he admits as he looks to the ground with an extremely sad expression. "You are all I can think about."

"I am so sorry to have caused you concern, Edmund, but I want you to know that I am fine," I tell him with a smile that I hope will bring him some reassurance. It is hard to show him my happiness, for I know how painful it will be for him to hear that I no longer wish to escape Tobias, and that I now love him. However, he needs to hear this for his own sake. To let me go so he may find love elsewhere. "I want you to move on from me, Edmund, to find someone for yourself. She is out there somewhere, Edmund."

"Thomas Greyson told me about his behaviour at your ball last week," he says without expression, "he returned with a black eye and a split lip. I would never forgive myself if Tobias inflicted those sorts of injuries upon you."

"Edmund, your friend was not without fault," I reply with a sigh, "he grabbed me, and unfortunately, Tobias saw him do so. Whilst I do not condone Tobias's temper, I know he would never hurt me in this way-"

"How does he hurt you, Emily? Does he still talk to you with disdain? Does he make you-"

"I love him, Edmund!" I cry out before I can stop myself. The look of pain on his face all but kills me, and I instantly hate myself for being so tactless.

"I see," he sighs with a stiff upper lip, almost looking ready to roar at me, though, I know he won't. He is Edmund, my friend, the softest boy I know. "I see."

"Edmund…" I reach out to place a hand on his arm, to steady him while he looks so lost. He stares at it and simply slumps even lower, almost readying himself to cry. "I am sorry to love my husband, Edmund, but surely you must see it is for the best?"

"Of course," he smiles, even though he could not look any further from feeling any kind of happiness.

"I wish you well, Edmund," I tell him, only to find myself whimpering, "and love, Edmund. I wish for you to have a love you can have for yourself; a love that will be all yours and yours alone."

"And I am glad you have found yours," he says with a nod,

signalling that it is time for us to part. I remove my hand as we look at one another for another moment or two, knowing that this may well be the last time we see one another. It is sad, but something that is needed to let him move on without me.

"Goodbye, Edmund," I say quietly. He does not say it back, just smiles, nods, and eventually walks away.

"Oh, Emily," Elsie says soon after, clutching at my shoulders when I allow myself to cry a little over our lost friendship. "Shh, he'll be fine, I promise you. Come on, let's get these silly dogs walked so you can return home to your husband."

Tobias

It is official; I am truly lost to Emily. The woman has me frequently checking my pocket watch, only to feel giddy when I realise she is due back any minute now. When I hear the front door open, followed by the sound of my butler muffling some sort of greeting, I smile to myself and begin to get to my feet. Alas, when the door to my study opens, it is not my beautiful wife walking through to gift me with kisses, it is Frederick. I cannot help but slump back inside of my chair with a disappointment I cannot hide. Fortunately, Frederick does not take my reaction to heart, he simply emits a hearty chuckle over my lack of enthusiasm.

"I'm sorry, Tobias," he says with a smirk before taking up the seat opposite to mine, "am I not who you were hoping for? Am I not as pretty to look upon?"

"Apologies, my friend," I smile sheepishly, "my wife and I are still in that blissful period of falling in love."

"And I hope it long continues, though..." He sighs and looks pensive for a moment or two, which only causes my chest to tighten with anxiety.

"Speak clearly, Frederick, but..." I pause, looking a little threatening toward my lifelong friend, for it sounds as though he is about to speak ill of my wife; something I will not allow anyone to do without consequence. "Choose your words wisely."

"I was invited for a walk along the Thames with Thomas and Victoria Greyson this afternoon," he explains, "I saw Emily there."

"With her sister," I cut in, warning him not to say anything that might impinge on her good name. "They went to walk the dogs together."

"Her sister was present, but Emily wasn't with her; not directly, anyway. I do not believe she is anything but loyal and trustworthy, but I would not be your friend if I did not tell you what I saw."

"What did you see?" I growl through my teeth, with the skin across my hands tightening as they clasp together in fear.

"She was with Edmund Barton, and her hand was resting against his arm while they spoke. She was crying, and when he left, she held on tightly to her sister and whimpered."

I let out a long-held breath as I lean back against my seat, contemplating all of what he has just said. The tips of my fingers rest against my lips, where they begin to run back and forth in an attempt to try and calm myself. I had told her not to speak to him again, to not go near that young pup, and yet she has. Does she not realise how hurtful such a betrayal is to me? After all we have been through, does she not know what shame that would put upon me if people were to find out that she had gone against my wishes? Does she have feelings for him?

Calm your fire, Tobias, this is not as bad as you are building it up to be.

"Tobias," Frederick calls out, interrupting my runaway thoughts, just as he always does when my tempter threatens to consume me. "You have no need to doubt Emily. It was most likely innocent; a chance run in with an old acquaintance."

"Of course," I agree with an unnatural smile for him. "I have no reason to doubt my wife."

"Good," he says, and physically slumps with relief, "I am glad we have all of that out in the open. I love Emily like a sister, you know that, but my loyalty will always lie with you, my friend."

"How about a drink at the gentlemen's club tonight?" I suggest, perhaps needing a break from losing myself inside of Emily. "Surely, you must need a strong one after having spent the afternoon with Thomas Greyson."

"Quite!" he confirms with a laugh. "But what could I say when he offered me a private walk with the lovely Victoria?"

Before I can answer him, I hear Emily walking through the door with a yelp at the same time as Monty comes running in with his wet fur spreading mud and water everywhere. Frederick ignores the commotion, and instead, watches me watching her with eyes now tinged with suspicion. I do not want to doubt her, to question her honour, but I cannot help my reactions. When I look at Emily, she smiles at me, just as she had done so before she left this morning. *Innocent?* Of course she is.

"Frederick, how lovely to see you," she greets him with a

carefree laugh, "and husband, of course."

She leans in to kiss me, and I smile at her, almost completely forgetting what Frederick had just told me.

"Emily, darling, you would not mind if I took Frederick out for a drink tonight?" I ask and she gifts me with a smile and a soft shake of her head. She looks so beautiful, I almost regret the suggestion, so lean into whisper, "I shall make it up to you when I return."

"Tobias!" she chastises me with a teasing tut. "We have company. Besides, I may well be asleep by the time you arrive home. I know how late men stay at such places. I should warn you though, you might come home to find another man in your wife's bed!" She giggles but it only has me clutching hold of her wrist more tightly, looking at her with such an expression, it is painfully clear I expect her to explain herself immediately. "I am talking of Monty, the dog," she whispers, now looking at me with nothing but concern.

"Forgive me," I reply, feeling beyond foolish for letting that flash of anger catch hold of me. "I am just so afraid of losing you, Emily."

"Frederick," she says, still looking at me with worry, "would you give me a private moment with my husband?"

"Of course," he replies, eyeing me as he gets to his feet without hesitation. "I shall see you later, Tobias. Emily."

"Goodbye, Frederick, be sure to put on your coat, is has begun to rain," she says to my friend before he disappears through the door. As soon as he does, she turns on me completely, and with her wide eyes melting my heart and causing me to feel guilty for ever doubting her. "Talk to me, Tobias."

"Who did you see at the park today, Emily?" I ask as I pull her into me for comfort and reassurance. She instantly sighs, long and heavy, before eventually resting her head against mine.

"I saw Edmund and we spoke," she admits. "It was not planned, and it is only because Elsie asked me to. I did not purposefully go against your wishes."

"Do you love him?" I ask her outright, holding my breath before she relieves me with a smile against my skin.

"Yes, but not in the way I love you," she replies, then pulls away to look straight into my eyes. "I love him like I love Monty. I told you this, Tobias."

"I know," I say on a long sigh before kissing her again. "I just…I cannot lose you like I lost my mother and my sister."

"Tobias, you will not lose me!" She tuts and holds on tighter, just as do I with her. "But you must always talk to me. Do not push me away as you did before."

"I am learning not to, my love, I am trying so hard," I murmur against her soft hair.

"I know," she whispers back, "it is why I love you so much."

"And I you," I tell her as I lift her into my arms. "Let me show you how much I adore you, my Emily."

I take her to bed before leaving for the club that evening, taking comfort in the sight of her waving me off from the window. Her smile warms me like no other; how could I have been so foolish as to doubt her?

Chapter 18

Emily

Mary and I have been playing cards in my bedroom for the past two hours, but she is a terribly poor student. Not only does she not understand the rules, but she frequently questions which card is which. In the end, we are laughing too much to even care what is happening with our card game.

"Forgive me, Emily, I fear I shall never get the hang of this," she giggles with me. "Some of us were not meant to play such games."

"Sometimes the trying is more fun than the achieving," I tell her while taking note of the rain still beating down against the glass. It hasn't let up since I returned home with Monty earlier on. "But you have made me laugh and taken my mind away from missing Tobias. Goodness, Mary, what has become of me?"

"You have fallen prey to love, child," she teases, "which wasn't an easy feat with His Grace."

"I know, and I am thankful for it," I admit with a goofy smile upon my face, "even if it does make me ridiculously lost to another."

"Ridiculously happy though, Emily," she says with a sleepy

smile and a yawn, "which you more than deserve!"

"Thank you, Mary," I whisper, sharing a tender and warming moment with someone who has become a good friend. Speaking of friends, I suddenly realise the other man in my life is missing. "Where is Monty?"

Mary begins looking around along with me, when Simon, Tobias' butler, walks in with his usual expressionless face.

"Your Grace, Monty is outside, refusing to come in," he says with little to no tone in his voice, "I wonder if he might listen to your calls."

"Of course, let me put on my gown and I will come to the front door," I tell him. He nods, then walks away at a heavy and slow pace, leaving Mary and I to giggle over his lack of any sort of personality. "I will go and fetch the dog, you put the cards away," I suggest, just as I would have with Elsie. She is indeed, fast becoming as close to me as my sister. "I think you are right about cards; next time we shall try chess."

"The game with little wooden people?" she questions me with a furrowed brow, and I emit a small laugh over her cluelessness.

"Yes, and horses," I tell her and laugh even harder when she pulls a face at me. "Unless you have changed your mind and want me to help you climb a tree?"

She says nothing but pulls a set of wide, shocked eyes at me. I wiggle my fingers at her, pull on my gown, and make my way to the door so I can attempt to get Monty back inside.

When I make my way outside, I can see the tall lights from the street, the carriages rushing by and splashing up the puddles that have settled on the road. There is no wind, but the steady beating of rain is relentless. I can already make out the oozing mud beneath the grass and the percussion of raindrops falling upon the leaves. The sound of which is making just as loud a noise as those falling upon the tiles beneath my feet.

"Would you like your coat, Lady Hardy?" Simon calls out in his monotonous tone of voice.

"No, Simon, I will be ok," I call back, wrapping my gown tighter around my waist. It is still summer after all, and although it is very wet, it is not at all cold. "Monty!" I shout out before making my way across the path. "Monty!"

Miraculously, I hear a rustling coming from the bushes up ahead, followed by a muffled whimper. I begin to step toward the muddied grass, trying to lift my skirts as much as possible so as to avoid the splash of mud. However, it is a futile action, for the hem is already sodden with water from the grass.

"I say, Emily, is that you?" an older, gentlemanly voice calls out to me. I recognise the friendly voice, so immediately turn to face it. "Why, it is you! What the devil are you doing outside in this God-awful weather, child?"

"Lord Bartholomew, I should ask you the same question," I counter, but grin widely as I watch him wandering over with his companion, a weedy looking gentleman who hovers close to his side. "All the darn carriages have been taken due to the rain. I wasn't about to wait for one when I live so close by. Now you; what on earth are you doing outside in the dark wearing only your dressing gown?"

"Rescuing my dog," I reply casually, talking louder than usual so he can hear me through the noise of the storm. "I think he has got himself stuck in the undergrowth, or perhaps the fence."

"Can't your man servant get him out? Where is that husband of yours? Torturing some poor mortal somewhere?"

"Do not be wicked, Lord Bartholomew!" I laugh. for he's a gentle old man really, one I have grown up with. "Besides, he will not listen to anyone but me or Tobias. You know me, always one to get my hands dirty."

"Yes," he says with wide eyes that soften into a smile. "Well, let's get the poor mutt out then, shall we?"

I smile my thanks before trying to navigate my way across the mud, thinking how my nightgown is sure to end up completely ruined at this rate. It does not matter though, particularly when Monty is in pain and in need of help. As soon as I approach the poor boy, I see the cause of his concern. He has gone and got himself caught up in a bramble bush, much like I had when I was twelve years old. He tries to wag his tail when he sees me, but then whimpers when the thorns cut even deeper inside of his skin.

"My Lord, will you hold him still while I try to pick the thorns away from him," I call out to the gentleman who is standing over us. He does what I ask of him after pushing his cane into his companion's hands. My knees are now completely sunken inside of the dead leaves, and my soaked hair is plastered against my face. It takes a good ten minutes or so to pick out every last thorn, but when Monty finally becomes free, he leaps onto the grass and begins shaking and leaping about as though he had been imprisoned for years.

"Very well done, my dear," Lord Batholomew calls back to me, "though, I think you should return inside and get yourself dry."

"Thank you, Barty." I smile widely, having just used the nickname I used to call him as a child. "I could not have done it without you."

"Quite," he says with a dramatic roll of his eyes before gifting me with an affectionate smile. "Goodnight, child!"

"Come on, Monty, get that ridiculous bottom back inside and let us take a look at those cuts!"

Tobias

It is late, and I have grown tired of drinking. However, the rain outside is stopping me from leaving and getting home to my wife. Frederick has been good company but his reluctance to make his intentions known to Victoria's father is now frustrating me. The thought of taking responsibility, as well as having lived a life as a rake, are holding him back. Both are excuses I cannot be bothered to listen to anymore. The only justification with which I can agree on for his procrastination, is the fact that she comes with a brother who literally makes my skin crawl with rage. Hopefully, he'll take on his own wife, along with Edmund Barton, and leave any thoughts of Emily far behind. I check my pocket watch one more time, something my drinking companion notices and laughs at me for.

"Counting down the minutes, you lovesick fool?" he teases.

"Jealousy is such an ugly colour on you, Frederick," I tell him with a smug smirk upon my face. After all, I will be going home to a beautiful woman in my bed, whereas his will be all alone and cold, or with a complete stranger. Neither of which sound at all appealing.

"Go," he instructs me, "for if I have to see you looking at your pocket watch one more time, I shall throw it across the room!"

"You are right." I smile as I get to my feet to put on my coat. "My wife calls-"

"Your Grace!" a familiar, but unwanted voice shouts over, causing me to sigh in frustration. "Your Grace, a word?"

"Good evening, Lord Greyson," I reply through tight lips and a bemused expression, "make it quick for I am about to go home to my wife."

"It is your wife I came to speak to you about," he says with his face furrowed in concern. My instant thoughts are of something awful having happened to her; even Frederick has got to his feet. "Away from here; you will not want others to hear this."

Frederick and I look at one another before giving him the nod to show us the way out. Once at the doorway, he gestures to our coats, then signals for us to go outside where it is still pouring with rain. Without any further word of explanation, he opens the door to the carriage that is already waiting for us. I assume it belongs to Greyson but keep my questions to myself, for my thoughts need only be of Emily. As soon the wheels set into motion, I lean forward, looking directly at him, and with a scowl upon my face. I am no longer able to exercise anymore patience with this man; I need to know the reason for why he has caused such scene.

"Explain yourself, Greyson," I growl at the same time as Frederick leans forward too, "and be blunt."

"Apologies, Your Grace, but I was witness to something that is going to cause you much pain and anger," he says, prompting my heart to begin thumping wildly about inside of my chest. "I was returning home from my card game when I noticed Edmund Barton walking through the park with...er...with your wife."

Frederick shoots his gaze at me, but my eyes remain solely focussed on the man before me. However, my hands have pulled into tight knuckles and every muscle in my body has tensed up with fury.

"She was alone with him?" Frederick eventually speaks, for I cannot.

"She was, and they were holding hands," he says with a guilty looking expression. It stupidly has me clutching onto a sliver hope that the man is simply pulling tricks again.

"You lie!" I growl through my teeth.

"I understand your doubt, Lord Hardy, you have made your feelings towards me more than clear in the past. It is precisely why I have brought you here," he replies, then gestures over to the park, still black but with a streetlight illuminating the entrance. "I am only warning you for the sake of my sister. It is no secret that Lord Brown and Victoria are forming an attachment, and the very last thing I want to happen is for Frederick to be connected to any sort of scandal. His friendship with you threatens that if you allow your wife to…cuckold you."

"My wife will not cuckold me!" I snap before bursting out of the carriage with the both of them soon following on from behind me.

I wrap my coat around my person before reluctantly standing still, waiting for Thomas to lead us to where he had seen Edmund, supposedly with Emily. The rain is still pelting down, and completely drowning out the sound of anything else. He walks at a pace, though not fast enough, given how angry and anxious I am feeling over the prospect of seeing the betrayal of the one woman I trusted my heart to.

Minutes later, Thomas throws out his arm to stop us from going any further. He then points towards a dark corner full of bushes and trees, where the distinctive shapes of two bodies lie resting against the trunk of an enormous oak. I study them for a while, but when I finally force my eyes to make sense of what is happening before me, I do not think I have felt any more broken. It feels as though every breath in my body has left me, and all that remains is a shell of a man.

"Emily…"

Right before my eyes, I see a young couple in the throes of passion, up against that old oak tree, in amongst the dirt, getting wetter and muddier with each thrust that he drives inside of her. The blue of her dress shimmers in the wet, whilst the straps of her dress have fallen to reveal her flesh, and though I cannot see her face, I can see long blond curls and a raised scar across her shoulder. It is the very same one that she had told me about only days ago. I close my eyes to it, but it only has me hearing his moans of her name all the louder.

"Tobias," Frederick whispers against my ear as I fall to my knees, with my hands gripping and tugging at my hair in grief. I let out something akin to a howling dog, with a painful shock running all the way through my body.

"Emily, I have to go to her…" I shriek, trying to shuck his hold off me whilst I take in the sight of Edmund's hands all over her body, their faces fused as one as they rise and fall together. "Look what he's doing to her!"

"Tobias, it does not look like he is forcing her," he mutters angrily against my ear. "The lady is disloyal and does not deserve your compassion, nor your downfall if this were to come out. Be the businessman that you are, the one who puts logic before emotion."

"Your friend is right, Lord Hardy, if this gets out, she will not be the only one to fall from grace, so too will you. To be cuckolded by someone far beneath you, far younger, will have the gossipers talking, and not in a good way!" Thomas, a man I have always hated, urges me. "Come, let us leave so you can think of what to do when you are feeling less emotional."

"Let us return to my house, Tobias," Frederick offers, pulling at my arm as he tries to get me away from what will be permanently etched upon my eyes forever more. "Come, Tobias!"

With one last look at the couple who are still kissing in the most obscene way, all the while writhing against the rugged trunk of the tree, and with so much animalistic passion, so much wanting and desire, I fear I lose control of my emotions and begin to run. Only when I feel I am far from the risk of seeing them again, do I allow myself to vomit, to expel all the disgust of what I have just been witness to. Memories of making love to her only this afternoon, of us telling one another how much we feel, how in love we are, float in and out of my head to taunt me. They turn to dirt, to wet mud on the ground with naked bodies and audible gasps of pleasure, of grunting and moaning as he pummels inside of her.

I shock a few drunken fools when I let out a single growl of rage and begin hitting and kicking at the carriage in which we had arrived. I do not even know how Thomas and Frederick manage to escort me all the way back to Frederick's Batchelor lodgings across town. Though once there, Thomas makes his apologies and leaves before I truly lose hold of my senses, no doubt suspecting that this time will be soon approaching.

"Tobias," Frederick murmurs as he passes a glass of something strong, wet, and amber to me, "try and calm the storm.

We did not see her face; it might not have been Emily."

"Do you really believe that, Frederick?" I growl through my teeth, barely able to contain the mounting rage inside of me. When I look at him, his sorrowful expression says more than enough. "It would still be wise to go home, talk to the staff, check her clothes, look for anything that confirms her deceit."

"I could have stomached this had she done it to me when I was cruel to her," I admit with a distraught sigh, "but to seek revenge in such a venomous way is something I never would have thought she could do. Turns out, I seriously underestimated just how clever and vindictive she is. A true wolf in sheep's clothing!"

"What will you do, Tobias? If she truly has betrayed you, what will you do?"

"Besides tear her limb from limb?" I reply on a whimper as my heart cracks that little bit more. The sound of my breaking urges me to gulp back the whiskey to try and soothe the sting; alas, it hardly makes a dent in the pain with which I am feeling. "I will learn from my mistakes."

"Explain," he sighs, no doubt bracing himself for the worst of my temper.

"I will become the Tobias I was before she coerced me into having feelings for her, and I will send her back to Kent. She will be kept far, far away from Edmund Barton, her family, and more importantly, from me."

He says nothing, just leans back and looks worried for my state of mind whilst I pour another glass of numbing liquor.

Chapter 19

Tobias

I barely slept, for obvious reasons, so as soon as the sun began to rise, I dressed myself and left before Fredrick would know I was even gone. I chose to walk, even though it would take me a good hour or so to get to my house across town. I even passed through the park, to see the evidence of their betrayal, to torture myself and build up my rage so I might look on her without softening. So, if nothing else, I could play the part of the stone-cold husband as I did so well before, like I should have remained.

The ground is waterlogged, but the skies are now clear. With the silence of early morning, I stand before the place where Emily and her real lover had laid together last night. The leaves are disturbed, though look no more unusual than they would have had she not cut out my heart with a blunt blade and thrown it away with the horse manure on the street. If you had not seen it, you would not think anything untoward had happened. I would be at home with my loving wife, maybe even making love to her as we have done so frequently over the last few weeks.

The door is opened for me before I even reach the top, letting me stride with purpose inside of the house. Simon nods his head before shuffling back to let me through. I offer him no words, just march myself up to the master bedroom where I should find my cheating wife. Everyone who passes me by sees the thunderous look on my face and scurries away as soon as is humanly possible. Part of me wants to throw the door open and confront her, but the more sensible side of me stops this rash course of action. Instead, it allows me to think for a moment before carefully turning the handle.

The room is still dark with only a sliver of light filtering in through the gap in the drapes. On the bed, she lies hidden under the covers that rise and fall with each of her breaths. She makes no sound, and the gentle curl in her hair is falling over her shoulders. The way she is tucked up tight, as though cold, has me walking over to sit beside her, where I momentarily eye her like the woman I had left behind yesterday; the one I was so desperately in love with. I watch her for a few minutes before placing my hand through her hair, sighing sadly when I feel it is still damp below my fingertips. How could you betray me when I gave you everything?

My hand clasps tightly around her locks, so much so, my mouth clenches up with fury, frustration, and hurt. It is only when she moans a little that I force myself to let go, to rise to my feet and go in search of further evidence of her deceit. With quiet feet, I pace around the room to find her clothes from the night before. It does not take me long to find them draped across the armchair, still sodden and muddied from having been immersed in the ground. Here is the evidence I need to prove that she had let Edmund Barton fuck her like the whore she is.

Within seconds of picking up the white cotton nightdress which I had left her in last night, now tarnished with black mud, I rip it to shreds. I leave the remnants of it scattered all over the floor so she might find it and know that I have discovered her shameful secret.

Emily

The cold wakes me up and I shiver from it. I rub at my arms, all the while feeling like someone has taken a mallet to my head. My nose is running with what feels like a cold taking over. I silently curse Monty for getting himself stuck last night, however, I then chastise myself for being so unkind, for it wasn't his fault. My clothes from last night are thoroughly ruined but I was much too wet to worry about giving them to Mary. Instead, I had wrapped myself inside of a blanket and fallen asleep within minutes of my head hitting the pillow. I do not recall Tobias coming home last night but the sound of him shouting at someone downstairs has me leaping up to go and find him. I really am beholden to him for my happiness now. Who would have thought it from someone like me? A boy of a girl, a lover of climbing trees, and a hater of all things girly and frilly, now completely in love with a man who once made me tremble in fear.

"Come in!" I call out to Mary when she knocks on the door to help me dress. She enters looking a little flustered, and I frown at her for some sort of explanation. "Something wrong, Mary?"

"I am not sure," she whispers as though someone might overhear us, "but your husband is in a frightful mood. He's already snapped at three of the serving staff, including poor Simon."

"Oh dear," I reply, having absolutely no idea as to what could have caused him to change so drastically since yesterday. I had hoped his evening with Fredrick might have set his fears to rest after our conversation. "I have not seen him since he left me yesterday. I wonder what could have happened."

"No idea," she replies whilst picking out a dress for me to wear. "We're all hoping you might be able to tame his temper."

"I shall try my very best, Mary," I giggle, "perhaps it does need a woman's touch."

"Emily, what on earth has happened to your nightgown?" she gasps as she fastens me in with the familiar pinch that comes from wearing a stay.

"I know, it really is quite ruined after rescuing Monty last night," I sigh with a smile, for it is a rather amusing story when I think of it now. "Perhaps that will make him smile."

"But it has been torn to shreds!" I feel my brow screwing up in confusion; it wasn't like that when I left it there last night. However, she soon shows me the evidence of her observation in the form of ripped pieces of damp cotton resting inside of her hands. "How strange," I exclaim, picking up one or two pieces to study as if I will find the answer somewhere inside of them.

"Perhaps Monty got in during the night?" she suggests, and I smile and nod my head, feeling relieved to have come to a conclusion over the mystery.

"Come on, Mary," I say as I smile at her, "let us go and soften that husband of mine."

I hear him before I see him, snapping at some poor maid who soon comes rushing out of the room with a pale complexion and a look that tells me she is close to tears. I tut at Mary, thinking how this really isn't any way for him to behave, no matter what has caused him to be in such a foul mood. When I finally enter the dining room, his angry eyes shoot up at me, and not even my smile can make him break his murderous expression. It freezes me in shock, and for a moment, it reminds me of how he used to look when he had felt so much contempt for me. I look at Mary who simply shrugs her shoulders before walking over to stand near my chair, which she pulls out for me to sit in.

"Good morning, Tobias," I say cheerfully as I walk over to kiss the top of his head. His whole body clenches up under my touch, and I feel something run down my spine. It feels horribly like a warning of something awful to come. However, I shake the feeling away and begin making my way over to my chair. "Something vexes you, husband?"

He says nothing, just stares at his paper, only moving to eat or drink his tea. I look at Mary again, but she still looks no wiser than I am for his sudden cold demeanour.

"Have you seen Monty this morning?" I ask, trying to speak as though nothing has changed since yesterday. "He managed to get himself into quite a pickle last night. And then the naughty dog came into our room and ripped one of my dresses to pieces!"

Nothing. Not even a look over his paper at me. Not even a clearing of his throat.

"I tried to teach Mary cards last night, but she is an awful student, aren't you, Mary?" I giggle at her, and she laughs back at me, though it sounds more awkward than jovial.

"I fear you are right, Your Grace," Mary replies with a smile upon her lips, however, it is as nervous as mine, for we can both sense something building.

"How was your evening, Tobias?" I venture, still sounding relaxed and happy, even though I feel anything but, what with the way his fingers are gripping hold of his paper with white knuckle force. I hold my breath when he eventually lowers his paper to fold it up with over-the-top precision. My mouth hangs open in confusion, when all of a sudden, he looks murderously at me; it has me feeling cold all over again.

"Leave!" he snarls at Mary, to which she nods, takes one more look at me, then walks away to leave Tobias and I completely alone. I suddenly feel terrified again, and the tremble in my hands returns to warn me of what is about to happen. He notices them straight away and smirks, but with an angry expression still upon his face. It is so intimidating, I pull them back in a futile attempt to hide my trembling from him.

"Tobias, talk to me," I whisper, "what has you acting so alien towards me?"

"I am not acting in any way you have not seen before," he replies coldly. "Indeed, I have decided I must have taken leave of my senses over the last few weeks. Why, it is positively folly to have fallen in love with a vapid, little girl, who still trembles before me."

"I am only trembling because of your sudden fury, Tobias," I try to argue, though have no real strength behind my words. "What have I done to cause you so much derision?"

"Did you not defy my orders yesterday when you ventured to go near..." He pauses to take a sharp inhale of breath, "...Edmund Barton, the man you really harbour feelings for?"

"Yes," I reply sheepishly, "but we discussed this, and I thought you understood, that you knew I only felt as much as I feel for the dog towards my childhood friend. I love you and only you!"

"It changes nothing, I'm afraid." He shrugs, and I see his wrath suddenly melt away into something else, something much more terrifying - his indifference. "I have no need of you until you turn twenty. Until then, you are to return to Kent. I will remain in London until you are of this age. When I have the time, I will return to exercise my conjugal rights. As soon as we have conceived, I shall return to London again."

"Tobias, please!" I gasp over his harsh words, but he only slams his hand upon the tabletop, instantly silencing me through shock.

"Do not think this anything other than a marriage of my convenience, Emily," he shouts, "you are nothing but a means to an end!"

"W-why are you being so cruel?" I whimper, being no longer able to hold back my tears. "I fell in love with you, Tobias, I gave you all of me!"

"And yet, I do not want it," he calmly replies before picking up his paper again. "Your 'gift' is worthless to me. Now, I suggest you run along and pack your things. A carriage will be waiting to pick you up in an hour or so."

"Am I to travel alone?" I mutter bitterly, for I am now filled with just as much anger over his utter disrespect for me.

"You will take that insufferable maid with you, Mary, but other than her, yes," he replies without any kind of feeling in his voice. "Monty will be staying with me."

"And that is all you have to say on the matter?" I sob, half through devastation, half through rage.

"There is nothing more to say on the matter," he replies before returning to read the paper again.

"Then I shall leave," I reply as I shakily get to my feet which instantly threaten to give way. "I hope you have an enjoyable stay here without me."

"Oh, I am certain of it," he says as he noisily turns a page, "there are plenty of beautiful distractions for me to sink into."

Those final words are the ones that completely break me, and I have to rush from his presence as soon as possible. Once outside the room, I close the door and fall into Mary's arms where she is already waiting for me. She leads me away crying and confused, having absolutely no idea as to why he has changed so drastically from the man who had left me yesterday.

Once inside of the master bed chamber, I collapse onto the bed where I curl up as tightly as possible. I let all my emotions pour out of me whilst Mary sets to packing up my things. She tries to talk to me, to soothe my nerves, but all I can hear, and all I can see, is a muffled concoction of everything that has come to pass since last night. The shadows of figures rushing about, all of which are trying to get everything ready to take me away, dart in out of my vision until at last, it is time for me to leave.

"Emily," Mary whispers to me, "it is time."

I do not know how I got from that bed to the carriage outside, but as soon as I step into the fresh air, I look over to where Monty had got stuck and begin to cry again. Mary comes over to wrap her arm around me, to help guide me into the carriage. A wonder, for my feet are hardly able to move. I look up to the window of Tobias' office where I find him standing with his hands fixed behind his back, staring at me with a determined expression. It is one which is full of nothing but a desire to see me gone.

Just as the carriage door is closed upon me, I notice two gentlemen marching up to the front door, ready to make their arrival known with the brass knocker. As if sensing my eyes upon them, they both turn to look at me through the glass. One is Frederick Brown, a man I have grown friendly with, however, now he only looks upon me with disappointment and detachment. He turns away quickly, as though to look at me will infect him with something unpleasant. When I can no longer meet his eyes, for they are now pointed firmly towards the door, I notice the other man. It is a man who makes me feel instant discomfort, especially when he gives me a smug smile. I have no idea why Thomas Greyson is suddenly at my husband's door, as though he is friendly with him, but something tells me he has had a hand in my husband's sudden change in personality.

I have one last glance up at my husband's window, and even though he is still there watching me, he may as well be already gone. I have lost the man who I had fallen in love with.

Chapter 20

Once month later

Tobias

"Tobias?"

"Tobias?!"

"TOBIAS!"

Frederick is now yelling at me and causing a scene in the middle of the busy gentlemen's club. To be fair, I cannot blame him for it, I am so far past drunk, I can no longer make any decipherable words escape my mouth with which to answer him. This is pretty much the standard for my behaviour nowadays. I am lost to liquor and a sad collection of memories which continue to filter in through my mind, both during the day and all through the night. It is only in these foggy hours of inebriation, that I feel like I can begin to forget about her, about how I feel, and how she has destroyed me.

"Lord Greyson has given me his blessing to ask Victoria to marry me," he says with a well-deserved smile on his face.

I try my hardest to be happy for him, to put aside the pain that strikes me whenever he talks of marrying his own lady. But it is hard when mine is living so many miles away from me and will continue to do so forever more. I lied to Emily when I said I would be back to impregnate her; I could never do that to her. No matter how badly she has hurt me, my mother's influence on the first eight years of my life, was enough to teach me to not treat a woman I love with so much disrespect. And I do love her. She is dead to me, but I do still love her.

"Try to be a little happy for me, Tobias," Frederick says with that friendly smile still on his face, one that will always remind me of Monty. That is, how Monty used to be. The dog is marginally more miserable than I am. The pathetic thing mopes about and can barely lift his tail anymore.

"I am, my friend," I smile half-heartedly at him, "and I am sure she will be true to you, unlike my harlot of a wife."

"I am sorry, Tobias," he says with a sad sigh, "have you heard anything from her?"

"No," I huff before draining my drink, which blissfully burns at the back of my throat. "Not that I would bother to look at any correspondence from her."

"Something still seems off about the whole sorry affair," he replies, sounding a little cryptic. "I got to know Emily, to see the kind of girl she is, and that girl would not have done what we witnessed."

"Fredrick, the evidence is stacked up against her," I scoff, "the hair, the scar, the wet and muddied clothes when I returned home. Edmund, for God' sake, her childhood sweetheart!"

"Speaking of…" he mutters while looking over to the door where Edmund and Lord Bartholomew have just walked in together. I instantly sit up tall with my hands already tightly wrapped into fists of fury. The younger of the two smiles with his teeth, and I picture myself knocking them out of his mouth with one punch. "Calm yourself, Tobias."

Unfortunately for my friend, I have sobered to the point where I am up on my feet and pacing towards where they are now stood chatting with a few other gentlemen. Fredrick is at my side, ready to rescue me from my own wrath. With a face like thunder, the two men turn to look at me, feigning innocence and confusion.

"Your Grace," Lord Bartholomew nods, "Lord Brown."

Edmund says nothing, merely nods to both of us before continuing to drink his liquor. However, as I continue to state at him with murder in mind, he knits his eyebrows firmly together and ceases his drinking completely.

"Your Grace?" Lord Bartholomew questions me when I refuse to take my eyes away from his godson. Neither do I offer any sort of explanation for my glaring. "Are you well?"

"No, not well at all," I growl through my teeth, "I am quite *un*well!"

"Ah, I hear the flu is doing its rounds," he mutters and begins to go into detail about his wife's recent bout of influenza. He rambles on about how it had made her bed ridden, and how she had kept him up all night with her coughing and sneezing. I only half listen because I am still staring at the cad before me.

"Did you catch it from your wife, Lord Hardy?" Lord Bartholomew addresses me, snapping me out of my vivid thoughts of murdering the man in front of me.

"What?!" I gasp with such an expression, he pauses his drinking and looks back at me with the same level of confusion.

"Emily?! Did she give you your cold?" he asks as though I have any clue as to what the hell he is blithering on about. "I warned her she would catch something in all that rain," he all but chuckles to himself, "but of course, there's no telling your wife anything, is there?"

"I have no idea what you are talking about" I declare. "Though, maybe your godson would have a better idea, seeing as he and Emily are so close."

"Not anymore," Edmund finally says through his conniving mouth, "not since you commandeered her against her will!"

"Watch what you say, boy!" I growl as I step closer with a look of pure venom.

"Now, then, dash it all!" Lord Bartholomew says as he tries to step in between us. "Edmund, you should not speak to Lord Hardy in such a way, and Lord Hardy, you are a grown man who should know better. Besides, you got the girl so give the boy some slack, ay?"

"Did I, Edmund?! Did I get the girl?" I grit through my teeth, trying to edge around the portly man in front of me so I can get up close to the miscreant behind him.

"Er, Lord Bartholomew," Frederick suddenly pipes in, now trying to clasp his hand over my shoulder, which is trembling with rage, "when did you see Emily last? She has been in Kent for at least a month."

"Yes, that's about right," he replies with a smile, "shuffling about in the rain late in the evening. Do you remember that night, Edmund? Absolutely ghastly for a summer's evening."

I know the night he is speaking of for it is the same night she betrayed me, something Lord Bartholomew has all but confirmed by his seeing her 'shuffling about in the rain' at night. No doubt on her way to meet with her lover. Edmund looks sheepishly to the ground and trundles uncomfortably on his feet, thus telling me he knows exactly the evening his godfather is referring to.

"You spoke to her, then?" Frederick continues, only frustrating me further with his ridiculous line of questions; ones that only remind me of Emily betraying me in that park.

"Of course," he smiles proudly, "I helped her don't you know."

"You helped her?" I suddenly turn my murderous look onto the old man who I always thought was innocent enough, yet here is now admitting to helping my wife betray me.

"What else could I do? She was clearly in need of it, even if she wouldn't ask for it herself," he replies.

"Come on, Tobias, we need to go before things get even more heated," Frederick mutters inside of my ear. "Remember why you sent her away in the first place! You do not want her humiliation of you getting out for everyone to hear."

With reluctance, I let him pull me away, leaving behind the two men to congratulate themselves on their deceit. For destroying anything Emily and I ever had or would have had together. I am not ashamed to say I fall apart as soon as I arrive home, alone, like I always will be.

Emily

Thank goodness for the sunshine! If the sun had not been shining over the past month, I think I would have spent my entire time in bed feeling sorry for myself. Mary has been witness to my wallowing through all of the emotions; everything from misery, rage, right through to denial. The worst part of all of this is undoubtedly the not knowing, the never-ending questioning of what on earth caused Tobias to act so cruelly towards me. To throw me away so callously and without any sort of explanation. For weeks I spent hours turning it around inside my head, so much so, I could not sleep. I simply laid in bed from nightfall, staring at the ceiling, until the early morning sun began to rise, and the birds started to sing, all the while contemplating the ugliness that had come to pass. I spent so much time trying to find the answers inside of my head, it would cause a searing pain all through my body, and I would feel like throwing things about my room.

When things finally came to a head with Mary, being that I climbed the tree where Tobias and I had had our first picnic together, and refused to come down, she suggested I find something more productive to do with my time. Such an idea was initially met with a rather ungracious raspberry blown her way, but after spending some time thinking upon it, I finally decided to take her up on her offer.

About two weeks ago, she took me to the local village to meet some of the tenants on Tobias' estate. It was on this visit that I met one of the farmers whose wife was in the very late stages of pregnancy, and with two children to look after. It was after she struggled to get them home by herself that I offered to help look after the little ones. I say little, however Ethel is eight already, and Marley, a handsome little devil, is just shy of six years old. I take them out for walks across the fields, the stream, or the woods, leaving their poor mother to put up her feet for an hour or two.

If I am not playing stick races, frog hunting, or climbing

trees with them, I am practising the piano, if only so I can feel some sort of connection to my father. I have not given my family the full story of why I was sent so suddenly back to Kent, and without my husband, but we have exchanged one or two letters with each other. To be honest, I would not know where to start with the whole sorry affair, so have felt it best to keep quiet. Though, from the tone of Elsie's last letter, I know she is suspicious of Tobias.

"Your Grace, I am sorry to disturb you, especially when you are playing, but Lady Elizabeth has arrived, and is in quite a fluster," Mrs Keppel says as she comes in to where I am playing one of my father's favourites. She is looking especially out of sorts over this unexpected arrival. Elizabeth is no doubt already giving them all a stern talking to for whatever reason.

"Show her out onto the terrace for tea and I'll be there in just a moment or two," I reply, and with a reassuring smile for poor Mrs Keppel. I offer her a rub of her shoulder to try and steady her nerves, which appears to work, if only a little.

It is probably for the best that I come to a stop now anyway, for I was about to play a melody that I had performed to Tobias, back when he still cared for me. Sometimes, I wish he had never changed at all; that he had remained the monster that he once was, and now is. At least my heart would still be intact.

Moments later, I am washing away my bout of sadness by walking in the sunshine, alongside the wildflowers that are full of bees going about their business. I can already see Elizabeth up ahead, tutting over something or other, and gesturing to something on the table with a bemused expression. I cannot help but smile even wider over the familiar scene, revelling in the normalcy of it; that is until she turns to face me. She looks so deadly and unnaturally serious, that I instantly brace myself for the sort of telling off my mother had given me when I had ripped my dress on those bramble bushes all those years ago.

"Aunty Elizabeth," I finally greet her.

She merely gestures towards the chair beside her, silently ordering me to sit in it. Her expression is even more intimidating that that of the one my mother wore, so I waste no time in adhering to her rather blunt invitation.

"Emily," she says with a no-nonsense tone of voice and her hand rigidly set on top of her cane, "I am going to ask you something of great importance and I need you to answer me clearly and honestly. And do not lie to me child. I know when someone is lying, it is all in the eyes."

"You sound like your nephew, Elizabeth," I whisper but without a hint of a smile, for I do not think she is in the smiling mood.

"Did you, or did you not, engage in a physical act with your childhood friend, a man by the name of Edmund Barton?" she asks, staring at me so intensely, I feel she is looking right into my soul. The question itself is even more perplexing, for I have absolutely no idea as to what she is talking about. Surely placing my hand upon his arm is not a cause for such dramatics from either my husband, or this lady who has always seemed so sensible.

"Do you mean when I placed my hand upon his arm? When he was upset because I had told him I was in love with my husband and that he should move on?" I look at her in such a way that tells her that the action has not in any way warranted the fuss both she and Tobias are making.

"No, not that," she says, still looking at me gravely, "I mean 'the' physical act. The one I had to tell you about when I first came to visit you."

She stares at me intently whilst I try to let that piece of information sink in.

"I beg your pardon?!" I eventually reply, sounding half shocked and half outraged over such an accusation.

"Because that is what Tobias believes he saw you doing, on the very night before he sent you away," she explains, "or so says Lord Brown, who had witnessed it too."

"I did no such thing and anyone who says otherwise is lying!" I spit before getting to my feet in outrage. "Of all the things to be accused of, I am disgusted you would even suggest such a thing!"

"Emily…" she calls after me, but I am in no mood to talk to her, or indeed anyone right now.

"Do not follow me!" I shout back as I march myself away so quickly, there is no possible way she could catch up with me.

"Emily!"

Tobias

I know Elizabeth will have gone to see Emily after she forced Frederick to tell her what had come to pass between Emily and I. Let her. Finally, Emily will be made aware of the fact that I know of her betrayal. Let her squirm in her guilt and humiliation for being caught in such a compromising position; it is no longer my concern. So long as she stays in Kent, hidden from decent society and out of my sight, I do not care. I have now entered a state where I straddle the fine line between love and hate. I had always believed people foolish for saying both emotions are so closely related, but now I understand the connection completely.

It is late afternoon, and the sun is beginning to make its descent towards the horizon. Watching the light fade, I feel a strange sort of peace for the first time in weeks. Perhaps it is from knowing that Emily will finally be made to face her crime. However, it is not long before my tranquil reflection is blown away by the sound of someone knocking loudly upon the front door. I wait for the angry footsteps that have entered onto the tiles to finally meet me in my study, for I am the only one here to visit now that my wife has been banished. When the door to my study bursts open, I remain seated, resting back against my chair with my hands lying firmly on top of the armrests. I sigh over the sight of the lady who has come to give me her form of wrath, no doubt on her sister's behalf.

"Apologies, Your Grace," Simon says to me from the door, holding onto his chest and panting over the strain of having to rush after the ball of angry energy now standing in front of me. "She-"

"Do not concern yourself, Simon, Miss Rothschild is my sister-in-law. I am sure we can have an adult discussion without your presence," I tell my poor, pale looking butler, who wastes no time in giving me a small nod before walking out again. Monty looks up at the commotion half-heartedly, only to then flop back to the ground again. I eye him with concern for he isn't even trying to look happy anymore.

"Miss Rothschild, please sit down. It is always nice to see one of my in-laws."

"I will not sit, Your Grace!" she huffs at me, only to begin pacing up and down with carefully controlled footsteps. "You have done a great disservice to my sister, many times in fact, however I would like to know what it is that has caused you to treat her so abysmally this time? She believed you loved her, that things had changed, yet the very next day you send her packing to live a life away from all her family and…and you!"

"You need to talk to your sister about that, Elsie," I reply bluntly, for I am in no mood for skirting around the subject, or for baring all to a girl I hardly even know. "Or perhaps you should speak to Edmund Barton, for it concerns him also."

"Is this all to do with her talking to him?" She looks at me like I am the villain, though it is nothing I am not used to. "Because if it is, then you should blame me. I was the one who made her talk to Edmund, to reassure him that she was safe with you, that in actual fact, she was happy with you."

"I could blame you, Elsie, but it will not change matters for your sister," I reply coldly, "she is disloyal, and I have no desire to be in her company."

"Well, then, she is surely blessed to be far away from you, Your Grace," she says with a disgruntled look on her face, one that makes me feel guilty for but a moment.

"Then we are agreed," I declare with a shrug of my shoulders, acting more than a little obnoxious towards her. To my delight, it causes every muscle in that pretty face of hers to clench up in anger, consequently making her lose her dainty lady like persona. It is the first time I have ever felt any kind of respect for her.

"What is wrong with your dog, anyway?" she says out of the blue, and with her arms crossed and her mouth set in a definite pout.

"I beg your pardon?" I look at her with a thoroughly perplexed expression, for I have absolutely no idea why she is suddenly taking note of the dog.

"I have three dogs, brother-in-law, and I know that dog there, is not right," she says, pointing at Monty, who cannot even lift his head up, just looks up at her with the whites of his eyes showing. Even I can see he is a lot worse than he was before, so I follow her over to take a closer inspection. She brushes back some of his black fur, but he does not even try to respond to her attention, something he normally craves more than his dinner. It is only when she hits his back that the poor hound emits a sad whimper and lifts his head to see what we are doing.

"Were you aware that his back is covered in scars and scratches? Look!" She points to a scattering of marred skin covering his spine, looking very similar to the scar on Emily's shoulder. "And here is the poor boy's problem, an old wound has come open."

Sure enough, he is bleeding from a deep cut, which now looks like it is need of cleaning. I rub behind his ears, desperately wanting to know what on earth could have done this to him. He has been at my side ever since Emily left, so there is no conceivable way that he could have been attacked by something without my knowledge.

"Simon!" I shout out for my butler but have to repeat myself several times. The poor man's hearing is beginning to worsen with age. When he walks in, he looks over to where we are crouched before the dog but shows no sign of finding our behaviour at all out of the ordinary.

"Yes, Your Grace?" he finally answers.

"Do you have any idea how Monty came to have these

marks on his back?" I stand to look at poor Monty before momentarily thinking of Emily and how it would kill her to see him in such pain.

"Not recently," he replies, "though, when Lady Hardy was here last, he had got stuck beneath the bramble bush outside. Lady Hardy had spent a good ten minutes trying to set him free."

"Emily?" I look at him with shock in my voice, for this changes that night somewhat. "My wife was out in the rain trying to rescue Monty?"

"Yes, My Lord," he confirms, "I had tried to call him in and mowhen he did not return, we felt he might respond better to hearing Lady Hardy's voice. It soon became clear he was in a little trouble. Your wife went to assist…with Lord Bartholomew and his gentleman companion."

"This gentleman companion, what did he look like?" I rush out, trying to ascertain if it was Edmund.

"Tall, very slim, fair hair and with a moustache," he replies, describing someone completely different to Lord Barton.

"That would explain the wet clothes, the damp hair," I mutter to myself, "Lord Bartholomew helping her."

"What are you talking about, Tobias?" Elsie interrupts, now standing to look at me with the same disdain as before. "I do hope you are going to do something about him."

"Of course," I reply, even though I am still thinking about that night and Emily. "Simon, call my physician; he should be able to do something."

"And my sister?" Elsie asks angrily. "Will you do anything about her suffering?"

"No," I finally reply after taking a moment or two to think about it. It still doesn't change what I saw - the hair, the scar, his calling out her name. "Good day, Elsie. Simon, will you see Miss Rothschild out."

"Of course." He nods before looking awkwardly at Elsie. She takes a moment or two to stare at me with a most venomous set of narrowed eyes before marching herself out of my study.

Chapter 21

Emily

After having run away in a dramatic fashion, Mary eventually came to find me. It was not until the sun was getting low in the sky, the bugs were floating around on the air, and the birds were flying back into roost for the night. I could see it all so clearly from my perch up in the tree. The same tree I had gifted Tobias with my first kiss, one I had given away freely because I had wanted to. I told him it was because he had tried to climb the tree, but I think we both knew it was nothing about the tree. No, it was about him opening his heart up to me. How wrong I was.

"Up in the tree again, Your Grace," Mary says to me as she leans back against the trunk below, "you must feel safe up there."

"I do," I declare with confidence, "no one can get to me here. Not even their judgement can reach me up here, in my new hiding place."

"You know, I heard what Lady Haysom said," she admits softly, causing me to close my eyes over the shame of it. "It must have been hard for you to hear that, Emily."

"You mean to hear that my husband and his best friend told

Lady Elizabeth, a woman whom I hold in the highest esteem, that they witnessed me consorting with another man, out in the open for all to see?" With every word more tears spill over my cheeks, and it feels as though my heart cracks open that little bit more. "Or that I was never given the chance to defend myself? To even know why he treated me so lowly. Instead, it has been spread about behind my back."

"Oh, Emily," Mary says as she wraps her arms around my shoulders and lets me fall against her chest. It feels a little better to face the hurt with someone I can call a friend.

"Mary?" I eventually pull away slowly to look at her, silently questioning as to how she is suddenly sat next to me in the tree.

"I have three brothers, Emily," she explains with a giggle, "how do you think I got away from them when we were playing pirates?"

"Oh, Mary, do you know how much you mean to me?" I laugh with her. "You are my guardian angel; I do not know what I would have done had it not been for you being here with me.

By the time Mary and I have returned to the house to face Elizabeth, her features have softened, and her hands are now reaching out for mine. With a quick glance at Mary for reassurance, I walk over to the older lady and embrace her with the same comfort as I would have done before she had accused me of doing unspeakable things with Edmund behind my husband's back. Mrs Keppel smiles with relief in her eyes before informing us that dinner will be ready within the hour.

"Mary, shall we leave Lady Haysom and Lady Hardy to have their conversation in private," she says, prompting Mary to follow her across the morning room. However, I stop them just before they vanish through the open door. I can tell by Mrs Keppel's perplexed expression that I have stumped the poor housekeeper.

"Please, I would like Mary to stay," I explain, "she knows the truth of what happened that night and I would like her support."

"Of course, Lady Hardy."

Mrs Keppel bows her head before leaving the three of us to discuss the awkward situation at hand.

"Emily," Elizabeth begins as soon as we have been left alone, "I apologise for my tactlessness earlier on, but when I heard the accusations from Frederick, I was rather taken aback. You should know that I told him the very idea was preposterous, but when he said they had witnessed the…er…the, er…act, my first thought was to go and question the girl herself."

"I appreciate your consideration, Elizabeth," I reply, for not many other women in Elizabeth's position would have afforded me the same curtesy. My husband certainly did not. "But Frederick and Tobias are mistaken. I did not venture from our London residence that evening, and I certainly did not see Edmund Barton."

"Then, forgive me, Emily, but what on earth has occurred?" She looks at me with true confusion in her eyes, but I can only offer her a long sigh, for I do not fully understand myself.

"Mary and I had spent most of the evening trying to play cards," I tell her, and when she looks at Mary, my faithful friend smiles and nods her confirmation. "Just before bed, Simon came to inform us that Monty was refusing to come inside, so I put on my gown and went to investigate. Simon remained by the door, but Lord Bartholomew saw me calling for the poor dog who had managed to get himself firmly stuck in the brambles and undergrowth. He helped me to release him, by which point we were all thoroughly soaked and covered in mud. I gave Barty my thanks and bid him goodnight. I more or less retired to bed straight afterward, which Mary can attest to."

"If I may," Mary steps in and I smile at her reassuringly, "Lady Hardy was never left alone that night, and even if she had been, no one knows more than I how much she feels for Tobias. Had I not been with her, I still would not believe her capable of such a betrayal."

"Thank you." I smile at her at the same time as she steps back. I sometimes forget she is part of the staff and not my real sister.

"I see," Elizabeth says, still sounding rather grave and confused. "So who was it the duke, Lord Brown and Lord Greyson saw?"

"Lord Greyson?" I blurt out with surprise in my voice. "What has Lord Greyson got to do with any of this?"

"It was Lord Greyson who alerted your husband to your indiscretion," she informs me, "he was the one who saw Edmund with 'you' walking into the park."

"Does it not strike you as rather odd that the man who Tobias had fought at our ball not long before, is now the same man acting all concerned for my husband's marriage?" I question her, and she nods along with me.

"You are right," she says, then places her hand to her lips as though deep in thought. "Emily, we must get you back to London to explain all of this to Tobias; to clear your name and prove your innocence!"

"Prove my innocence?!" I cry out, suddenly feeling furious again. The anger in my voice is so obvious, both Mary and Elizabeth look a little shocked by it. "I can assure you I am going nowhere!"

"Emily, my dear," Elizabeth says, looking nothing but concerned, "don't you want Tobias to know you have been true him? To know that you still love him?"

"Tobias can believe whatever he wishes. As far as he is aware, I am still in the dark as to why I was sent away with nothing but his contempt to keep me company. I have spent the last five weeks in exile, wondering what on earth I could have done to warrant such punishment. I did not sleep or eat for the first two of those weeks, and I have been in a constant state of mental anguish over his treatment of me. If Tobias wants to feel abused, to vilify me, so be it. I will not bend and scrape to his poorly judged view of what he thinks I may or may not have done. Let him live the life he so dearly craves, one full of loneliness and bitterness, for I am better without."

"Emily, please, he was shocked, destroyed-"

"And yet he said nothing!" I shout, rising to my feet for I can already feel the threat of tears burning at my eyes. "I was never afforded the opportunity to defend my honour, so why should he?"

"Emily, you have to come with me!" Elizabeth reaches out for my hand, but it only causes me to step even further away.

"Your Grace..." Mary calls out for me with concern.

"No!" I snap. "If you will excuse me, I think I need to be alone. I-I am no longer hungry."

"He loves you, Emily!" Elizabeth calls out as a last attempt to talk me into going with her.

"No," I whisper sadly, "no he doesn't. Tobias does not know the meaning of the word."

Tobias

It has been a week since my physician saw to poor Monty, but he is finally on the mend. Today is the first day he has been allowed outside of the house. I decided I did not trust anyone enough to take him for this first, careful walk, so I have taken it as my personal responsibility to take care of him. The ridiculous hound tries too hard to move around as he would have done so before his nasty wound had reopened, but after a few stern instructions, he finds a pace that we are both happy with. He seems content to potter about my feet and sniff at a few plants here and there. I am also relieved to see his tail is now wagging, even if it is not to the same extent as it did before.

Just up ahead, I see Elsie with her three rat like dogs, all fluff and no substance, walking arm in arm with Lord Bartholomew and his wife. I brace myself for the verbal onslaught that I am bound to receive from my sister-in-law, probably with Bartholomew's contemptable expression to match.

"Your Grace," the man beams with his belly sticking out before him, "what an unusual sight to see you walking your dog along the river! Good God, man, what has happened to him this time?"

"An old wound came open and he needed a few stitches," I reply with a shrug, trying to look indifferent over Elsie's self-congratulatory smirk.

"That must have cost you a pretty penny! And for a dog, no less?" He smiles for he has just witnessed a hint of humanity from me, something I try at all costs to avoid.

"I reward loyalty," I reply sharply.

"Really, Lord Hardy?" Elsie scoffs, sounding less than convinced by my statement.

"Yes," I snap, eyeing her just as coldly, "but those who cross me should know I will show no mercy."

"I am afraid I have quite lost where we are going with this conversation," Lord Bartholomew flusters. "How is Emily these days? The last time I saw her she was a soggy mess. She is a good one, Lord Hardy," he declares with a jolly laugh, "you are lucky to have her."

"Come, Barty," Elsie smiles at him, thus completely ignoring my reaction altogether, "some people never know what they have. Good day, Lord Hardy."

As I watch them walk away, with Elsie whispering inside of Lord Bartholomew's ear, I consider her words. Could I ever consider forgiving Emily after what she did to me? Is she worth me trying to forget that awful night, of their flesh coming together, the moaning, and the lying? I look at Monty who is sat obediently by my side, his staring out onto the grounds before us, and for a moment, I envy his ability to love no matter what. To accept anyone without fear, judgement, anger, or hurt. To love unconditionally. Unfortunately, I am not Monty, and I cannot do the same.

Emily

"I do wish you would come back with me, Emily." Elizabeth smiles at me before leaning in to kiss me on my cheek. "Though, I have come to understand why you will not. My nephew is no different from many other men in his position - proud and foolish!"

She tries to laugh whilst I attempt to smile alongside her, but it still feels too raw to show any kind of mirth when it comes to Tobias. She cups my face with her soft hand and looks at me like a mother would when comforting her daughter, and it finally breaks me.

"Oh, Emily," she says and pulls me against her chest for comfort while I cry over a failed marriage, a broken heart, and for me.

"How could he think I would do that to him, Elizabeth?" I sob as I whisper to her. "To us?"

"Anger and hurt have people doing ridiculous things, Emily," she says against my ear, "Tobias has had to live with a lot of those feelings over the years."

No further words are exchanged between her and me but the expression on my face tells her I mean no hard feelings towards her. I will always welcome Elizabeth with open arms for she has shown me trust and loyalty, something her nephew could not. Mary is by my side when we finally wave her goodbye, and there we remain for good long while after she has disappeared altogether from sight. Whilst standing here, it suddenly occurs to me that I have no idea what to do with myself. Now that I finally know the reason for Tobias casting me off so abruptly, I wait for a feeling of relief to wash over me. But it does not come. All I can feel are the exact same emotions which Elizabeth told me Tobias has been dealing with his whole life.

"What now, Emily?" Mary asks.

"Nothing," I answer almost straight away, "nothing has changed."

"You do not want to prove he was wrong?" she asks, clearly shocked over my stubbornness to not profess my innocence.

"I can understand he had reason to doubt me from what he saw," I try to explain, "but he was so desperate to hold on to his bitterness that he sent me away without even first speaking to me. That is not love, Mary, that is something I cannot even begin to fight."

"Perhaps," she replies, and smiles as we fall into step, heading to the terrace for morning tea. "I cannot begin to understand it."

"Then you are fortunate," I tell her with a sad sigh. "Trust me, Mary, you do not want to feel as I do right now."

Chapter 22

Tobias

I have not been able to stop thinking about my run in with Elsie and Lord Bartholomew. Loyalty is something that I value highly, which is perhaps the reason for me only having one friend and a love for the mutt currently sitting beside me. I thought someone like Emily would give me that in a wife. Admittedly, she was merely a partner who was more a means to an end, but when it turned into something more, something unexpected, her loyalty was something that had attracted me to her even more so. Part of my anger is because of how wrong I had assessed her character.

I find myself staring out of the window pondering over all these conflicting thoughts, so when Frederick appears on my doorstep, I smile with gratitude for the relief. I remain in my stance, waiting for when he will burst through my door, hopefully to tell me good news about his engagement to Miss Greyson. It will be bittersweet to hear of his happiness, but I wish it for him, nonetheless.

"Tobias!" He bursts in with a smile so wide I can only assume the lady said yes.

"It went well then?" I ask casually before taking up my

chair next to Monty.

"Very," he replies as he sits himself down. "We marry three weeks from now; you are to be my best man."

"Of course," I reply with a single nod.

"And as such, I expect you to accompany me for celebratory drinks this evening."

"Only for you, Frederick," I reply as I pat Monty on his head, giving him permission to lie down at my feet. "I wish you every bit of happiness, even if I do not have it for myself."

"Thank you, Tobias," he says with a softer expression, "you are the king of friends, Your Grace!"

Hours later and we are sat together in our gentleman's club, at our normal table, where we have a good view of all who enter. The usual patrons are here this evening, including Frederick's soon to be brother-in-law, Thomas Greyson. I still eye him with deep suspicion; however, I have managed to bury the hatchet since he alerted me to my wife's deceit that night, and for his silence. We are not friends by any stretch of the imagination, but we have learnt to tolerate one another for the sake of Frederick. He turns to see us and lifts his glass in greeting, to which we do the same to him.

When he begins to walk over to us, I acknowledge his presence, then make my excuses to go and take in some air. After all that has happened today, I do not feel able to play nice, so feel it better to leave Frederick to accept his new family's congratulations.

Once inside of the entrance hall, I take in a few deep breaths, thinking of Emily and the magical few weeks in which we had been in love, in bed, and in a true marriage. It was everything I had ever wanted and more, but oh so fleeting. Was it worth the bitter and hurtful ending? I cannot honestly answer that question right now. As I ponder on that sad thought, something catches my eye, or rather, *someone* catches my eye.

"Emily..." the person calls out to someone who I cannot see, someone who is at the top of a staircase. They keep rooms for patrons to engage in personal affairs, usually inside the embrace of a woman's arms. A woman whose business is to provide a man with warmth that for whatever reason, he cannot get at home. But to bring Emily here? It is more than my temper can bear. As to how she even got back to London without my knowledge, does not even cross my mind at this point. I am more outraged over their continued affair and in a place in which I am known to frequent.

I creep up the stairs, not knowing if I want to see what I am about to, but also not wanting to alert them to my presence for fear of not catching them. The journey seems much longer than is possible, but they are stopping frequently to kiss and touch, so I am able to follow. Every time I hear the sound of lips slapping at each other, I feel my hands ball into tighter fists, if only to stop my volcanic eruption coming out prematurely.

"Emily, I need you now," he growls between embraces, "to be inside of you!"

"Shh, patience, Edmund," a voice that sounds alien replies to him, "let us get to our room first."

"Yes, you are right," he flusters, almost losing himself completely to his lust. "And remember to call me 'Your Grace'."

It is too much for me to remain silent, so I rush myself up

to the top and turn the corner, only to find they have already gone; they are now hidden behind a closed door. I find myself pacing while running my hands through my hair with a mixture of fury and anxiety, bracing myself to march in there and catch them doing God only knows what. Composing myself, I take in a deep breath and kick at the door where I can hear the breathy moans of 'Emily' being thrown about without any shame for bedding another man's wife.

As soon as the door bursts open with the thud of my boot against it, I see two naked bodies wrapped up together under one sheet. Edmund is on top, and a blonde girl is lying beneath him. Her arms are poised around his shoulders, revealing the tell-tale scar she sustained when she was only twelve years old and still innocent.

"Get your hands off my wife!" I growl through my teeth.

"What?!" The blonde suddenly turns to face me, the sight of which completely freezes me to the spot.

"Y-you're not Emily!"

"Your Grace!" Edmund gasps whilst trying to disentangle himself from the woman still lying beneath him. He flaps around the room, grabbing for his clothes whilst she casually covers herself up with the sheet, feeling no shame for any man seeing her womanly curves.

"What the hell is going on here?" I bark at Edmund, who is now, thankfully, covered enough so I am no longer able to see his unmentionables. "Where is Emily?"

"Emily?!" He looks at me as though I am talking in crazy riddles.

"Yes, damn it, you've been calling out Emily, just like you

did in the park when you defiled her almost a month ago!"

I step towards him with rage spilling over from the memory of that display. He shivers and stumbles back against the wall, all the while throwing up his hands in surrender.

"I have not been near your wife since the day she spoke with me alongside the river, when we decided to go our separate ways because she told me she was in love with her husband. Elsie had been with her the entire time! This is Polly." He pauses as he gestures over to the prostitute lying in the bed; she smiles and waves at me with obvious amusement. "I see her frequently because her hair and, well, surely you can understand why."

"The scar?" I gesture to where it is still showing as clear as day upon her shoulder.

"I'll do anything if you pay me enough," she says with a lascivious wink, "and Edmund is a valued and loyal customer. If he wants to call me Emily and give a small scratch to my shoulder, so be it."

"You cut her to make her look more like Emily?" I ask in utter disbelief.

"I am not a proud man," he mutters, "I am a destroyed one after you took her away from me. No one else knows of my rendezvous with Polly, so what is the harm?"

"You do not realise the *harm* you have caused!" I roar at him.

"You did not seriously think that Emily would have done such a thing with me after she had promised herself to you, do you?" he asks with the same look of horrified disbelief that I had just sported. The sight of which has me feeling incredibly nauseated over how grave a mistake I have made.

"Is that why she was sent back to Kent so suddenly?" he asks, stepping forward as I slump with shame. "You thought it was her in the park? That she would have given herself so willingly in such a public place?"

I look at them both with such an expression, it leaves no doubt as to what I believed.

"Clearly, she was mistaken," he says, looking almost angry with me, "you could not have loved her at all. You did not even know her!"

"I did…I saw…" I try to argue but nothing more comes out of my mouth.

"And when she defended her innocence, what did you do then?" he challenges me whilst stepping forward again.

"She…she did not know the reason for my exiling her," I mutter ashamedly, "I simply told her I did not want her anymore."

A heavy silence falls upon the room, one of shame, hurt, and anger. The atmosphere turns heavy, but all I can do to relieve my discomfort is run my hands over my face. I refuse to shed tears before this man, even if I have already shamed myself in front of him.

"How did you happen upon Polly and me in the park that night?" he questions me out of the blue. "How did you know we were there?"

"Lord Greyson," I reply, not really thinking about that night anymore. My thoughts are only of Emily and what I have done to her.

"Thomas?!" he cries out in shock. "Thomas Greyson brought you to us?"

"Oh my, I think Tommy has been a very naughty boy!" Polly giggles from the bed where she has taken to tapping her leg against the mattress. *If only I had seen your face that night!*

"He is downstairs now, drinking with Frederick," I reply, still sounding like a ghost of myself.

"The dirty cad!" he growls. I look up suddenly, for I don't think I have ever seen this pup looking so vengeful. "It was Thomas who introduced me to Polly, who arranged our meetings and gave her the scar!"

His words reignite a bitter storm from deep inside of me, and so, without any other words, I take to the door and march out of it, readying myself to confront the man who has sought to destroy my marriage. Edmund, to my surprise, isn't far behind and is looking ready to give his own form of vengeance upon Lord Greyson. The sound of chattering and laughing from the main drinking room has me pausing in my quest to go and wreak havoc.

Once inside the room, I speak quietly to the barman and agree to a plan of sorts.

"Gentlemen," he announces, thus silencing the room, "if it would please you, the Duke of Kent has promised a round of brandy for each and every one of you. If you kindly follow me into the reception room across the hall, I will be opening a few of my best bottles."

The whole room cheers in drunken joy before making their way out the door, all except Frederick who is now eyeing me with concern over both my murderous expression and my new right-hand man, Edmund. Thomas is still sitting beside him, making no attempt to move. Instead, he chooses to remain seated, where he smirks to himself. He is a cad but not an unintelligent man. He has surely come to the correct conclusion over the situation at hand.

When the last patron has exited the room, I walk over to Thomas Greyson and eye him with the contempt he deserves.

"Explain yourself and your despicable actions. And do not bother to try and fool me, Greyson, I have no patience for liars."

"On the contrary, you have been more than patient with me over the last few weeks," he says as he continues to grin smugly to himself. "It was almost too easy to exercise my little plan for vengeance."

"Vengeance?!" I snap over his audacity, and with my fists now growing itchy, desperately wanting to throw themselves into his villainous face.

"Vengeance," he confirms with a nod of his head.

"On what grounds?!" I gasp. "For hitting you when you insulted my wife?"

"Oh, dear me, no, old boy," he laughs with his teeth, "vengeance for the love of my life."

"Who, damn it?"

"Genevieve," he replies with his face suddenly turning as thunderous as mine. However, that one name turns my fury into utter confusion at the same time as about a thousand questions begin forming inside of my head.

Thomas

Genevieve 16, Thomas 18

The summer was coming to an end, and I would soon be sent back to school, most likely before the week was over. Genevieve will be without me but at least Tobias, her brother, should be home to protect her in my absence. Give it less than two years, when I will be twenty, and we shall be married. I will take her far away from this place and far away from him.

I fear he is making her weaker every time he shouts at her and calls her names, the like a lady should never have to hear. She tries to reassure me, to tell me it is ok, that she is used to no better from him, but I know the effect it has on her. I have seen the fits that follow, the exhaustion that has her passing out for hours following one of his visits. He only comes to see her when he is drunk and feeling the effects of depression after having lost his wife. He comes to lay blame on Genny to appease his own frustrations, to make himself feel better. He never sticks around to see her shudder against the floor, to see her eyes spin back inside of her head, or see how her limbs contort into the most unnatural of positions. I have. Whenever Tobias is away, I am here to make sure she is safe, looked after, and loved.

Genny and I had met at one of my parents' soirees when we were both still children. She wore a pretty pinafore with curls in her hair, and I wore a set of clothes that I longed to rip away so I could run across the fields and climb trees. Her brother appeared to be just as stiff as their father, apart from when he was around Genny. He clearly loved and protected her, and the way she spoke of him told me how much she cared for him too. It only took that first meeting for me to decide that Genevieve Hardy was going to be my wife someday. I would venture out on my horse so I could meet her in the woods edging their estate. We would have picnics, race sticks, and when we were older, steal kisses from one another.

I did not see any hint of a fit until our third or fourth meeting. It was at another family event, only this time, it was at her father's house. When we arrived, it was clear to a lot of people that Lord Hardy was already past drunk. There was no hiding it, no matter how much Tobias tried to. The man was slurring his words and talking with far too much volume. He would flip between laughter and carefree conversation, to being ridiculously angry over things that did not warrant such an aggressive reaction. Genny soon grabbed hold of me so we could escape to the parlour, where a grand piano sat in pride of place.

She giggled at first, telling me she was not very good at it, that she wanted to be but was not allowed any lessons. Her mother had been a proficient player, and this piano had belonged to her; it had been a special gift from Genny's father. She turned sad, like she always did when she spoke of him. It was as if she knew how little he thought of her.

"He hates me," she said sadly as she began running her fingers softly across the keys, "he blames me for her death."

"I am sure that's not true, Genny," I tried to comfort her, for what else could I say to such a statement.

"It *is* true, Thomas," she laughed without any real mirth behind it. All the while, she stared hopelessly at the keys, as if she was longing to connect with them in some meaningful way. "He tells me so nearly every time I see him. Always has done. I am afraid, Thomas."

"Why, Genny, why are you afraid?" I turned her shoulders to face me, so I could see the tears pooling at the bottom of her eyes.

"His temper is getting worse, and Tobias will be going away to school soon," she whimpered, "what will I do then?"

"Does he hurt you, Genny?" I asked, now full of concern

for her safety.

"He never touches me," she whispered, "but they tell me I have a weakness, that-"

"What the bloody hell are you doing at her piano?!" A voice shouted out with so much venom in it, we both leapt to our feet in fear. "Don't you ever touch her piano with your bastard fingers!"

He stormed over to my poor Genny, and I saw the tremble in her fingers, in her entire body, even her mouth. My voice dried up and my feet refused to move, for this man seemed so big in comparison to me. After all, I was a mere boy. He towered above her whilst tears streamed over her cheeks, and I swear I could see him smiling with satisfaction. Genny was right; he truly hated her. The sweet, beautiful girl with curly locks and a sunny smile was the object of this man's hatred.

"You are not my daughter," he growled at her, "my daughter died at birth like she should have instead of my wife. You're the demon who killed her!"

"Father!" I heard Tobias crying out as he ran up behind him. "Father, leave her!"

"You're not worth the effort," he practically spat at her, now with his eyes rolling around in a drunken stupor. "You're no better than a murderer, a parasite!" He shoved her away at the same time as he turned towards Tobias. Fortunately, I was quick to catch hold of her before she landed on the floor.

"You're my only child, Tobias," the man slurred, then began to whimper, all the while pawing at his son who was trying hard not to lose his temper. "Make me proud, Tobias, dear God, make me proud!"

"I will, father," he reassured him, but remained looking at Genny who was lying inside of my arms. "Now go and join the party; people are asking after you."

The girl in my arms had turned rigid, and her back began to arch in an unnatural arc. I tried to look into her eyes, to silently ask her what was wrong, only when I did, her eyes were rolling back. Too far back.

As soon as the wicked man had disappeared, coughing, and slumping his drunken old body along the tiled floor outside of the door, Tobias flew down and leant in close to his sister, taking no note of me whatsoever. He began to run his hand over her hair whilst she shuddered and flung her limbs around.

"Genevieve," he whispered in a soothing tone of voice, "it's ok, Genny, I'm here and you're going to be ok. Just do what you need to do, Genny."

Only then did he look up at me, as if silently reassuring me with his eyes that this is something he has seen before, and to remain calm. I knew from that look that if I panicked, it would only make her condition worse. I was scared, terrified for my friend, but I stayed still whilst she worked through whatever it was that she needed to.

When the shuddering finally past, and her body eventually fell limp within my arms, Tobias reached over to cup her face and study her eyes. They were no longer rolling back and appeared to be looking at him. He nudged at her arm whilst calling her name, then waited for a response.

"Gen, are you with us?" he asked and she nodded. The relief on his face and within his tense muscles was more than obvious.

"Wh-what just happened?" I stuttered, which earnt me a hard stare from the boy.

"Nothing," he snapped, "it was nothing and you are not to mention this to anyone, do you understand?"

He looked so angry, but also worried, so I instantly nodded, promising to never mention this to another single person.

A few days later, I had met Genny in our usual spot in the woods and she explained what she could to me.

"I have always suffered with it, mostly when I am upset or frightened. I go somewhere, away, and when I come to, I have no idea I have been absent at all. Only Tobias and Mrs Hassel, my governess, have witnessed it. Tobias once asked about it when he was at school, but he was told such behaviour was an affliction of the brain, one that needed bleeding out, or for the patient to be locked away for their own safety. He is convinced they will say I am mad or need experimenting on. He told me it would be better to keep quiet, to not let anyone know about my condition. Seeing as my father refuses to let me out beyond the Hardy estate boundary, most likely because he likes to think I do not exist, it is not a huge concern. But now you know, Thomas. You will keep my secret, won't you?"

"Of course, Genny," I reassured her as I held her close to me, "I won't tell a soul. And I will be here whenever you need me to be."

And I was, as much as I could. When I wasn't at school and would not be missed, Genevieve and I were virtually inseparable.

But that summer, when we were so close to being able to be together as man and wife, the same one when I was to be sent away to further my education, fate decided to intervene in our plans. It forever changed the course of our future, and in the cruellest of ways.

The evening before I was due to leave for London, we had sat underneath the tree near the stream in the woods, watching the sun go down. I held onto her whilst she nestled between my legs with a blanket wrapped around us. No one would see us here, no one ever came here. I fluttered kisses over her neck, her back, her shoulder whilst she giggled. We both knew this was the last time I would see her for a long while, and I feared for her safety without me.

"Next year I will make my intentions known," I whispered against her ear, "and I will buy you the biggest diamond I can find, one to match the sparkle in your eyes, Genny."

"And where will we live, husband-to-be?" She grinned as she planted a soft kiss on the back of my hand.

"Far away from here, and far away from your father," I reassured her. I studied her as she lay against me with her eyes closed, as if she was revelling in the image of what I had just said. "And I will love you like no other."

"More than Romeo did Juliet?" she teased.

"Romeo has nothing on me when it comes to loving you," I told her before we kissed, much too passionately for a lady in her position, but she had nobody to fear, for I would marry her this very moment if anyone were to catch us. "I do not want to leave you, Gen; in fact, I won't! I refuse to!"

"You must!" she insisted. "You need to get your education so you can work in your father's firm and keep me in the life I have become accustomed to," she laughed at me. I laughed too, for

Genevieve may come from a family of considerable wealth, but her life was hard and full of hurt and anger. She cared for the finer things in life as much as my horse did. "Besides, Tobias comes home tomorrow so he will take care of me. Please, Thomas, you must" she said before pausing to kiss me sweetly on my lips, "so we can live happily ever after."

"Ok," I conceded with a heavy heart, "but if I find that you have found another whilst I am away, I shall take that dram of poison just as Romeo did!"

"Never!" she whispered. "You are my only Romeo!"

Chapter 23

Tobias

"But you did not return home that night did you, Tobias? You did not return home until the following day when it was already too late," Thomas growls at me with tears of grief running over his cheeks.

"I had decided to stay one more night to celebrate with my fellow classmates," I explain, remembering it as if it were only yesterday. "I thought she was safe in her governess' care. I was told she had died days before I had returned home, with Ms Hassel leaving not long after."

"Her governess had been let go at the beginning of the summer because your father had refused to pay for Genevieve's schooling. She was going to tell you when you returned. She insisted on waiting because she had me to look after her in the interim. However, she died the night you were due home, when I had already left for London. One of the maids, Martha, told me that your father had visited Genny that evening. He was heard shouting at her from three doors down. I can only guess that she fitted, like usual, but was left entirely alone. She died alone, Tobias, alone!"

The room turns deathly silent for too long a while to feel at all comfortable, to not think of my poor sister dying in the confines of her room, all alone. I should have been there, to catch her when she fell, to tell my father to leave her alone, to be the man my mother wanted me to be. And then, there is Emily. All this time she has been innocent, been true to me, but I was too quick to believe her betrayal, too bitter to give her the chance to prove me wrong. I do not deserve her. Just as Genevieve did not deserve my father's wrath or her death, but at least she had the love of a man. A man who has made it his life's mission to ruin me. The same man who has dishonoured my wife, was the same one to keep my sister going as long as she did.

"I had no idea Genevieve even knew you," I eventually say to the room. "Did my father?"

"Your father?!" he begins before smiling wickedly with self-satisfaction. "Your father was allowed to live in his bitterness and misery for another year or two after he killed my Genny. However, when my father and I were invited on a hunting trip with him and a few other gentlemen from the area, I am afraid the temptation to avenge Genny's death was much too great. His death was no accident, Tobias. After I shot him, he lay dying, which was incredibly gruelling to watch, but oh so satisfying. He begged for mercy but instead, I told him everything. He tried to talk to me, to put his rancid breath to use, but alas, it was too much for him to manage. I watched him take his last breath with only thoughts of my beautiful Genny, picturing her as the bride she should have been to me."

"I am sorry," I tell him without thinking about it because I truly mean it. "But Emily-"

"At first, I left you alone, Tobias, you were miserable enough without my interference," he continues, "but when Emily came along and I saw the way you took her away from Edmund, you revived my need for vengeance. I had visions of doing the poor girl a favour by keeping her from developing any real affection for you. However, when I saw how you looked at one another at your ball, I had to know for certain if there were any true feelings there. So, I cornered her, knowing you would catch me, and touched her arm. It was so easy to see you had finally fallen for her, and that she had done the same for you. Knowing that you could find happiness was not an option I could let you have, Tobias, you had to pay the same way your father did, how I had too. If I was to be miserable without the woman I was meant to be with, so would you. It is unfortunate that Emily had to pay some of the price for your selfishness."

"And what do you think will happen now, Thomas?" Frederick speaks up for the first time, all the while I remain shocked to silence. "You have admitted to murdering a man in front of all of us, what are you proposing happens next?"

"I have my affairs in order, Lord Brown," he says with a strange look in his eye. "Victoria was my last piece of business; I thank you for that, Frederick. Unlike your friend here, I believe you are the finest of men. Loyal, caring, and with a good temperament for my gentle sister. But as for me, I am ready to be reunited with Genevieve once again. I will die with a smile on my face, Tobias, will you?"

"Mr Barton, will you call for the constable?" Frederick calls over to Edmund, but I put up my hand to stop him. "Tobias, surely you cannot let this pass without consequence. Think of what he has done to you, and to Emily!"

"He loved and protected my sister when I could not," I explain, "for that, I will let him go. For hurting my wife, I will give you until Monday to do whatever it is you feel you need to. After that, I will be passing your name over to the relevant authorities. And as for hurting me…it is no less than I deserve."

With those last words, I turn to leave, nod to Edmund, and begin my walk home. How I managed to finally get to my house probably had more to do with Frederick than my conscious thought or ability to function properly. Whatever he did, I know I need to thank him when I wake up to the burning headache that I am sure to have. I do know, however, that I cried. I wept for Genevieve, for my mother, for Emily, even for Thomas. I can only imagine how hard it has been to live with his pain for so long, knowing that he will never again be with the woman he truly loved.

The following morning, Frederick and I find ourselves slumped inside of my study, trying to make sense of all that has transpired. I have no idea what to feel first - grief, resentment, pain, anger, relief, guilt. The unsavoury mix has me frequently sighing along with the bitter taste of bile that is threatening to erupt.

"Will you go to her, Tobias?" Frederick eventually breaks the silence with this inevitable question, but I give him nothing but a sigh in response to it.

"A bloody good question!" Aunt Elizabeth declares as soon as she bursts through the door with a dramatic tap of her cane. "She is innocent, Tobias!"

"I know, Aunty," I reply with yet another sigh. "Lord Greyson concocted the whole illusion of Emily betraying me."

"I don't follow," she says, clearly shocked to have me agreeing with her without any kind of a fight. I get to my feet so that I might go and look out over the London Street that is already shaded in an autumnal hue. Frederick begins to recount the whole sorry story to my aunt whilst I close my eyes to it all.

"I see," she says gravely, "our poor Genevieve."

We all fall back into a melancholy silence, though with our duo now being a firm trio of misery and confusion over such a sorry situation.

"But why are you still here, Tobias?" Elizabeth finally asks with her brows firmly knitted together. "Why are you not headed for Kent as we speak?"

"For what, Elizabeth? To try and beg for forgiveness from a woman who deserves so much more than me? For a love my sister had stolen from her because I was too selfish to come back when I had promised her?"

"For love, full stop, Tobias!" she tuts at me. "What good does it do to have you here feeling miserable, and Emily over there, being just as miserable? I swear Genevieve will be looking down on you and shaking her head, right alongside her mother. Whether Emily likes it or not, you are the one her heart belongs to, as does yours to her, so why torture one another by living separately when there is no one to stand in your way?! Do you think Genevieve would have stayed away from Thomas if she were alive and well? And would he have let anyone stand in his way from being with her? Good God, no!"

"She has a fair point there, Tobias," Frederick adds.

"Of course, I do, I am always right," she snaps, and I watch him try not to smile. "You do more of a disservice to your wife by staying here feeling sorry for yourself, and to Genevieve, for that matter. She loved you too, and the last thing she would have you doing is stubbornly punishing yourself by remaining heartbroken. You did not kill her, Tobias! It was a horrible, unfortunate situation, one that was likely to have claimed her earlier in life anyway. If anyone is to blame, it is your brute of a father. Though, it sounds like he did."

"How will I ever get her to forgive me?" I ask them both. "I did not even give her the chance to explain herself. I was no better than Father in my treatment of her."

"Surely, once you explain about Thomas and Genevieve-" Frederick begins to argue, but I cut him off before he can even finish.

"Please do not think me dishonourable and cowardly enough to use the death of my sister to excuse how I have treated Emily," I tell him, and even Elizabeth is nodding along with me. It is perhaps the first time she has ever agreed with me. "It would cheapen all concerned and I will not lower myself into doing such a thing."

"You are right, Tobias, this is on you and you alone," Elizabeth adds. "Though, you have your work cut out for you, Nephew. Do not expect to find Emily weak and floundering without you. You will have a fight on your hands with that one. Then again, I suspect that is one of the many reasons you chose her in the first place."

"I know," I admit with a smile, one that tells her I will fight tooth and nail for that girl, right up until my dying breath.

"Go then!" she orders whilst pointing at the door with her cane and a set of wide eyes.

"Thank you, Aunty," I murmur before kissing her head and rushing to make my way back to Emily.

Chapter 24

Emily

"Emily!" Marley shouts at me with the biggest grin on his face. "I've found one, I've found one!"

Before he has even finished declaring his find, he is bounding over to me with a large, warty looking toad in his hands. His poor sister, Ethel, begins screaming and running in the opposite direction. I, on the other hand, crouch down to take a closer look at the funny-looking creature who appears to be a little shellshocked. We study it together but when it croaks very suddenly, Marley yelps and lets it hop out of his hands and onto the ground. I watch with fascination as it scuffles along the damp earth until it reaches the stream and hops in.

"Is it gone?" Ethel shouts out from a fair distance away from us and I have a giggle to myself.

"He's gone!" I call back whilst Marley pouts over his newfound friend now having disappeared. "I think it is time I got you two back to your mother. The sun is beginning to dip so it must be near your supper."

"Oh!" Marley whines just as Ethel runs over to grab my

hand. "Will you take us tree climbing tomorrow?"

"It is Sunday, tomorrow," I tell them, "I think you will be expected to spend some time with your parents. Take your mother in now for she'll soon be very busy with your new brother or sister!"

"Ok," he sulks.

"Shall we sing a song on the way back?" I suggest, to try and cheer him up. "How about *In and Out the Dusty Bluebells*?"

"That's my favourite!" Ethel beams.

"You only learnt it yesterday!" Marley argues, so I begin singing before an argument can ensue.

About ten minutes of marching later, we pull up to their small cottage on the outskirts of the village, singing at the tops of our voices and eventually skipping over the hill. Smoke is billowing out of the chimney and there is a distinct smell of food cooking from inside. Mabel can be counted on to have her children's dinner cooking at the same time daily, just before the sun hides behind the trees. Their father, a blacksmith by the name of Eric, saunters outside while wiping his hands on an old cloth. Alas, he still looks blackened by soot and smoke. He smiles affectionately at Ethel and Marley as they run to him for giggles and hugs.

"Your Grace," he says with the customary nod of his head. His cheeks have turned pink, as they always do when he is in my company. Though I do not think of myself as a duchess, especially after everything that has happened. However, I suppose to all intents and purposes, I am one. "I do hope these two are being well behaved for you."

"Oh, I do believe it is they who are keeping me in check;

isn't that right, Ethel?"

"Emily and Marley found a toad and I ran away until it was gone!" she informs her father, screwing up her little nose in disgust. Eric, bless him, sports a thoroughly aghast expression just for her.

"Away with you both, your supper is already on the table. You best be washing those hands if you've been playing with toads," he shouts at their retreating forms before laughing with me. "And say thank you to Lady Hardy."

"Bye, Emily!" They both wiggle their fingers to wave me off just before they enter the cottage.

"Why, Eric, I thought we had gotten past you calling me such titles," I say, pretending to chastise him.

"Aye…yes, but when the Duke of Kent himself comes to call in search of his wife, I feel it best to call you by your formal name," he says with a soft smile.

"Hello, Emily," a familiar voice calls out from behind Eric. I feel my heart begin to thump rapidly in response to that voice, for it sounds like a sad memory I do not wish to torture myself with. Eric gifts me with one of his awkward nods, turns to nod at the man behind him, then returns to inside of his house.

With my voice frozen in shock, I watch Tobias walk towards me as though creeping upon a wild animal that is getting ready to buck at any moment. This might well be the case given everything that has come to pass between us. However, for the moment, it is still taking all my mental capabilities to simply accept that he is actually here.

"You look well, Emily," he says as he ventures forth a few more steps, "and making good use of your time I see. I should have expected nothing less from you, Emily. You are always so good with people."

He looks at me intensely, silently urging me to say something to him - a greeting, a reply, anything. But I have nothing to say. Absolutely nothing.

"Emily...?" he whispers as he reaches out for me, but my natural instincts have me stepping back. I notice my hands are beginning to tremble for fear he is going to turn on me again.

"Your Grace," I eventually reply with a nod before turning around and making my way home on foot. He does not follow me; he knows better.

I do not see Tobias again until dinnertime. As I make my way down into the main dining room, just like I have for the past month or so without him, I shake my hands about my skirts to try and rid myself of their shaking. Usually, it would be just Mrs Keppel, Mary, and I, with perhaps the odd butler floating about in the background. These meals were informal affairs and if not for Mrs Keppel's refusals, I would have had them eating with me. Tonight, I walk in to find the usual row of serving staff, a full table of every sort of food imaginable, and Tobias standing by my chair, waiting to assist me in doing something I am quite capable of doing by myself.

I slowly make my way over in silence, offering him nothing more than my stern expression. He chooses to ignore it by grinning hopefully at me. Hopeful for what, I have no idea anymore. The man is an enigma, one I am through trying to crack. It does me no good at all to let down my barriers when it comes to my husband.

"You look very beautiful tonight, Emily," he offers before pushing me in. I feel his fingertips dust across my shoulder at the same time as he takes a small inhale of my hair. My body instinctively stiffens and my jaw ticks with mounting anger.

"I take it you know the blacksmith's family well?" he asks, changing the subject and taking himself over to the chair right next to mine. His proximity means I am unable to take my eyes away from his. "They call you *Emily*, do they not?"

"I have been offering my help to their mother. You can see she is near the end of her pregnancy, and with two small children to take care of, it is very hard. I merely offered her what I suddenly have an abundance of - time."

"Oh, quite!" he nods in agreement. "It is very gracious of you to help those in need."

"Not really, Your Grace," I begin, watching him wince over my use of formalities, "it is merely human decency to be kind to one another."

"Emily," he says my name on a sad sigh, one that knows I am commenting on more than just the Porter family. "I know what you must think of me, and you have every right to, but please, will you give me a chance to explain myself, and to make it up to you?"

"I have no idea what you are referring to, Your Grace," I reply with a sweet smile, then watch as his face clenches up in frustration.

"Please, Emily, do not call me that," he whispers, and looks at me with such hurt, I almost feel like relenting. "You have always called me Tobias, even before we... I mean, I..."

All I offer is a smile because this only reminds me that he is not worthy of forgiveness, not for a second time. I had believed his apologies the first time, but I shall not make the same mistake twice.

"Emily, I know you are now aware of what I thought you had done. I was wrong, I know that now-"

"No," I interrupt him, feigning confusion all over my face. "I have no idea what it is you thought I had done, for you never actually accused me of anything. In fact, I do believe even common criminals, murderers, thieves, and those held for treason are at least offered more than what I was."

He grabs my hands with both of his, looking as if he is struggling over his words for what to say next. Thinking of what he can possibly say to convince me that I should offer him any more chances. I merely eye their presence on me coldly before looking back into his eyes with the same contempt I had been shown on too many occasions to count.

"What do I need to do, to say, for you to forgive me? I will do anything to win back your love and affection," he whispers gravely. "I miss you, Emily."

"You do?" I ask, to which he looks to the table and nods with sadness. "What happened? Did you run out of whores to bed in London? After all, your parting words were to reassure me that you would find comfort in the arms of others whilst I was here, alone, and cut off from everyone I know and love. Even from Monty."

"Emily, I did not meet a single woman-"

"Excuse me, Your Grace," I cut him off as I make a stand to leave. He says nothing, just looks up at me with those sad eyes of his. "I have lost my appetite. It was the first thing for me to lose after I was exiled without reason; the second was sleep; the third was all feeling; the fourth was very nearly my mental state of mind. But that was when I fought back, Your Grace. I decided not to let you ever hurt me again."

I march away from him without looking back, ready to retreat to my room where I shall remain alone forever more.

Tobias

I left dinner not long after Emily, for my appetite has also depleted into nothing. Ever since I found out about Thomas, my sister, as well as my wife's innocence, I have not wanted to eat a single thing. I knew Emily would be no easy feat, but I did not realise she would be quite so defiant, so angry, and so hurt. She wears her indifference well, but I can see the rawness of the sadness in her eyes. It is who she is to be so emotional and so passionate. Try as she might, she could never show indifference over emotion. It is why I love her so much.

Before I give in and retire to bed, I make my way over to do one more thing for Emily; something I should have been compassionate enough to do when I had sent her away. When I arrive at her bedroom door, the same bedroom where my poor sister had once had to endure my father's wrath and die alone, I pause to listen. She is making snuffling sounds, as though she is crying, and it cracks open my heart all over again. History is repeating itself, only this time, I am the villain. How did I get to become the very person who I despised more than anyone else in the world. With a long sigh, I look at the dog who is about to be Emily's hero, who I once was to my sister, and pat his head with reassurance.

I knock upon the door and brace myself for her hard stare when she finally opens it. It is no surprise to see her eyes are red and puffy, and her overall expression tensed up in anger.

"Forgive me," I say quietly, "but he was so desperate to see you, I did not have the heart to tell him he would have to wait until tomorrow."

"Monty!" she cries with overwhelming joy taking over her entire face. "Oh, my gosh, look at you!" Monty leaps all over the place before shoving his waggling bottom against her legs, taking in all her love and affection with glee. Before long, she's down on her knees to embrace him with all that she has, and it makes me ache.

"I shall leave you to reacquaint yourselves," I murmur.

"Goodnight…Your Grace," she says without even looking at me.

Hours later, I am still staring at the ceiling with no signs of falling asleep, much like every night since that storm back in London. A night I would like wiped from history. But it cannot be undone. In the end, with no hint of sleep coming to claim me, I dress myself as much as is reasonable, and take a walk to somewhere I have not ventured to since my father's funeral. I have not felt able to.

The night is warm for autumn, and with a clear sky above and a dampness beneath my feet. The walk to my family's small burial plot is not far from the main house, though far enough away to let me pretend that it isn't there. The gate squeaks when I push it open, the sound of which has me dreading this even more. It tells me I have neglected this place, forgotten about the people resting inside of it, just like I did the night I had chosen to stay with my friends instead of being here to save Genevieve. So much guilt is swimming around inside of my blood, my entire body feels sick with it.

The gravestones, once fresh, clean, and grand, now stick out of the ground with moss and ivy eating away at the masonry work. No one has been here to make sure that they are kept looking respectable, just something else to add to my long list of guilt riddled thoughts.

"Genevieve, Lucy, Hardy," I read her gravestone aloud, "Beloved Daughter, Adored Sister, Beautiful Heart."

I personally had the gravestone made for her; the words are my own. I did not think of any for my father when I wrote down the details for the stone mason. By comparison, my father's gravestone is as impersonal as I could make it. It simply says his name and the dates of his birth and death. I could not think of single thing to say about the man, not anything to go on a gravestone at any rate. Even now, he only gets a few short moments of my attention before I return my gaze to my mother's stone, then back to Genny's again.

"I am sorry," I mutter into the darkness, and it sounds strange to my ears, unnatural even. "I have failed you both." Of course, I get no reply, not even one inside of my head. "Would you believe me if I said I tried to do the best that I could? My actions, my choices, when made, were made with the best intentions. If I had known what was to happen that night, that one night I did something for my own, selfish reasons, please believe me when I say I would have done everything in my power to get back to you, Gen."

I sigh heavily, trying to keep my tears at bay, but it does not work. They chase one another down my cheeks whilst I make the most ungracious of noises through my nose and throat.

"Genny, if I had known about Thomas, we could have helped you together!" I gasp for air to try and compose myself. "God, I hope you are with mother, Gen, that she is looking after you the way I could not. I am so, so, sorry!"

Nothing changes, there is no calming feeling, no relief from my guilt, just darkness, sadness, and loneliness. Eventually, I make my peace with their graves, nod politely as a gentleman should, and leave.

Chapter 25

Tobias

The following morning, much later than normal for me, I wake to hear Emily playing one of her melodies on the piano. It takes me back to a time when we were beginning to fall in love with one another, when we were both happy and hopeful. I do not yet know if there is any hope left for us, but I like to think there is. It takes me little time to get dressed and be on my way to that sunny parlour room, where I will find her there, completely lost in her music. However, once I am at the doorway, looking at her with the sun upon her face, I falter, wondering whether I should go and disturb her from her happy place. And I don't, not for a while, but when I see her looking so beautiful, and so passionate in her playing, I cannot help myself.

I walk as quietly as I can so as not to disturb her. I simply watch and indulge in the beautiful sounds being emitted through her fingertips. Without much thought process behind it, I slip myself around the back of her, so that her body is nestled between my legs and my arms are perched around her waist. It is much too much for her to ignore, and she falters a little in her playing, though it is only for a moment or two before she continues. She smells of vanilla and fresh air, of the outdoors, and everything delicious in my life. I cannot help but rest my nose inside the crook of her neck and press my lips to her porcelain skin. The thump of her pulse becomes quicker and her breath shallower. My other hand reaches up to close gently around her neck at the same time as my body closes in around hers.

Hope infiltrates my heart when she lets me kiss her, touch her, excite her. However, as soon as she has finished playing, I feel her entire body slump. She does not move away from me, but she does not move against me either; I know I have lost her. My lips stop working their way over her skin, my hands release her, and I wait for her to speak.

"Say something, Emily, please?" I whisper, the force of my breath blowing a few strands of hair against her neck.

"I do not know what it is you wish for me to say," she answers without emotion, sounding like a lady when she is being courted by a perfect stranger. It is too polite, too unnatural for my Emily, and that hope I began to feel slips away again.

"I want you..." I begin but have to take in more air to stop myself from whimpering. "I want you to forgive me, to want me again, to lie in my bed with me like you once did."

"Are you asking me, Your Grace?" she asks, and I shut my eyes to her calling me by my title. I long to hear her call me by my first name again. "Or are you demanding it of me as your wife?"

"I cannot demand this of you, Emily," I tell her as I reach for her hands, but she stands angrily before I can get to her.

"I think we both know you can demand of me whatever you feel like at the time."

She then turns to leave, but I find myself calling out for her to stop. It is a momentary impulsive decision to try a different tact, a gamble too. However, it is one I am willing to make, for I will do anything to cling onto her.

"Emily!" I shout sternly, then purposely wait for her to turn and face me before speaking again. "You are right, I can make demands of you as my wife."

Her shocked expression, one that is most likely hiding a multitude of names she would dearly love to call me, none of them pleasant, remains on her face all the while I walk slowly up to her with a determined look. When we are but a foot apart, I tuck my hands behind my back and stand up tall, readying myself to face her wrath.

"I demand you join me for a walk, as soon as you are ready," I say to her with confidence, "Monty will accompany us."

I watch her facial expression change a number of times, most of them with her mouth opening, as if readying to reply, only to close it again without any words. Eventually, she straightens herself and looks into my eyes with as much steely determination as she can.

"As you wish, Your Grace," she finally replies with a half-hearted bow. When she turns to walk away again, I cannot help but smile a little. Most men avoid women like Emily, or worse, try to beat that same spirited attitude out of them. However, I love my Emily for exactly who she is; to change her would be a true loss, one I am not willing to accept.

Emily

I am so mad; I could have screamed the whole way back to my room, where I reluctantly collect my coat for my enforced walk with 'His Grace'. Even the staff, who are so used to seeing me smiling and being blithe, move away when they see me stomping down the corridor. However, when I finally reach the bottom of the main staircase, Augustus, one of the footmen is waiting for me with a letter. I thank him with a tight, angry smile, which he does not deserve. However, it is one I cannot help, especially given the foul mood my husband has just put me in.

"Thank you, Augustus," I tell him before taking the letter up to my room where I shall leave it until after our walk. If it is from a member of my family, I would rather read it when I am not feeling so venomous.

By the time we have reached the boundary of the garden, and are walking out onto the sprawling fields, we have barely said two words to one another. And neither of those were worth anything beyond politeness. He smiles and walks casually, as though we are merely playing along to the standards set by society; something we might have done had he taken the time to court me properly. Monty is happy to sniff about and does not seem to pick up on how frustrated I am feeling in his master's company.

"Where would you like to go, Emily?" he asks with a cheery tone of voice. "To the village or to our woods?"

"The village, I think," I reply without hesitation, "I do not wish the woods to be tainted by ill feeling."

"Of course," he replies with a nod of his head, even though I can tell I have caused him pain through my unforgiving words. "Perhaps we might visit the Porters, seeing as they are so fond of you, Emily."

"You? Consorting with the tenants?" I mock him with a snide smile. "Whatever next, Your Grace?"

"Emily, I am also going to demand that you do not call me by my title," he replies stiffly, "my name, as you well know, is

Tobias, and I expect to be called as such."

"Very well...*Tobias*," I concede, though I cannot deny to sounding just as short with him.

"Excellent," he says with a satisfied smile, as though trying to lighten the atmosphere again. "I see there is a lot of mistletoe growing this year," he announces, pointing to the balls of it growing high up in the trees. "Did you know there is a tradition of kissing under a sprig of mistletoe? I learnt about it during my travels around Europe."

"No, I did not," I reply truthfully. My curiosity gets the better of me when I rise onto my tiptoes to get a better look. I have no idea why I thought the action would make it any clearer, but I suppose natural instincts told my body to do it anyway.

"The rule is, a gentleman may kiss a lady upon the cheek while he picks at one of the berries," he explains, "should she refuse the kiss, she will not receive a single proposal for an entire year."

"Well, I will never know, will I?" I reply with an exasperated sigh. "You plucked me before I had the opportunity to test such a theory."

"True," he says with a smile, "though, I would still like the kissing part."

"And I am sure there are many who would like to kiss you back, Tobias," I tell him without expression, "however, I am not one of them."

His eyes look at me with so much hurt, I almost feel guilty for saying such a thing. In fact, I even go so far as to open my mouth to apologise for my cruel tongue. However, the sound of someone moaning in agony has both of us breaking away from one another and looking straight over to the Porter's cottage. I instantly spy two worried looking children sitting on one of the logs outside the woodshed.

"Ethel, whatever is the matter?" I call over to her when we are close enough to be heard.

"Mama is having the baby," she explains. "Papa told us to wait outside cos it hurts."

"Who is in there with her?" Tobias demands in such a way, they cower beneath his large, intimidating frame. I roll my eyes over his inability to lower his voice to a more soothing level, even when in the presence of frightened children.

"Agnes Copper," Ethel whispers shyly, "the nurse from the village. She delivers all the babies."

"Do you think I should go in?" Tobias asks and I almost laugh when he loses all colour from his face. It is not an easy feat to stop such an action, especially when the children drop their mouths open in utter shock over such an idea.

"Goodness me, no!" I whisper shout. "The very last thing Mrs Porter needs is a duke traipsing about the place whilst she's in such a delicate position."

"Well, then *you* should go in," he flusters, "one of us ought to!"

"And what, pray tell, do you expect me to do once I am inside?" I argue.

"I-I don't know, boil water, or…er…hold her hand!" He points to me with a smug expression upon his face. "Mother had a whole host of people with her when she gave birth to Genevieve. Surely Mrs Farrier should have at least one other person to try and bring her some comfort."

"Ethel, where is your father?"

"Still at the Smithy," she replies. "Mama began moaning early this morning, but when Agnes said she had a way to go, he said he may as well go to work."

"Quite right," Tobias says in a haughty tone of voice, followed by an uncomfortable clearing of the throat. "No sense in a man being there when it is clearly a woman's area of expertise."

"You!" A red, flustered, and large looking woman cries out as she bursts from the cottage with perspiration covering her brow. "Oh, Your Grace!"

She begins to curtsey before us and it is about all I can bear.

"Oh, never mind all that; what do you need, Mrs Copper?"

"The baby is nearly upon us," she says, looking a little gobsmacked over my outburst. However, after Mrs Porter emits another deafening scream from inside, she soon gets back to the job at hand. "It's time to get the father!"

"Right, Tobias, take the little ones and go and fetch Eric while I go and provide some assistance to Agnes," I instruct him, trying to sound firm when in fact, I am feeling anything but confident over the prospect of childbirth.

"Very well," he replies before reaching out to take Marley's hand, just as Ethel begins leading the way. "Good luck!"

Reluctantly, I follow the older woman inside to where poor Mrs Porter is clenching her teeth and turning bright red, as if holding in a long breath. I walk straight over to where her head is laid up against a pillow on her bed and reach out to hold her hand. Agnes returns to her position between her legs to looks for signs of a head.

"Good girl, Maeve!" Agnes beams at her. "I can see the head and…oh, there's a lot of beautiful hair!"

"I cannot anymore!" Maeve whimpers, so I squeeze her hand a little tighter. "I am too worn out!"

"I am sure you can do it one more time," I offer, even though I have absolutely no idea what I am talking about. "You have already had Ethel and Marley; you must be able to."

"Oh my!" Agnes gasps, causing me to look at her with a worried brow. She looks back at me with the same concerned eyes, and whispers, "Baby's head is a tad large."

"Right?" I ask, hoping she has the answer to such a problem. I certainly do not.

"Hmmm, Duchess," she finally says as she stands, "I shall need you to come and take one of Maeve's legs and hold it out for me."

"I beg your pardon?" I ask with wide eyes and the feeling of bile climbing up my throat. "You wish for me to go down there, where I will see…" I lower my voice to a whisper, just like her own, "everything?!"

"I'm afraid so, Your Grace," she replies. I have to bite my lips together to try and stop myself from screaming. However, I know I will do as she has asked if it means helping poor Mrs Porter through this awful experience. "You can close your eyes if you need to."

"Right, yes, ok, fine. It sounds like a plan…of sorts," I

finally concede with an anxious nodding of my head.

I take hold of Maeve's leg and raise it up and to the side as I was instructed. This is all while trying my best not to witness anything that might have me refusing to have children, no matter what is threatened against me.

"OK," I say to Agnes with a firm nod, as if telling her to continue.

"Cor, bloody hell!" Maeve gasps as she winces and falls into clenching her teeth again.

"Push, Maeve, push with all your might!" Agnes shouts, and I do believe I find myself trying to push along with her. When she screams, as though she is in complete agony, I feel a need to cry, though I stop myself for that won't do anyone any good. "That's it! You've torn, old girl, but baby's head is out," Agnes giggles, though I do not think Maeve is feeling quite so happy at this moment in time. "On the next one, Maeve, he or she will be out."

We wait with bated breath for the moment when Maeve can push the thing out and I can finally let go of her leg and return to the safe end, next to her head. It comes sooner than I think, and I brace myself all the while she pushes with everything in her, right up until we hear the delicious sound of a new-born baby crying.

"Oh, Maeve, it's another wee boy!" Agnes laughs with joy, and I chance myself to open my eyes and look at the bloody, slimy, little creature yelling out with all its might. Maeve is crying and laughing at the same time but appears to be already over her ordeal of having to push the little thing out. Agnes wraps the trembling baby boy up with skilled hands before placing him to his mother's chest.

"Hey, bonny boy!" she coos, pressing a finger to his mouth so he can suck on it and calm his crying. "Oh, wee one, oh, wee one!"

"Oh my," I laugh in shock over what I have just been a part of. "I am amazed at all of you!"

"Maeve!" The sound of Eric calling for his wife with desperation has me feeling even more emotional than before. As I hear him fast approaching, I immediately stand out of the way in the hopes of making myself invisible to the room. The poor man practically flies over to his wife's side, where he proceeds to cover her in kisses of love and relief. He then peers inside of the blankets where his newest child has now settled onto his mother's teat. "Well done, girl, well done!"

"You have a son, Eric." Agnes smiles as she continues working between Maeve's legs, though I try not to concentrate on that area for too long.

"Ah ha ha!" he laughs with his hands clamped firmly on the sides of his head. "Another wee boy!"

"Delivered with the help of a duchess, no less!" Maeve informs him, prompting the whole room to now turn and look at me through smiles and tears. I blush with awkwardness and flap my hand in such a way to try and play down my part in the whole affair.

"My grateful thanks to you, Your Grace!" Eric nods before picking up the blanket with his son inside. He appears to have fallen fast asleep with a full belly after all that hard work. "With your permission, I would like to let you hold him, so he can tell it to his children one day."

"Oh," I gasp, feeling a little shocked over such an offer,

just as Tobias knocks on the door. "I am afraid I have never held an infant before. I wouldn't know how."

Tobias steps inside, safe in the knowledge that Maeve is now well and truly covered up with her blanket. He nods to the other three before walking over to where I am standing with a strange expression upon his face. He holds his arms out towards Eric, smiles at him in such a way that the man hands over his new son to Tobias. My husband takes the infant into his arms with such care and grace, he looks almost as well versed in caring for newborns as Agnes. He bounces him inside of his arms and smiles whilst walking over to me.

"I was one of the first people to hold my sister when she was born," he explains with so much emotion in his voice, I begin to think he might cry. "I held her a lot as a baby. My governess had told me it was one of my favourite things to do; she had had to practically fight her away from me."

I look at him with awe and wonder, then peer down at the tiny baby resting contentedly inside of his arms.

"Hold out your arms, Emily," he whispers, and I do. "Now protect his head with your elbow and use your arms to cradle him like this."

The baby fits naturally inside of my arms, and I instinctively begin to bob him up and down just as Tobias had.

"He is heavier that I was expecting," I laugh nervously, just as Tobias pushes back some of the baby's downy hair from his face with only his forefinger. "He is so warm."

"You're a natural, Your Grace," Agnes calls out with a smile on her face, and I laugh, though I have no idea why.

"It suits you," Tobias whispers to me whilst we look deep

into each other's eyes, when I feel something begin to melt away. Perhaps it is my anger; perhaps it is my stubbornness to refuse what I so dearly want; perhaps it is my fear that he will hurt me again. Whatever it is, I have an overwhelming desire to return to that tree with him.

"You know where I am, Your Grace," Agnes says before winking at me, "when the time comes."

I blush awkwardly but Tobias simply smiles with what looks like genuine happiness.

Chapter 26

Tobias

"Emily!" I shout after her when she practically flies across the field that leads straight over to the woods. She is marching as if on a vital mission whereby time is of the essence. I try to keep a little distance between us, for something is telling me to tread cautiously. "Emily, where are you going?!"

She says nothing, nor does she spare a glance back at me, but I keep following alongside Monty. We most likely looking like a couple of puppies following after their mother. We march through the field, past the bridge where we had played stick races, and right through to the tree we had picnicked under only a few months ago. Once there, she wastes no time in setting to the task of climbing that damn tree without any thought or reason for it. This is also where my following after her stops. Instead, I fold my arms and look at her with an amused look on my face. Meanwhile, after she finally reaches her branch to perch upon, she too, folds her arms and looks at me with a determined expression.

"Well?" I ask, with Monty now sniffing about in the background. He is no longer agitated by her strange love of tree climbing.

"I am ready to talk, Tobias," she says without any sort of a smile.

"Is there a reason for being in the tree whilst we do this?" I ask, feeling confused over her behaviour, even for her.

"I feel safer being at some distance away from you," she says a little cryptically, "this way we can just talk, nothing more."

"To what are you referring to, Emily?" I ask with a mischievous smile.

"You know very well what I am referring to," she says sternly, "your kissing me and trying to send me into a stupor is not going to happen whilst I am in this tree."

"I could climb it," I gesture, still with a smile on my face, one that has her rolling her eyes and sighing at me.

"Tobias, be realistic, you are more likely to fall on your back than get even close to me on top of this tree," she pouts, "besides, you are wasting time."

"You are right; I apologise," I tell her, knowing that this is the closest I have managed to get to her listening to me since I returned. It could be my only chance. "When I thought...when I believed you had been..."

"Tobias, we both know what you saw, and I can understand how you thought it might have been me; that is not why I am angry with you," she says with the sun beginning to set in the background, casting a warm glow over her already golden locks of hair. "I would have been equally suspicious had our roles been reversed."

"Then...?" I ask the obvious.

"You shut down on me, Tobias! You promised me only that afternoon to always talk to me, but at the very first obstacle, you were prepared to throw us away without even giving me any sort of explanation. I spent weeks feeling confused, hurt, embarrassed and completely heart-broken with no idea as to why. Do you know what that feels like, Tobias? To feel destroyed but have absolutely no idea what for. Then, when Elizabeth arrived to tell me what I was being accused of, to know I was being talked about like a common whore, well, it was the last straw, Tobias!"

"I know," I reply ashamedly, "I owe you so much, I do not even know where to start."

"Try," she snaps, "and if you feel uncomfortable, then perhaps you will understand a fraction of what I have been feeling ever since you sent me away."

"Believe me, Emily, I have been aching just as much as you since that day," I tell her truthfully. "I have been battling loving you, but it has only proved to be a fruitless exercise. I did not say what I thought had happened to anyone; never once, did I utter those words out loud, for doing so would mean it was true. I know I took you away from your family, treated you abysmally, only to fall for you when I tried so hard not to. Seeing what I saw, I could not help but feel like it was my punishment for hurting you, and for everything else before you."

"I do not understand," she says with her brows knitted firmly together, "what do you mean 'before'?"

"That is a conversation for another time," I reply, smiling tightly at her, "all I care about right now, is you. I was wrong to not trust you, Emily, so very wrong. My silence after, is a condition I have long held onto since childhood, when I had to keep secrets to save my sister from my father, and from other people who might want to do her harm. I have since learnt that keeping silent did not do her any good, neither did it for me or you, Emily. Know that I will always strive to be open and honest with you, for you are my wife." I pause to walk over to where her feet are dangling from the tree, and clasp hold of them inside of my hands. "I love you, my duchess, and if you forgive me, I will spend my life making it up to you, I promise."

She stares at me in such a way I know she is beginning to relent in her anger, but is yet to be convinced, so I place a kiss to each of her ankles. I cannot help smiling when I hear her inhale a large gulp of breath, just like she had on our wedding night. She then tries to cover her reaction by noisily clearing her throat.

"Typical of you to break with the rules, Tobias," she murmurs, "I told you to keep your distance, that we were only to talk."

"Would you like me to stop?" I smile up at her, still running my fingers over her feet.

"No…yes…Help me down, Tobias," she whispers, and I waste no time in adhering to her request.

"What else does the lady of the house require of her husband?" I ask when she is safely inside of my arms, all the while she is looking at my lips, as if waiting for me to kiss her.

"This is but a start, Tobias," she says quietly, "I am not yet ready to forgive completely."

"That is fair, but if I may?" I ask looking at her lips, desperate to kiss them but knowing I must wait for her say so.

"You may," she replies, then leans in to kiss me before I can even make my head make sense of all that is happening. Once our lips touch, I cannot even begin to try and hold back from giving into all my desire for her. We lose ourselves to it, so much so, I soon have her pushed against the tree, and with her hands pulling at my neck to get closer. It is only when I thrust against her, showing her what she does to me, that she breaks away with crimson cheeks and a loss of breath.

"Forgive me," I pant, "I did not mean to be so…so forward. I have just been without out you for so long. I know I must wait."

"Perhaps we should return to the house?" she asks but does not look at all convinced by her suggestion. If I so chose to push, I have no doubt I could have her giving into every one of my urges to have her beneath the sky in this very clearing, which will forever be *our* tree.

"Of course," I relent, then offer her my arm, which for the first time in weeks, she takes with a genuine smile for me. Hope blooms inside my chest, and I silently promise her to be the best husband I can be. To make up for my past failures to both her and Genevieve.

Emily

It is late, well past bedtime, and yet I have arrived at Tobias' bedroom door, ready to confront him after reading my letter from Elizabeth. When my hand lifts to the thick wood, I falter for a moment or two, with my heart racing in fear, excitement, anger, and sadness. I count to three, close my eyes, and breathe out once more before finally knocking.

I find myself stepping back when I hear the thudding of his feet coming towards me, his brow no doubt sporting a confused furrow, questioning as to who might be calling on him so late at night. If I weren't feeling so nervous, I would be laughing at how accurate I was in my mental image of him when he finally throws open the door. With nothing but a sheet wrapped around his hips, he pulls back the door even wider, and with his eyes still trying to adjust to my candlelight.

"Emily?" he asks, then looks left and right down the hallway to ascertain how much of an emergency this might be. When his eyes finally rest back on mine, I find all breath has left my body and I am unable to speak. "Is everything alright?"

I close my mouth and rapidly shake my head, for in all honesty, it is not. His face takes on a concerned expression before he reaches for my hand and pulls me into his bed chamber. He only relinquishes his grip when he has closed the door behind the both of us. I take the opportunity to wander over to the end of the bed where I perch, hoping I might be able to calm my nerves into something that will at least allow me to speak. When he stands before me, wearing only a sheet, I feel a heat spread through me. I cannot tell if this feeling is through excitement or embarrassment.

"Emily, please, I am worried," he says as he kneels to clasp hold of my hands. "Tell me you are ok, Emily."

"I-I am," I manage to push past my lips. "Tobias, your aunt wrote to me. She told me to tell you that Thomas Greyson was found dead this morning. They suspect he had taken some concoction inside of his whiskey the night before."

"I see," he says quietly, turning to one side so I can no longer look inside of his eyes. "I see."

"Tobias, I think she may have told me all that you could not," I barely say louder than a whisper, moving my head down so he has no choice but to look back at me. "Tobias, she told me about Genevieve."

"Emily, I couldn't-"

"I respect why you didn't tell me, Tobias," I reassure him, "I am not angry. In fact, I am proud of you for not using her to try and fix things between us. I would not have expected anything less from you. But I am also glad your aunt told me what you could not."

"You must think even less of me now," he says with such sadness, I almost let my emotions get the better of me.

"Tobias, why would you think that?" I finally ask on a whimper, no longer able to control my tears. "Genevieve was not your fault; how could it have been? She was sick, Tobias, and you did the best you could to protect her. Please do not blame yourself for what you could not control."

"I should have been there that night, to stop him, to help her-" he tries to argue but I cut off his words by placing my hand to his lips.

"You are a duke with status, power, and a nasty temper," I declare with a gentle laugh, and he smiles, "but you are not God and cannot be responsible for what others do. Neither can you control a sickness you did not even understand yourself. To come as far as you have, to have survived all that heartache, I think your mother and Genevieve would be proud of you, Tobias. I know I am."

"You are?" he asks me with wide eyes and his hands now trembling against mine. "Not everyone agrees with you, Emily; Thomas certainly did not."

"Thomas was obviously sick with grief," I tell him as I pull him in closer towards me and brush my fingers across his face. "He had his own demons to bear."

He nods slowly, sadly, before I throw my arms around his neck and hold onto him with all the love and support that I can offer. He has lived in loneliness and bitterness for so long, but now he is mine, and I can help to free him of this guilt with which he carries. I can try and make him whole again.

"I love you, Emily," he whispers over my shoulder, "and I never want to lose you again."

"Neither do I," I reply softly, "which is why I want to come back in here with you."

He pulls back so suddenly; I laugh a little. He smiles with hope and a pale complexion turning warm again.

"You do?" he asks whilst cupping my face inside of his warm hands. "You really do?"

"I do," I tell him and kiss him with a forgiveness I am now ready to let him have.

Our kiss turns more passionate, and I feel brazen with lust after having missed his warmth for so long. It is I who pulls away at his sheet first, who holds him close to me whilst shuffling back onto the bed. It is I who makes it perfectly clear as to what I want from him. For a moment, he pauses, looking at me as if waiting for permission, for absolute clarity on the matter, so I smile to show him he has read me right. After this, he is all hands and urgency to pull down at my nightgown and kiss any piece of exposed flesh that he can get to first.

Once there are no barriers left between us, he falls perfectly between my legs, kneading at my breasts with a gentle touch, as well as kissing my neck.

"Claim me back as your wife, Tobias," I gasp with a smirk to my lips, causing him to laugh at me. "Do not laugh at me; we must consummate our reunion, don't you think?"

"Whatever you wish, Your Grace," he smiles against my shoulder, right before he moves inside of me, and we both take a deep inhale together.

"Look at me, Tobias," I tell him as I pull him back up, "so you can be sure of this, of me, and make no more mistakes."

He moves slow and deep whilst we stare into one another's eyes, with mine telling him that I forgive him, and his saying he will never doubt me again. As we fall into kissing, with his fingers lacing through mine, he moves quicker, harder, and so intensely, I release not long afterwards. I watch his face clenching up for control, to keep himself from falling as long as possible, but when I smile and place a chaste kiss to his cheek, it is too much for him to hold back. He growls as he freezes inside of me, releasing himself with relief in his eyes, before falling to my chest where I hold onto him for as long as he needs me to.

Epilogue

Emily

The fire is burning for it is freezing. Even I have forgone my daily walk with Monty to rest a while in front of the hearth. Mary is trying her best to learn Chess, but in all honesty, I think she is a lost cause. I yawn for the second time in only minutes, causing her to laugh at me.

"Late night, Your Grace?" she asks with a devilish smile.

"That is none of your business, Mary," I reply before sticking out my tongue rather ungraciously. Inside of my head I beam, for most of my nights with my husband are late, even if I am more tired than usual these days.

Before Mary can make a poor strategic move with her knight piece, a dishevelled looking Monty comes running inside of the room with a puffed-out Mrs Keppel not far behind. He is whimpering and barking at me; it has my heart thumping in fear for Tobias. He had taken him out for a walk not long ago, and for the dog to return without him, looking so out of sorts, can only mean something terrible has happened.

"Mrs Keppel," I gasp, "please, my coat!"

"Of course," she cries whilst we all head to the door.

"Come on, Monty, show me where you left him!" I tell the

poor dog who has not looked this worried since he had gotten himself stuck in the brambles all those months ago.

I put on my coat whilst following Monty out the front door, towards the back garden, where he heads straight to the boundary and in the direction of the woods. Mary offers to come with me, but I tell her to wait behind and to call the doctor so he can be on standby. I look the epitome of calm on the outside, but inside, I feel like I am screaming. If anything bad has happened to my husband, I do not know how I will live through it. I have gone from dreading the day I was to marry him, hating him, being in fear of him, only to now succumb to loving him with all my heart.

I pace after Monty, ignoring how out of breath I become, and follow him deep inside of the woods, just about keeping afoot when I cross over the icy bridge across the stream. I end up in the small clearing we frequent for picnics and other…activities. When I look at the tree, *our* tree, I cannot help but burst into a fit of laughter. There before me, sat upon my branch, is Tobias Hardy, Duke of Kent, smiling smugly at me.

"What on earth are you doing?" I giggle, walking slowly towards him with my arms firmly crossed.

"Well, I remember telling you about a tradition involving a sprig of mistletoe," he replies. He then brings his hands out before him with the aforementioned plant being held between his fingers and thumb. "And you told me you would never get to test it."

"Ah-ha," I reply, "and we are still married, so I fail to see how we can still test this tradition of yours. Wait! Did you climb all the way up there to get it?" I ask, peering way up high to see where the ball of mistletoe is growing.

"Well, perhaps," he shrugs. "Though, I may have caught Ethel and Marley looking like a couple of monkeys up there and given them a few silver coins for this small piece."

"A few?!" I gasp. "They must have thought their birthdays had come early. I hope you told them to never be so reckless again!"

"Why, Emily, are you losing your edge?" He tuts at me before jumping to his feet and sauntering over with a slow, confident swagger. I smile at him as he leans in to kiss my cheek, picking at the berry from the greenery between his fingers. I giggle even harder when he moves into kiss me more passionately, all the while running his hand over my belly. "Must be your condition; it's making you soft."

"Never," I whisper. "I would still climb that tree before you even had time to blink."

"You will certainly not!" he says sternly. "You are beginning to show, my love."

"I shall have to write and tell my parents and Elsie," I agree as I place my hand over his. "Perhaps next week when we return to London for my cousin's wedding."

"Ah, yes, this wedding, will Edmund be there?" he asks with a strange expression on his face.

"He will," I reply. "I hear he is planning to go abroad for a while."

"Good, I have been meaning to ask him about some business I have in London," he says, now taking hold of my hand to lead me back towards the house. Monty naturally falls into a trot behind us, sniffing all around with excitement. "And Frederick and Victoria will be joining us for dinner the following day. I believe she too, is due soon. I do not think Frederick thought it would happen so quickly."

"Frederick, a father," I giggle at the thought. "Poor Victoria will have two children to look after."

We stop for a moment when we come to the small cemetery on the outskirts of the woods. Tobias has had it cleaned up, so it no longer looks overgrown and rife with moss and ivy. A sadness descends on him when I catch him staring at his sister's grave. I rub at his back for comfort, to reassure him that he is still not to blame.

"It was good of you, Tobias," I tell him, pushing my chin out towards the head stone standing next to hers. "I do not think many other men in your position would have agreed to such a thing."

"She loved him, and he clearly loved her," he replies, "had it not been for Gen's death, they would have been married with children of their own by now. If they could not be together in life, it was only right that they be together in death."

"Such beautiful words too," I tell him as I rest my head against his shoulder. "Thomas, Archibald, Greyson, Beloved Son, Protective Brother, Committed Husband."

We take a few more moments to let those words sink in before returning home. A home that I hope will be filled with love, trust, family, but above all, happiness.

Let's connect!

Facebook Taylor K Scott | Facebook

Instagram: Taylor K Scott (@taylorkscott.author) • Instagram photos and videos

Website (including my blog) www.taylorkscottauthor.com

Author Dashboard | Goodreads

Sign up to my monthly newsletter through my author website or through the link below:

Taylor K Scott Author (list-manage.com)

Other works by Taylor K. Scott:

Learning Italian

A romantic comedy, which is available now on Kindle Unlimited

The Darkness Within

An enemies to lovers romantic suspense.

Gabe

A contemporary romance standalone. This is the second book in 'The Darkness Within' series.

Claire's Lobster

An age-gap, romantic comedy novella

My Best Friend

A Friends-to-Lovers contemporary romance

Mayfield Trilogy

A dark, suspense romance.

2023

The Carter Trilogy

A set on contemporary romances, including 'The Gentleman', 'The Knight', 'The Fool' and 'The Devil'

If you enjoy historical romances, and you've grown fond of Emily and Tobias, then it might please you to know that I have started writing Elsie's story. It's in the early stages but here is a snippet:

A Marriage of His Choosing
Elsie

Now that I am out here, in the dark, the silence, I can better understand why my sister enjoys the outdoors. I never much indulged in its pleasures when I was younger, for I was always deemed to be the more responsible one. The eldest must set an example for her younger sibling, as well as represent the family by her actions. Emily, although a daughter of a viscount, was afforded a level of freedom that I was not, especially when she was so obviously our father's favourite. Not that I am especially bitter about the fact, more saddened than angry. However, a strange affliction of insomnia has caused me to wander from my sister's house, away from my husband, and in search of something I cannot even name, for I do not even know what it is.

A small, rickety bridge grabs my attention, it having a sliver of moonlight hitting at just the right angle. It looks as if a painter had arranged the scene for his latest masterpiece, and so I must go to it. The water sets my nervous, tense muscles at ease a little, almost clearing my head of all the troubling thoughts that have ailed me since marrying my sister's former admirer. To be a poor conciliation prize to both my father and husband is enough to trouble any woman's mind. I try not to feel ugly emotions, such as jealousy, but it is a strong ask when I have tried so hard to be what society deems the perfect lady, only to see my sister now living the life I was brought up to believe would be mine. It makes me feel wicked, superficial, and utterly miserable.

"Oh…" A moan coming through the trees across the path from me interrupts my daydreaming. It is so fleeting; I almost believe I imagined it. However, I soon hear a giggle which I recognise almost immediately. Emily, when she was reading books no woman should have any business reading, and when she was only fifteen years old at that. I know I should ignore it, turn around and return to the house, however, I cannot deny how curious I am.

Like a greedy thief, I creep among the trees and undergrowth, being careful not to step upon a twig likely to snap and give away my position, then take refuge behind a bush. I am taken aback by the sight of my sister and her husband lying all but naked underneath a large oak tree, with only a thin blanket to shield their entire bodies. Tobias, my brother-in-law, cages her beneath his broad body, with that same painter having bathed each and every one of his muscles in silvery moonlight. Her hands are braced against his shoulders and her leg hooked around his. Their hips look to be massaging against one another, causing her to pant and roll her eyes before closing them altogether.

"My beautiful wife," he gasps, "the stealer of all my thoughts!"

"Thoughts?" she giggles with a long moan at the end.

"So many thoughts…ahhh…" he trails off as she seemingly pushes him over and onto his back, so she is now on top, gyrating against him.

"Oh, my!" I gasp to myself as I watch his hands move to hold onto her naked breasts, quite clearly enjoying what she is doing to him. It is such a sight; I have to turn away. My breath has quickened, and my heart is thumping so hard, I fear it might leap right out of my chest.

"Lustful thoughts?" she whispers between pants.

"Ridiculously lustful thoughts!" he laughs before emitting a moan that sounds as though he is half in pain, half in rapture.

"I am…I am…" she cries out before she too, emits a moan similar to that of the one of her husband.

A silence ensues before they seemingly fall into fits of giggles. The sound of their kissing leaves me no choice but to turn and face them once again. Still naked, bar the sheet wrapped loosely around the parts that truly matter, I watch as he leans over her, brushing away her hair while looking so adoringly at her, so happy with her, I cannot help but feel that ugly pang of jealousy once more. The way they are looking at one another is so beautiful, I have no words with which to describe the scene that will do it any sort of justice.

"Emily, I love you more than anything," he whispers with a smile I do not believe any other person has ever seen on him. It is all for her, just her. "You and James."

"And Monty?" she asks with a teasing smile. He laughs, then kisses her forehead with so much tenderness, I cannot help but wish it were me lying there with him.

"Of course, my love, and Monty," he whispers, turning serious again. "I love you."

"And I you," she says, pushing back his hair with affection.

It is too much to bear, too much to watch without the need to scream in frustration. With as much care as before, I turn and run far away from all that it is that I so desperately crave for myself. I run back to the house where my husband lies sleeping. I am sure that if he had borne witness to what I had just seen, he too would be feeling beyond frustrated, wanting nothing else other than to be there with Emily instead of Tobias. As for me, it is not the man beneath the tree that I want, more the relationship that my sister has.

Printed in Great Britain
by Amazon

47400554R00185